HEALER
OF THE
WATER MONSTER

HEALER

OF THE

WATER MONSTER

• BRIAN YOUNG •

Heartdrum

An Imprint of HarperCollinsPublishers

Heartdrum is an imprint of HarperCollins Publishers.

Healer of the Water Monster
Copyright © 2021 by Brian Young
www.harpercollinschildrens.com
ISBN 978-0-06-299040-2
Typography by David Curtis and Erin Fitzsimmons
21 22 23 24 25   PC/LSCH   10 9 8 7 6 5 4 3 2 1

First Edition

For all the young Navajos
who are searching for themselves in stories.

PROLOGUE

'Ałk'idą́ą́, shinálí 'ashkii.

Ages before humans lived in our current Fourth World, it has been said that the ancestors of the Navajo left the mists and clouds of the Second World for the shimmering waters of the Third World. First to crawl onto the land were the beings of thought, First Woman and First Man. Second were the beings of land, Coyote, Turkey, Deer, Turtle, Cougar, Bear. Finally, the beings of air, the many birds and winged bugs, flew into the crisp, salty air. The beings of thought, of land, and of air gazed at their new environment. A sheet of rippling blue water brimmed to every horizon. Unlike the shadowy and dark First World, tiny islands where land beings could walk dotted the vast sheet of water.

Beings of water originated from this world. Among them

were the mighty water monsters, giant lizards whose toes were as thick as the trunks of fully grown pine trees. These water monsters governed the torrents of this water world and kept the waves tranquil. Most powerful of them was Mother Water Monster, who offered both her domain and nourishing waters to these unfamiliar beings.

The beings of thought, of land, and of air lived in harmony with the beings of water for an age. Coyote, who became curious and envious, watched the water monsters and their influence over the rising and falling of waves. From afar, he often spied upon them. They would hum and then either slam or gently bob their thunderous tails on the sheets of water, causing ripples. These ripples would grow into waves that would bring moisture onto the islands. The moisture that sprayed into the air would condense and form clouds pregnant with rain.

One evening, after all had closed their eyes to sleep, Coyote snuck away from his companions. Using his knowledge of the ways from the First World to hide himself, he folded a nearby shadow like a blanket and draped it over his furry body. He came upon Mother Water Monster's nest without the slightest disturbance. There, Coyote found an infant, no bigger than a fully grown sheep, and kidnapped it. He returned to the beings of land, eager to begin learning the ways of the water monsters.

◊ ◊ ◊

The next day, the land beings discovered that their islands had shrunk in half. They helplessly watched the danger around them grow as the once-gentle tides now foamed with fury. Tidal waves were rising and, like starving mouths, swallowing morsels of land down dark blue throats.

First Woman and First Man set to saving everyone and planted four seeds. With songs and prayers, the seeds sprouted, grew, and shot upward. The first three grew into trees that stopped short of the ceiling of the Third World. The fourth seed, a river reed, ascended and pressed against the rocky ceiling of the Third World. Still it continued to grow, but instead of growing upward, it grew round and thick. Soon, it was thick enough that its leaves were big and strong enough to support the weight of all the beings. One by one, they scaled the reed as quickly as they could. At the ceiling, the beings discovered a small hole through which they could escape the livid waters beneath them.

Before they could leave, First Man and First Woman had to make sure to carry as many seeds as possible. They had no idea if the next world would be able to feed them. The seeds they carried fell out of their hands, and no other animal could carry the seeds because they had only feet and paws. It was then that First Turkey offered to keep the seeds in her feathers. When the waters rose, First Turkey almost didn't make it, as the weight of all those seeds slowed her down. First Turkey was the last one to climb up the reed that grew to the top of the sky. The foaming waters touched the tips of her tail feathers, turning them white.

Seeing their imminent escape, Mother Water Monster commanded a cloud to condense and form a thick sheet of ice that covered the hole, barring their exit. Before the waters could claim them all, Coyote presented the kidnapped infant back to Mother Water Monster. The sheet of ice melted, and everyone crawled into the hole that would lead them to the glittering walls of the Fourth World, wherein we, their descendants, now reside.

T'ááłá'í

ONE

A WAVE OF DESERT HEAT knocked the wind out of his lungs when Nathan finally stepped out of his father's SUV. Nathan stretched his arms upward, and then bent his elbows and knees. The hot New Mexican sun singed his exposed skin. He quickly pulled his shirt down to hide his belly, which pushed uncomfortably against the waistband of his stretchy shorts. His limbs tingled and tickled, reawakening from the five-hour drive to his paternal grandmother's mobile home on Diné Homelands, forty-five minutes north of Church Rock.

Nali, his grandma, rushed out of her mobile home, which sat in the middle of a wide, dry valley, waving her arms in large circles at him. Her flower-print skirt billowed behind her. "Ooo, shináli 'ashkii!" she yelled.

Nathan rushed over and hugged her. Nali always smelled like lavender and sage, which Nathan was glad to inhale over and over again. Her wrinkled hand rubbed and squeezed his shoulder. Even through his shirt, he could feel the comforting calluses on her palms and fingers. "How I've missed you," she whispered. The last time he had seen her in person was when she had visited him at his mom's apartment in Phoenix for his eleventh birthday three months ago. For his gift, Nali had given him a small deer-hide pouch filled with corn pollen, which she said was called tádídíín.

"I missed you, too, Nali," Nathan said.

"Shinálí 'ashkii! You're getting just tall! I should call you shinálí hastiin now, huh! Tell me, what does 'hastiin' mean?"

Nathan tried his best to remember the few Navajo words he knew. "Well, ''ashkii' means 'boy.' You mentioned I was getting taller. Does 'hastiin' mean 'man'?"

"'Aoo', exactly! You are growing. Pretty soon I'm going to have to look up to talk to you. And after that, I'm going to have to put any girlfriend through the grandma test. She's going to have to butcher, cook, and chop wood. If any of them fail, I'm going to say, 'Nope, get rid of her!'" Nathan blushed at the thought. "Is there a girl?" Nali asked, looking deep into his eyes. Her eyes had a sliver of silver outlining her deep black pupils, like a midnight crescent moon, and her white hair speckled with strands of black was pulled into a tight traditional Navajo bun that was held together by a bundle of white yarn. Nathan briefly thought of Joyce, who he sometimes saw at lunch. "Oh, there is!"

"Stop it, Nali!" He laughed to hide his embarrassment.

"Speaking of cooking, what do you think of frybread for an early dinner?" Nali said.

"It's like you speak my language," Nathan said.

Nathan's father was carrying two cases of bottled water toward the mobile home. He placed them down and hugged Nali. "Hi, Mom."

"'Aoo', yá'át'ééh shiyáázh." Nali looked at both of them and smiled. "My handsome men. You sure you can't stay for a meal?"

"Can't. Leandra's plane will land as soon as I get there."

Nali sighed. "When you pick Nathan up, you're staying for a meal. End of discussion." Nali went to the firepit that was in front of the chaha'oh, a traditional rectangle shade hut made from oak stumps, branches, and leaves, and started a cooking fire.

"Nathan, don't forget your stuff," his father said.

"I gotta go to the bathroom first," said Nathan.

"Don't forget it's the outhouse. Because there's no running water—" his father started to say.

"I know! Jeez," Nathan interrupted, leaving before his father could say another word. He didn't need another reason to be frustrated with his father.

Nathan stood in front of the wooden outhouse. His nose could already smell it. Out of everything that he would be giving up for these next possibly two months, a flushable toilet was definitely in his top three, alongside internet and Hot Pockets. He could get through it. He had to, especially if it meant avoiding his father's girlfriend, Leandra.

Originally, Nathan was supposed to stay with his father while his mom went to document a growing protest against a company laying pipelines across designated tribal lands. Having some quality father-son time would have been cool. Even Leandra's weekend dates with his father wouldn't have been that bad.

Then his father got the idea of going to Las Vegas. No complaints there. But his father told him that Leandra was joining them. That destroyed all hope Nathan had of spending time with his father, because he and Leandra would be kissing, holding hands, and doing other annoying couple things.

Nathan braced himself, inhaled deeply, and entered the outhouse. A swarm of bothersome flies buzzed in front of his face and landed on the tips of his ears, on his cheeks, on his shins, on his elbows. Their microscopic furry feet tickled everywhere they landed. He reminded himself he could do this. He could make it through two months of this. That's how long it was going to take to get enough measurements for his science experiment. He already regretted tricking his parents into letting him stay here.

Two weeks ago, at the end of May, when his father first suggested Las Vegas, Nathan told his parents that he wanted to spend time with Nali at her mobile home, where she stayed when she wasn't teaching high school Navajo language classes in Farmington, New Mexico. His mom was driving to drop him off at his father's that weekend, and they were talking about where he was going to stay.

"You do know there's no running water or electricity," Nathan's mom had said. She bit her lower lip and breathed loudly through her nose, things she did whenever she was uncomfortable or unhappy.

"I know, Mom," Nathan said, rolling his eyes.

"There's no cell reception—" Nathan's mom said.

"Jeez! I've been there before," Nathan said. It was like she didn't remember Nathan had already spent time with Nali at the mobile home. It wasn't just her. His father, too! They both forgot things like this, because they never paid him any attention.

"I don't know how long this protest is going to last," his mom said. "It could be weeks. It could be months."

"I can do it," Nathan said, texting his best friends, Weslee and Steven, on his brand-new smartphone, which both his parents got him for getting straight As on his report card. It had all the bells and whistles like AR support and 5G capabilities. Not that 5G meant anything for Nali's mobile home site.

"Why don't you just spend a few days with Nali and then stay at your father's?"

"Because." That was all he could come up with at the moment.

"You're going to have to tell your father. I don't think he'll be too happy."

Nathan didn't care that his father wasn't going to be happy. If his father had cared about him one bit, he would not have invited Leandra to Las Vegas in the first place. He called his father to tell him about his summer plans.

"You're telling him now? Can't you wait until you see him in person?" his mom asked.

His father answered, "Son? Everything all right?"

"Yeah," Nathan said. "Mom says that I have to tell you that I want to go to Nali's instead of Vegas."

"Wait, what?" his father asked. In his mind, Nathan could see his father's expression of surprise and concern, eyebrows raised, mouth shaped like an O. "I don't know how to respond. I mean, did you ask your mother?"

"She's okay with it," Nathan said.

"I'm okay with what? What am I okay with?" his mom said.

"That doesn't sound like her," his father said.

"With me going to Nali's for the summer," Nathan said to his mom, his hand placed over the microphone of his phone to make sure his father didn't hear.

"I never said that. You should go with your father to Vegas," his mom said at the same time his father was saying, "You should still come with me, Nathan. This is supposed to be our time together."

Nathan said to his mom, "He says that it's okay with him and that he trusts me."

"What does he mean by that?" his mom asked, raising her voice. "Trusts you? I trust you."

Nathan whispered into the phone while his mom was distracted, "Mom said it's all up to you whether I go or stay." Nathan's father didn't like to be put in the position of making a decision like this, especially when it came between him and Nali.

"Tell your father that he's acting immature, and I don't appreciate it," his mom said.

"Tell your mother to stop putting all this pressure on me," his father said.

"So can I go?" Nathan asked both of them. There was an uncomfortable silence. He knew they were on the verge of saying no. He had to sweeten the deal. The first thing that popped into his mind was that they never said no to anything school-related. "I want to do another science project for the Arizona Science and Engineering Fair."

"Science project?" they both asked.

"I've been brainstorming one for next year's fair," Nathan lied. He knew that they weren't going to communicate to confirm the existence of the project.

"Right now?" his mom asked. "It's summer."

"Yeah, it involves, uh, her cornfield," Nathan said, trying to maintain his cool. If he sounded too desperate, this would all fall apart. "If you want, you can talk to each other."

"No, that's fine," his mom said.

"Don't worry about it," his father said at the same time.

Over the next few days, Nathan drafted an experiment that would compare water consumption between Nali's heirloom kernels that had been passed down to her through many generations and store-bought kernels. He then talked with Nali, who was more than willing to have him at the mobile home. With her help, they were able to convince his mom and father to let him stay at Church Rock for as long as the project went.

Now he rushed out of the outhouse and inhaled fresh air, rubbing the areas that still tickled from the flies. He miscalculated his momentum and lost his balance. Throwing his hands forward, his palms pressed into the hot, soft sands. Once the dust settled, a cool breeze blew between his wrists, hovering just above the desert floor and carrying pink cactus flower petals. Nathan watched the wind suddenly change direction and circle above a five-fingered footprint that was as large as a pizza box. The tips of the claw marks dug deep into the loose dirt. The breeze smoothed the sands, erasing the print. What in the world could make a footprint as large as that? He looked for more footprints and the string of cactus flower petals. There was nothing but the wide expanse of flat desert, which reached toward the edge of the horizon, where massive sandstone plateaus stood that were as faint and round as orange clouds. Clusters of sagebrush and gnarled oak trees peppered the sunbaked desert floor.

"Nathan! I have to get going!" his father yelled.

"Yeah, sure. I'll get my bags and bring them into the mobile home," Nathan said to himself, unsure whether or not he had seen a large footprint at all.

Moments later, Nathan entered the mobile home with his bags and the kernels his mother had bought for his science project. Though it was still pretty warm inside, it was way more comfortable than being outside. The mobile home was narrow and long. The living room extended into the kitchen area to his left. Beyond the kitchen was Nali's room and an empty area where washing machines would have gone. Nathan's father was stacking the cases of water there. To Nathan's right was a hallway that led to a nonfunctioning bathroom and the only other bedroom, where Nathan was going to be sleeping.

Nali had redecorated since he had been here. There were two large bookshelves stuffed with books. Most of the book spines were faded and frayed. At the very top of the bookshelves stood Nali's collection of yé'ii figures, which were carved out of twisted branches of cottonwood. Their wooden faces, frozen in their various expressions, stared down at Nathan. Clothed in leather, some wore tiny pieces of turquoise in their necklaces, earrings, and bracelets. Among her collection of wooden yé'iis were eight large glass jars filled with seeds of different colors and shapes. There were so many colors, they looked like jelly beans. The largest jar had "Corn" written on a strip of masking tape. There were also beans, watermelon, squash, and other vegetables. Nali had said that these seeds were from her own childhood, when the entire Church Rock valley was carpeted in grass that grew as high as her knees.

On the walls, Nali had hung photos of Nathan, his father, and Uncle Jet. One of the photos was of him at last year's Science and Engineering Fair. He held a blue ribbon in one hand and a Geiger counter in the other. For last year's experiment, he had compared the background radiation around the mobile home with the background radiation in the Phoenix valley. There was a noticeable difference. Phoenix had twice the amount of background radiation. In his conclusion, Nathan hypothesized that the higher levels in Phoenix were due to the presence of hospitals and cell phone usage. The nearest hospital to Nali's was thirteen miles away in Gallup, New Mexico. In the picture from the fair, both his mom and father were at his sides. They didn't argue once that day. Nathan missed those moments when they didn't fight.

Next to that picture was one of Uncle Jet posing in the middle of a desert just as sunny and dry as the one outside. Wearing his Marine fatigues, Uncle Jet proudly held a black rifle across his broad chest. Nathan wanted to look like Uncle Jet when he grew up, tall and muscled, instead of being short and chubby. After being honorably discharged seven years ago, Uncle Jet lived out of his duffel bag in California, Nevada, and even Colorado. Last Nathan had heard, Uncle Jet was working as a security guard at one of the casinos in Albuquerque.

Nathan's father entered, carrying the last of the ten cases of bottled water. His father hustled to the kitchen and dropped it on the plastic tiles. "All right, I'm gonna hit the outhouse and then I need to head out. You still have time to change your mind."

"I'm good," Nathan said in a tone that meant he was done talking. His father sighed and then walked outside.

Nathan waddled his way down the hallway to his room, the straps of his heavy duffel bag scraping his neck. Once in, he let the bag fall onto the floor and hunched over to fish out his phone's charging cable. He pulled out the cables and out of habit plugged in his phone to charge. The battery was at 30 percent and there wasn't a single cell reception bar. When the familiar *ding* didn't happen, he remembered there was no electricity. Still, this was much better than being around Leandra.

Nathan sat down on the stiff mattress that was tucked against the wall underneath the room's window. To call this a mattress, he thought, would be like calling a cracker a piece of bread. On the wall panel opposite the window was a fist-sized crater.

"Nathan! I'm leaving!" his father yelled. Nathan lurched outside to say goodbye to him, even though he was still mad. Why didn't his father understand that Las Vegas was supposed to be for just the two of them!

"Well, son, I'm heading out," Nathan's father said.

"Okay," Nathan said. He looked at the ground, avoiding his father's face.

"Absolute last chance. Las Vegas? Pools? Video games?"

"I said I'm good!" Nathan practically shouted.

"Is it because of Leandra?" his father asked.

Nathan could feel his father's eyes trying to look into his. "No," Nathan said, not caring how sharp and angry the word sounded. In the side of his vision, he saw Nali walking toward them from the firepit.

"Okay." His father patted his shoulder. His lips pulled into a sad grin. Nathan moved away. "Well, you got more guts than I do. I couldn't handle more than a few days here. One thing is for certain. You're going to have plenty of material for the 'What I Did Over Summer Break' essay."

"Sháh!" Nali butted in. Dough caked her rough knuckles. "You heard him. He's made up his mind and you need to respect it. Ha'át'íílá! Jó Vegas go diniyalá! Ni' 'at'ééd niba'! Leandra's going to have to wait when she lands. I didn't raise you to make women wait."

His father pulled him into a hug. "This doesn't count as my time with you, okay?"

Nathan pushed his father away from him. "Sure." Folding his arms over his tummy, Nathan looked at the empty cornfield, where rows of parallel plots looked like dark brown scabs. Anywhere that wasn't his father's eyes.

Nathan heard his father enter the shiny SUV and drive away.

A heaviness developed in the back of his throat. Like thick paint, it slowly dripped all the way down into the bottom of his stomach. He forced himself to not care and to not cry. Nathan finally looked. The dust cloud behind the SUV was still thick like morning smog in Phoenix. Despite his frustration with him, Nathan already missed his father.

Nali's rough hand rubbed the back of his neck and the base of his hairline. He smelled the sweet scent of flour. As if moving on its own, his hand reached out and held hers. Their hands squeezed bits of dough. The dust dissipated and there was no more trace of his father.

"All right, young hastiin," Nali said in an excited voice. "Txį'. Ch'iyáán 'adaal'įįgi bóhoo diłááł. Do you remember how to knead dough for frybread?" Nathan immediately craved frybread, with its crunchy exterior and soft interior. Nathan didn't remember how to knead the dough. But it was okay because Nali was patient and always allowed him to make mistakes.

Naaki

TWO

NATHAN WOKE IN THE MIDDLE of the night, shocked
that he wasn't in his own bedroom. Instead of the humming
motors of cars driving on the pavement outside his bedroom
window, he heard the sigh of the midnight breeze and the chorus of chirping crickets. He shivered. The thin, patchy blanket
didn't protect him from the cold desert night like his thick blanket at home did. There were mosquito bites on his forearms that
ached to be itched.

He felt childish for missing Phoenix, for wanting to be with
his mom in her apartment, or with his father in his apartment,
and for wanting to go back to the time when loud arguments
hadn't fractured their family. He could not stop himself from
saying, "Mom!" It was much louder than he intended. Hopefully, he hadn't awakened Nali.

His eyes watered. His vision blurred. The emptiness near the back of his throat returned and, like a whirlpool, it pulled everything into the shadow below his heart. He shoved his face into the pillow so that he'd be able to keep his tears a secret. Then he smelled a gentle fragrance of lavender and sage. Recognizing her smell, he said, "I'm sorry I woke you, Nali."

"It's okay. I was already awake," she said. Her blurry figure came into focus. She smiled underneath the bluish starlight that shone through the window above the mattress. She sat down next to him. Her long silver hair flowed down her shoulders.

"Hazhóó'ógo, shinálí," Nali said, almost singing the words. Her smooth and pretty voice warmed him. Her rough palm moved across his cheek and then across his brow. "Everything is going to be okay."

He told her, "I miss my mom and dad."

"Oh, shinálí," Nali said, smiling. "How about we make some tea, huh? You can make the fire. Doing physical things takes away the loneliness and longing." She stood up and pulled him off the mattress.

After putting on his sandals, Nathan met Nali in the cool, dark kitchen. A small oil lantern sat on the kitchen table, lighting up both the kitchen and the living room. Its wick emitted a gentle hiss and soft yellow light as a tiny petal of flame danced inside its glass hexagon.

Nali bit her lower lip, something she did whenever she was thirsty. She stood on tiptoe and reached into the back of the cabinets. Nathan noticed the quarter-full water bottle on the table.

Nali must have been in the kitchen getting a drink when she heard Nathan's crying.

"Aha! Here they are!" Nali withdrew two bulging Ziploc bags, one filled with bundles of lavender tied with white yarn, and another filled with loose leaves of gray-green sage.

They walked to the front door. Out of habit, Nathan grabbed the nearly empty bottle and threw it into the trash can. His mother didn't like it when trash was left on the table.

"Sháh!" Nali raised her voice, scaring him. His body tensed up. Her unexpected yell reminded Nathan of slamming doors and long nights of silent solitude in his old room playing video games. "Pull that out of the trash. Water is not trash," she said.

His cheeks warmed with guilt as he fished the bottle out of the trash can. Embarrassed, he placed it back on the table.

"I've been saving these especially for us. Txí'," she said, like she hadn't yelled at him just seconds ago.

She exited the mobile home. Nathan followed, wondering if she was still mad at him.

The cold air stung Nathan's cheeks as he stepped outside. A dim new moon shone among stars that sparkled like shards of light on the ocean. Satellites moved in straight paths in the cloudless sky, like ships passing each other without ever colliding.

Nali led him to the chaha'oh on their right, holding the oil lamp. Even though he was familiar with the layout of the mobile home site, the elongated shadows made the chaha'oh appear sinister. Even Nali's hogan, on their left, looked spooky. Bathed in shadows, the traditional home structure resembled a sleeping monster. Its rounded top looked like broad shoulders. In front of the east-facing entrance of the hogan, the metal fence posts of the cornfield poked out of the dry earth like splinters. She stopped and pointed to the woodpile. "Níléidi chizh ła' nidiijah shinálí, behind the chaha'oh. Go gather some wood chips."

Bits of wood chips crunched underneath his sandals when he entered the woodpile. Sawed circular tree trunks were stacked on their sides, creating a massive wall behind the chaha'oh. Under the light of the stars, he collected slivers of wood that would be perfect to start the fire. He also kept an eye out for any large footprints like the one he'd seen earlier. Something with feet that big would be hard to miss.

He returned to the firepit and arranged the pieces into a pyramid-like structure in the firepit. He crisscrossed their thin, pencil-like bodies so that the fire would be able to get oxygen, just the way Nali had taught him. Nathan enjoyed that the steps to building a fire could be repeated over and over again and the result would always be the same. It was dependable.

Nathan held the lighter to the wood. The heat from the small fire expanded and retracted with the tempo of a heartbeat. The fire bloomed among the wood chips. As the flame grew in heat and height, Nathan added bigger and bigger pieces of wood.

"Done," Nathan proudly said.

Nali finished washing the charred kettle. "'Áłtsé, we need water first."

"I'll get it, Nali." Nathan took the lantern and kettle from her. He hurried to the tanks.

The two plastic water tanks sat by the side walls of the chaha'oh, on the bed of an old truck whose front half was missing. Their spouts hung off the tailgate. Nathan lifted the lantern. "DRINK-ING" and "CLEANING" were written in black paint on the exteriors. He opened the spigot of the tank marked "DRINK-ING" and felt the weight of the rushing water push the kettle downward. In a few seconds, the kettle was full.

Something grunted on his left. Nali was setting up chairs by the fire to his right. He closed the spout and raised the lantern to inspect the branchy walls of the chaha'oh. Something was on a leafy branch. It was a large horned toad, certainly the largest Nathan had even seen. Spikes poked out of its seven- or eight-inch body. But was it standing on its hind legs? And wearing a small turquoise necklace? Nathan tiptoed and lifted the lantern higher. The shadows of the branches warped and twisted, and the horned toad disappeared.

"Nali!" Nathan screamed.

"What's going on over there?" Nali asked.

He regained his footing and looked again. "There's a huge horned toad, I mean a cheii!"

"A cheii? Hurry, grab it and put it on your heart!"

"I think it was wearing a turquoise necklace," Nathan said.

"Turquoise necklace, is!" Nali walked over and grabbed the lantern from Nathan. With the light, they both searched the branches. Nathan wondered what Nali would say. One of the branches shook. Then, suddenly, a chipmunk jumped from one branch to another. It faced them and angrily chirped.

"Wah!" Nali said. "It's just a chipmunk."

"No, it wasn't that. It was the largest cheii in the world, I swear! And it was standing on its back legs like this." Nathan locked his knees and raised his heels off the ground.

"Hágoshįį. Whatever it is, just leave it be," Nali said in a tone that was similar to the one Nathan's mom and father used when they talked about adult things in his presence. That annoying tone made Nathan feel small and ignored.

"It wasn't a stupid chipmunk," Nathan whispered. He took one last look at the branches, hoping to see whatever it was again before he returned to the firepit.

Nathan placed the kettle onto the charred rectangular cast iron grate that was next to the firepit. Nali used a metal poker to scooch bright embers underneath the kettle, rustling up embers that floated like fireflies. Nathan sat in the chair next to Nali.

"Are you excited to begin planting tomorrow?" Nali asked.

"Yeah, sure," Nathan said. He thought about the horned toad and the massive footprint. Aside from those two events, this month was going to be so boring—and it was all his father's fault.

"You don't sound excited," Nali said.

"I am." He wasn't. He truly wanted to be in his own bed right now or playing an online round of battle royale with Weslee and Steven.

"It's okay to not be comfortable out here." She must have sensed Nathan's lack of enthusiasm. "It's tough living and not everyone finds it relaxing. We have a long summer, and if you keep that attitude, it's going to be even longer. Be patient. Give it time. For me?"

"Okay, Nali." The kettle started whistling. Nathan inserted a sprig of lavender and two sage leaves into the kettle.

"Are your friends working on their projects over the summer, too?"

"No, just me."

"Oh? What are they doing?"

"They took off." Weslee was going to summer camp and Steven was going on some family vacation to Disneyland or Disney World.

"What about your other friends?"

That question stung. He didn't really have any other friends. Weslee and Steven were the only ones who didn't call him "Butterball." He folded his arms over his stomach and wished it would go away.

The tea should be ready, Nathan thought. He poured steaming liquid into the mugs that Nali had brought out. Nali blew on the tea in her cup, took a sip, and grinned.

"Mmm, shił łikan. Hágo, come over here." She pulled Nathan closer to her. He rested his head on her soft shoulder.

She continued to take small sips of her tea. Nali inhaled deeply and said, "Look at all the sǫ', Nathan. 'Sǫ" means 'star.'" She pointed up with her lips. "Nínít'į, in the Navajo way, each and every sǫ' has a story behind it."

"That's a lot of stories," Nathan said.

Nali chuckled. "Yes. Only medicine men and medicine women are able to remember each story. The medicine folk say that the sǫ' sing their stories to each other. Once you know their stories, they'll sing to you as well."

Nathan gazed into the sky and stared at the Milky Way cluster. "Do they sing to you?"

"Sometimes, when I pay real good attention. 'Iishjáshįį, if you really pay attention, you'll notice other things, too. Out here, away from the big cities, the Holy Beings have a much easier time connecting with us."

"I saw a big footprint earlier."

"'Aoo'. Sometimes like that. Sometimes like little cheiis that wear turquoise necklaces." She smiled at him. "Respect them and let them do their thing while we do ours."

Normally, he would have shrugged off Nali's comments, but then he had seen the footprint and the horned toad that wore a turquoise necklace. "What do the sǫ' sound like?"

"Like birds when the sun rises," Nali said.

"Cool, I guess."

"Yes, sir, very cool! But sǫ' are also very shy. They sing only to their friends. Once you know what story each one represents, they'll be your best friend and they'll sing for you."

"Okay, Nali. Sure," Nathan said. He yawned.

"Once you earn the stories, you'll realize that the brighter the star, the bigger the story. In my heart, I believe your story is going to be as big as the sun."

Nathan rested his head against her shoulder again. Nali always knew what to say to make him feel all right about himself. Perhaps these next two months weren't going to be that bad.

Nali pointed to the stars above and called certain clusters by their Navajo names, while Nathan's fire consumed the last bits of wood. Nali asked Nathan to tell her a story of the Hero Twins. Nathan did his best to recount the story of the Hero Twins, who felled the Giant known as Human-Eater. Not long into the story, the fire dimmed into embers and then the embers extinguished. Nali ushered Nathan back into the mobile home and toward his hard mattress. She told him that they were going to have to wake up early so that they could work in the cornfield before it got too hot. Nathan fell onto the mattress and into a peaceful sleep.

Táá'

THREE

THE NEXT DAY, NATHAN STARTED his science project. The first part was to plant Nali's traditional kernels and then the modern, store-bought variety. The sun was barely brimming over the horizon and the air was still chilly when Nathan thrust the shovel head into the dry cornfield. Dust erupted as if the earth was exhaling. Birds darted through the air, chirping as they chased bugs with open beaks. Lizards scurried across the dirt leaving slashes in the earth. Yawning, Nathan tossed the cinnamon-colored sands to the side. He walked two steps to the right of the hole in a clockwise curve and thrust the shovel again into the cornfield.

Nali held her jar of colorful seeds against her hip. Singing in Navajo, she bent over and scattered a handful of red, blue, and purple kernels in the hole. Even though he couldn't understand the song, Nathan enjoyed the melody. There was a structure that he noticed. She repeated certain words like "naadą́ą́'," and "nahałtin," which were "corn" and "rain." She pushed the soil over the seeds and patted it.

"What are you singing, Nali?" Nathan asked.

"Blessing songs and rain songs," Nali said. "'Ałk'idą́ą́, our ancestors planted in this spiral pattern. They would place every kernel individually and sprinkle tádídíín onto each one."

"Sounds like a lot of work."

"You bet!"

By the time they finished the traditional kernels, the air had warmed considerably. Sweat crept into his eyes and stung them. He rubbed the corners of his eyes and then looked at the pattern. It was the most uneven, wobbly spiral Nathan had ever seen. Whatever, he was done.

"Why don't we take a break before we begin your store-bought kernels?" Nali asking, massaging her lower back with her knuckles.

"That sounds cool." Nathan aired out his palms, trying not to upset the blister that was forming.

They walked to the chaha'oh. Nali handed Nathan a bottle of lukewarm water.

Nathan gulped down a mouthful. It was so quiet that he could hear his throat squeeze the liquid downward. Self-conscious, he tried to drink more quietly. "Do you really think there's going to be a difference between the traditional and the store-bought kernels?"

"What do you think? It's your science experiment. Tell me your hypothesis."

"Probably not." Nathan examined his variables. The soil was the same for both. The amount of sunlight was the same for both. Because of the ongoing drought, Nathan would have full control of the amount of water both groups received. At the end of the project, Nathan would measure both groups to determine which was better suited for droughty conditions. "Right?"

"We'll find out soon enough." Nali finished her bottle of water and went back into the cornfield.

Nathan left his bottle on the table and hurried after her. He gripped the shovel handle firmly and got back to digging. He hoped the traditional kernels grew taller than the modern store-bought ones. "Traditional" and "modern": those would be the perfect names to label the two groups of corn.

Nathan and Nali planted the modern kernels in four rows of twelve. Nali didn't pray or sing for them. As a result, planting these bright yellow kernels that were uniform in shape and size didn't take long. The sun was at its highest and its most furious when they finished; its heat sizzled the back of Nathan's neck.

Nali wiped sweat off her neck. "Shooyá, k'ad 'ałtso. Dichin nísin. I want pasta for lunch."

Nali's definition of pasta was an off-brand Chef Boyardee. The only time Nathan ate stuff like that was when he spent time with Nali. His mom did not like to eat food that was suffused with GMOs or not organic or a whole bunch of other phrases and words that Nathan didn't really pay much attention to. She said it was bad and Nathan obeyed for her sake.

"Sounds like a plan."

"Hágoshį́į, go wash up," Nali said, pointing to the water tanks. She gathered the shovels and went to put them back in the hogan.

He couldn't wait to soak his blisters in water. Nathan walked to the water tanks. He kept alert for any weird footprints on the ground or jewelry-wearing horned toads in the branches of the chaha'oh.

Nali had simply placed a large bowl on top of a wooden stump next to the Cleaning tank on the eastern side of the chaha'oh and called it the washing area. To make it fancier, she also had hung a cracked oval mirror on a nearby branch. The gross brown water inside the bowl made Nathan nauseous. He poured it out and refilled the bin with some fresh Cleaning water.

It made no sense why Nali would want to live here when she had a perfectly good home in Farmington. There, she had electricity, cell phone reception, and, most important, air-conditioning. Here, there was absolutely nothing to do, except get bored to death.

Once his blisters calmed in the water, Nathan splashed water on his forearms and his face. The water evaporated almost instantly; his skin became dry again. He gripped the soap bar and his pain reawakened with piercing stings. Still better than hanging with Leandra, Nathan reminded himself. To think, his father actually had asked Nathan to hug her. Seriously, he'd rather kiss a spider!

◊ ◊ ◊

The air inside the mobile home was at least twenty degrees cooler than outside. Here, in northwestern New Mexico, the heat was dry, and all you had to do was step out of the sun and the temperature dropped dramatically. In Phoenix during late summer, however, you couldn't escape the humidity. Your clothes stuck to your body like you had stepped out of a sauna.

Nathan walked to the table and sat next to Nali. There was a bowl set out for him filled with off-yellow pasta swamped in bright orange sauce. It didn't look very appetizing. Nathan tasted a spoonful and immediately spit it back out into his bowl. It was salty, sweet, and weirdly tangy. There was a lingering plastic aftertaste, too. "Gross."

Nali lifted the pasta to her face and sniffed. "It smells normal." She placed the bowl back in front of Nathan.

"Maybe it's spoiled?" Nathan said. He pushed the bowl away from him and wondered what else Nali had to eat. It was just too hot to cook outside right now, so it would have to be something quick and easy like a sandwich.

Nali got up and walked to the area where she kept all her aluminum cans for recycling. She pulled the pasta can out and looked at it. She said, "'Éí dooda, expires in two years. You're being picky."

"Don't you have anything else to eat?"

"Yaa! Just eat it."

"I'm gonna make myself a sandwich." Nathan didn't care

if he had upset Nali. He was starving and this was not what he wanted to eat. Nathan got up from the table to look for the ingredients for a peanut butter jam sandwich. But he found that Nali had only the cheap brands.

"Don't you have anything else?" Nathan asked, disappointed.

"We can pick up some food you like tomorrow in Gallup. But for now, you're going to have to settle," Nali said.

"Ugh! Why do you live out here so far away from everything? Wouldn't it be easier to just live in Farmington?" Nathan grabbed the peanut butter, jam, and bread.

"That's true, shináli." In between spoonfuls of food, she said, "I choose to live here: 'Éí biniinaa, this land was passed down to me from my own great-grandma. She survived the relocation times, when the whites rounded up all us Navajo and took us to Hwééldi. When she returned, the US government gave her a piece of paper saying that this land, kwe'é sikéhíjíí, right here where we sit, belonged to her." Nali rested her hand above her heart. "I was about your age when she told me, as she was passing, that she survived relocation times because she wanted her grandchildren, her grandchildren's grandchildren, to be able to live here, the area where my clan, your father's clan, originated. 'Éí biniinaa, that's why I live here in the summers."

Nathan sat beside Nali and ate the sandwich he had just made, feeling embarrassed about his bratty behavior. The dry peanut butter had torn the flaky bread and the syrupy jam was spilling over. It tasted old and stale.

"We're going to have to fill up the water tanks. Your corn is going to need water if it's going to grow in this drought," Nali said. She pushed the bowl of pasta in front of Nathan after he finished his sandwich. He forced the sludge into his stomach. Nathan could deal with lackluster sandwiches and awful canned pasta, especially when comparing his discomfort to the struggles of his ancestor who had survived Hwééldi.

After they hitched the water tanks to her truck, Nali drove northward toward the mountains. On the drive, they listened to KTNN, a station that was only in Navajo and that played old country songs that sounded grainy. It was deadly how boring it was.

While Nathan powered his phone with his car charger, he checked his phone to see if either Weslee or Steven had responded to the text he had sent a few miles back. Nothing. Maybe he couldn't receive their texts because of poor cell phone reception. Or maybe they were too busy having fun to even think about him.

Nathan opened a game on his phone, but it wouldn't start because he needed the internet to log in. He couldn't do anything except listen to these boring country songs. "Ah!"

"What's going on?" Nali asked.

"I can't do anything!" Nathan said.

He tossed his cell phone onto the console and then folded his arms. He looked outside and saw a tall metal fence with looping razors at its top. They drove past large metal signs that read "Warning," "Church Rock Mine," and "Radioactive Area." Nathan didn't care to read more than that.

"Ha'át'íílá? You're going to break your new cell phone!"

Nathan groaned and picked his phone back up. There were no cracks on the screen, thanks to the heavy-duty phone case that his father insisted on buying.

Nali turned up the music louder and the DJ was quickly speaking in Navajo like an auctioneer. Then a Navajo song, similar to those Nali sang in the cornfield, came on. Nali drove into hilly terrain and higher altitudes. The trucked veered off the dirt road and into pathless wilderness.

Half an hour later, Nali parked so that the water tanks were next to the hand-operated water pump. The two of them stepped out of the truck. Nathan looked at the spiny canopy of the tall, thin pine trees that grew toward the cloud-patched skies. Round brown acorns weighed down the thick branches of oak trees. A tiny chipmunk snatched an acorn and leaped to another branch. A robin landed on the earth and overturned leaves, searching for chubby bugs.

"Lots of animals here because of the groundwater," Nali said.

It seemed to take forever to fill up both water tanks, and each minute that they pumped Nathan wanted more and more to go back home to Phoenix. Living without running water and electricity was just awful.

It was around six thirty when they returned to the mobile home. The sun inched closer to the western horizon. Nali immediately started cooking dinner on an open fire. Nathan grabbed a bucket and gently poured water over each of the seeds. The blisters had grown and pulsed in red painful flashes whenever the handle rubbed against them.

Nali was nowhere near done with making dinner after he watered the cornfield.

"If you're bored, go chop some wood," Nali said.

There's nothing better to do, Nathan thought. He put on some gloves and grabbed the ax. He swung its metal head into the stump in front of him. Tiny shards of twigs were flung in every direction and the stump split in two. Chopping wood wasn't bad. Once Nathan found a flow, it was slightly fun. Nathan lost track of time, and before he realized it, he had chopped a large mound of firewood that needed to be stacked. His armpits were sweating, and parts of his shirt stuck to his shoulder and stomach.

"Da'ósą!" Nali yelled from the cooking pit.

Nathan could smell the amazing aroma of fried potatoes and Spam. He sat down on a pile of stacked firewood to catch his breath. Then tiny furry legs tapped his bare forearm. He jolted his hand back and screamed.

"Nathan?" Nali shouted.

There was a brown spider, as large as a strawberry, crawling right beside him. Nathan jumped away, lost his balance, and fell onto the ground. The spider turned slowly to face Nathan, raising one large leg at a time. Nathan grabbed a nearby piece of firewood. He approached the spider and was going to slam the freaky abomination out of existence when Nali yelled, "Wait, Nathan! 'Ałtsé! Don't hurt him!"

Don't hurt this monster? It had to be killed! And then doubled-killed, just to be sure!

"Cheii Chizh, we mean you no harm. Quick, call him cheii. If you do, then he'll have to treat you like his grandson and he won't hurt you."

Nathan stared at the brown spider. He was supposed to call this thing cheii, like the horned toad. Why in the world would he do such a thing! With reluctance, Nathan addressed what would most certainly be in his nightmares that night: "What's up . . . Cheii Chizh?" The spider remained motionless. All eight of his eyes reflected Nathan's terrified face.

"Cheii Chizh, go about your way. We're sorry we disturbed you," Nali said. As if it understood, the spider crawled away and into the heart of the woodpile.

Nathan knew that the spider was back there, probably craving a taste of his hand. "Why did you let a thing like that live?"

"Cheii Chizh doesn't bite. You know all those bugs that do bite, like mosquitoes? Spiders eat them. So, in a way, spiders protect us."

"They're not going to bite me?"

"Not in a million years. You just called the head honcho cheii. He's gonna treat you like his grandchild."

"What if it comes back?" Nathan asked. His voice quivered. His hands were jittery. Nali must have seen how horrified he was. Seriously, if it was a millipede or a scorpion, Nathan could deal.

"Stay on the other side of the pile; Cheii Chizh won't bother you."

"How do you know that?"

"They like dark shadows. So, stay where the sun is shining."

"They? You mean there's more?" Nathan's breathing sped up. Nope. That was it. No amount of persuasion would convince him to approach the woodpile. Nathan drew the line at more than one spider. No more chopping for the day, or for the rest of his time here.

Later, Nathan sat inside the mobile home kitchen. He gathered mounds of fried potatoes, canned sweet corn, and Spam with Nali's fresh tortillas. The food took away some of his frustration. He realized that today he had been a jerk to Nali. But he didn't know how to say sorry to her. So instead he asked, "Hey, Nali, where's Uncle Jet?"

"Your uncle has a job in Albuquerque." Nali sighed deeply. "Hopefully he can hold on to this one. Did you like the food?"

"Yeah. It's good." Nathan sensed that Nali didn't want to talk about Uncle Jet.

"I'll tell you what, yiską́ągo', tomorrow, when we're in Gallup, let's stop by the library and get some books to read. For both you and me."

In Gallup, he would have reception and could reconnect with the world. "Sounds like a plan."

"I know this isn't easy living. But I do appreciate you spending your summer with me, shinálí. I cherish our time together."

"I do, too, Nali." Nathan felt like this was the time to say sorry for his attitude earlier. But it was very hard to do.

Early the next morning, Nathan went to water the cornfield while Nali did her morning prayer with corn pollen. When he arrived, he was surprised to find narrow slits in all the traditional planting spots they dug yesterday. Nothing had happened to the modern planting spots. There were also tiny footprints. Nathan poked his finger down, expecting to feel the pointed end of the kernels. There was nothing. All the seeds he had planted in the traditional group were gone.

Dį́į́'

FOUR

A BREEZE BRUSHED AGAINST NATHAN'S ankle, erasing the weird tiny footprints, just as it happened with the larger ones. Who or what would take the kernels, and for what purpose? Nathan had a feeling that whatever had done this wasn't natural. He stood up and went to Nali, who was standing on the eastern edge of the cornfield, praying.

"Nahadzáán shimá. Yádiłhił shítáá'. Díí'ko hozhó dooleeł. Shiyáázh Jet shá bik'é jidlíído'." Her eyes were closed, and she pressed her beaded tádídíín pouch against her chest.

Nathan didn't want to interrupt her. But she kept praying and praying and praying. It felt like an hour had passed when Nali finally said, "Hózhó náhásdlį́į́, hózhó náhásdlį́į́, hózhó náhásdlį́į́, hózhó náhásdlį́į́, amen." She then sprinkled corn pollen to the four directions.

"Nali, something stole the traditional seeds."

"Huh? Stole them? What did?" she asked.

"I don't know."

"Probably that chipmunk we saw earlier."

Nathan shook his head. It wouldn't have been able to dig such strange holes that were like narrow tunnels. A bird couldn't have done it, either. Even then, why did it leave the modern kernels alone, and take only the traditional?

"I don't think it was an animal," Nathan said.

"You're going to have to replant," Nali said.

"Really?" Whatever stole his seeds, Nathan hated it.

After breakfast, Nathan searched the cornfield, looking for more evidence of the thief. There were no actual footprints, not even a slight scratch. How could anything dig in this way? The closest thing Nathan could think of was an anteater with a long tongue that could slither down narrow crevices. Still, there had to be footprints. In any case, he was going to have to get the shovels from the hogan and begin the whole process again.

Nali stepped out of the mobile home with her big jar of multi-colored corn kernels and a cup that was steaming in her other hand. She took loud sips on her way over to him.

"Nali, look at this." Nathan pointed at the crevice.

"Huh, what do you know? Well, it ain't a chipmunk."

"I told you."

"That you did. Here." She handed him the jar and turned around to head back into the mobile home. "I'm going to get ready for Gallup."

Nathan didn't want to dig the holes again. The blisters on his hands had finally popped, and whenever he squeezed his hands, the sting wasn't as sharp.

"Whatever," Nathan said. He wasn't going to re-dig the entire traditional spiral design again! He opened the jar and slid his hands in between the cool, smooth kernels. He pushed the kernels into the slits and then stomped as hard as he could to collapse the holes. When he was done, he said a very quick three-word prayer: "Bless these seeds."

As he left the cornfield, Nathan looked at the feeble fence. The posts along the edges were leaning in various directions. The smooth wires that connected each post had snapped and were lying on the ground below. Clearly, the fence was not protecting the cornfield and would have to be replaced. He screwed the lid back on the seed jar and went to the mobile home.

On the drive to Gallup, Nathan couldn't wait to hear his mother's voice again. But he didn't have reception until they reached the highway. Immediately after the wheels sped onto the smooth pavement, his phone got a bar of service and Nathan received several texts from his mom, Weslee, Steven, and even his father.

"You kids and your toys," Nali said, with a quiet chuckle.

Nathan quickly wrote a few replies. When he texted his friends and his mom back, he felt a little proud to tell them he was able to chop wood and haul water—things they couldn't do. Nathan assumed his father was probably too busy with Leandra to want a text from him. Even the thought of her name made his face scrunch up. His father wouldn't have noticed his text anyway. So, he didn't bother sending one.

Nali drove through Gallup to the main public library, where Nathan checked out a science-fiction trilogy about kids who were drafted by the government to fight an interstellar war against aliens. Before they left the library, Nathan charged his phone and used the internet to update all his games as well as download new ones that didn't require reception.

At the grocery store, Nathan was able to grab his favorite snacks and cereals. He wanted to buy some fresh cold milk, but Nali said that because she didn't have a refrigerator, he would have to use powdered milk.

On their way to get the powdered milk by the baking supplies, they passed a stand containing packets of seeds. Nali reached for a packet of watermelon seeds.

"I love watermelon," Nali said.

"You wanna plant it with the corn?"

"That's not a bad idea. But watermelons take three months to harvest. You and I will both be back in school by the time they're ready."

"How about other plants?"

"Now we're talking. We can do beans and squash. I'd love more than anything to have a full garden again."

"Hey, Nali, if something is stealing the seeds, do we need to fix the fence?"

"'Áyóo nanitł'a," Nali said. "It'll be hard to do. But I'm willing to do it if you are."

"That'd be cool."

Nali smiled. She tossed several seed packets into the cart. "Yes, sir, very cool. Let's have lunch here and then head back. Are you craving anything?"

"Burgers and fries!" Nathan said.

"Well, I can't grow those in the cornfield!" Nali said.

Nathan got carsick while reading the first book of the trilogy that he had checked out. So, he instead played a video game on his cell phone that didn't need reception.

"Did you text your zhé'é back?" Nali asked out of the blue.

Nathan shifted uncomfortably in his seat. He didn't want to text his father. "No."

"Aren't you going to tell him that you're doing okay? Parents love to hear from their kids that they are fine. It's very hard for a parent to not hear from their kid for a long time."

Her voice sounded sad. Nali had mentioned that she hadn't heard from Uncle Jet in a while. Was Nali thinking about Uncle Jet?

Nathan wondered if this was how his father felt. As mad as he was at his father, as much as his father deserved it, Nathan didn't like intentionally causing his father the same sadness that Nali was feeling.

"I'll text him." He opened the chat with his father. He didn't bother reading what his father had said and sent out, *I'm fine.*

"I'm sure your zhé'é will appreciate your text, shinálí." She turned the truck off the pavement, and they were back on the bumpy dirt road.

Nali drove for a few minutes before she asked, "Are you mad at your zhé'é?"

"No," Nathan said. He blew off the heads of several hostile aliens.

"Are you sure?"

"Yes," Nathan said. He didn't hide the fact that Nali was annoying him.

"When you're ready to talk, I'm here to listen."

Nathan wasn't mad at his father. At least not directly. Yeah, he had messed up his summer. But Leandra was also to blame! She always interfered and got in between them. She was so . . . Nathan couldn't finish that thought without saying an adult word. Why couldn't his father dump her?

"It's okay to be mad with your zhé'é, you know."

"I'm not mad at him!" Nathan yelled. Nathan shut off his phone. He looked out the window and at the mobile home in the distance. Couldn't Nali see he wasn't mad at his father? He was mad at Leandra! It was how she distracted his father from seeing how his mom. . . . There was someone sitting on the steps of the mobile home. "There's someone over there," Nathan said.

"You can tell me what's . . . My word!" Nali gasped. She parked the truck. Her hands covered her open mouth.

Nathan looked at the man. His hair had grown and was tucked

underneath a faded black baseball cap. His black leather jacket, that had a round US Marine seal on its right arm, hung over his right shoulder. His skin was darker than in the picture in the mobile home's living room. Uncle Jet smiled broadly at Nathan.

'Ashdla'
FIVE

NATHAN JUMPED OUT WHEN NALI parked the truck closer to the mobile home. He sprinted toward him and said, "Uncle Jet!"

Uncle Jet stood up, placed his black leather jacket on the duffel bag at his feet, and walked toward Nathan with his arms open for a hug. "Hey! I wasn't expecting you here."

Nathan wrapped his arms around Uncle Jet. He smelled like dried sweat and beer.

"I missed ya, too, buddy," Uncle Jet said, and hugged him tightly. Uncle Jet then held him at arm's length. He said, "You're growing, little man! Last time I saw you, you were this high." He held his hand at Nathan's rib cage. "Shoot, you're going to be taller than me."

"I hope so," Nathan said.

"Nathan," Nali said by the truck. "Bring the groceries into the kitchen."

"Mama." Uncle Jet's eyes met Nali's. For a moment, they stared at each other—Nali's eyes narrow and angry, Uncle Jet's wide and ashamed. He ran his fingers through his hair and forced a smile through clenched teeth. "It's good to see you, Mama."

Nali approached Uncle Jet. Her nostrils flared and her eyes narrowed. Uncle Jet wilted under her angry expression. Nali was going to yell at Uncle Jet at any moment.

"Did you lose your job?" Nali asked. "Did you get kicked out of your apartment?"

"Jeez, at least hear me out before you jump down my throat," Uncle Jet said.

"Nathan, groceries. Now," Nali said in a stern and scary voice.

"Okay," Nathan said.

He grabbed as many bags of groceries as he could from the back of the truck and hurried inside.

It took a moment for his eyes to adjust to the dark interior. Nathan heaved the groceries onto the kitchen table and went to the window. Nali's knuckles dug into her waist and her brows were furrowed. Uncle Jet was looking at the ground beside her, his head slouched in between his shoulders like a turtle's.

Nali's voice was getting louder. "I've listened, time and time again. It's always the same excuse. Enough! Act like that while Nathan is here, and I'll take you to jail myself." Nali jammed her finger into Uncle Jet's chest.

"For what? What did I do?" Uncle Jet asked. He stepped out of view.

"You punched a hole in my wall, so to begin with, destruction of property. . . ."

There was a loud thud behind him. Nathan turned around and noticed a wooden yé'ii figure on the floor in front of the bookcase. He went over to pick it up. Nathan looked up at Nali's wooden yé'ii collection on top of the bookcase. Row upon row of frozen faces peered down on him, and twice as many eyes scrutinized him. Nathan grew conscious of their gaze. He tugged his shirt down and pushed his glasses back onto the bridge of his nose. Nathan placed the wooden yé'ii that had fallen off back by one of the jars of seeds that was filled with thin pumpkin seeds.

"What else was I supposed to do?" Uncle Jet's voice echoed in the mobile home.

There were still a few bags of groceries in the truck that Nathan wasn't eager to get. He didn't like being near adults who were fighting. He decided to put these groceries away in the meantime. Hopefully by the time Uncle Jet and Nali were finished arguing, he could go back outside and get the last few bags.

He felt responsible for their argument, even though he knew that Nali and Uncle Jet were not arguing because of something he did. But it still felt like when his mom and father were together and fought all the time. As much as he tried not to, Nathan choked up.

◊ ◊ ◊

The sun slipped behind the western plateau. Shadows dripped like dark purple paint down the fiery orange sides on the rocky plateaus in the distance. Darkness quickly stretched across the land, blanketing miles of sand. The air grew cooler with each passing minute. The fire Nathan had started to cook dinner shone brighter than the feeble glow of the setting sun.

Nali quietly stared at the small amount of potatoes and Spam on her plate. Uncle Jet, on the other hand, ate and ate! He shoveled mounds of food into his mouth, chewing for a few seconds and then washing the large lumps down with gulps of bottled water.

"Shiyáázh, you're going to clean up my hogan," she said suddenly to Uncle Jet.

"I am?" Uncle Jet responded. Food fell out of his mouth.

"Once it's clean, you can sleep in it," she said.

"Wait. What?" Uncle Jet looked at Nathan and nudged his shoulder. "All right! You got yourself a deal."

"Then you're going to start fixing up that truck of yours sitting in my front yard."

"Your front yard?" Uncle Jet looked at the vast space around the three of them. "Where exactly does your front yard end?"

"Don't get smart with me," Nali said. She sipped from her cup of lavender tea. "After that, fix up the cornfield fence."

"Now, why would I do that? There's no rain," Uncle Jet said.

"When the drought ends and the rains return," Nali said, "I want to have vegetables again."

"You know what? No," Uncle Jet said. "I'm not going to fix the fence. It's a waste of time. In all these years, the rain hasn't returned. And you know what—it's not going to!"

Nali pulled the food away from Uncle Jet.

"Oh, that trick again." Uncle Jet dusted himself off and walked to the hogan. "Whatever."

"Eat your food," Nali snapped at Nathan. He wasn't as invisible as he had hoped. He slowly sipped his bottled water, feeling her stare.

"Shinálí, I don't mean for my anger to go to you. Your uncle has a way of getting under my skin," she said, in a much calmer voice. Nali looked toward the distance, where Uncle Jet had stormed off.

"What did he do to make you angry?"

"Ever since his tour of duty, he's been different. But it wasn't always this bad, not until his father . . ." Nali shook her head and pressed her knuckles against her lips. "This is not your problem, shinálí. Focus on your project and let me handle your uncle."

Nathan remembered when his paternal grandpa, James, passed away three years ago. His father took his passing pretty hard and cried for weeks. "Is there anything I can do?"

She prepared a plate of food and handed it to him. "You can take this food to him. He's probably still hungry."

Nathan stood up and grabbed the plate.

"Shinálí, don't tell him I told you to do this. His pride will get the better of him."

◊ ◊ ◊

Nathan stepped into his uncle's footprints. His stride wasn't as long as his uncle's, so he had to stretch his legs and carefully balance. Uncle Jet sat in front of the hogan, staring at the rising, slim moon. When he noticed that Nathan was heading toward him, Uncle Jet quickly put out his cigarette. The trails of cigarette smoke floated upward and disintegrated.

"Sup, little man."

"I wanted to bring you more food." Saying that wasn't exactly lying, but it still made Nathan a little bit uncomfortable.

"Your grandma put you up to this?"

"No. I snuck it away." Now he *was* lying. He twisted his right foot into the sand.

"You don't lie much, do you?" Uncle Jet smirked. "Probably better that way. But for now, let's pretend that you did sneak it away and that your covert operation was a success." Uncle Jet took the food from Nathan. "Let's keep that bit of intel between us."

"Uncle Jet, why is Nali mad at you?"

"It's probably easier to name the things she isn't mad at me for."

"Are you mad at her?"

Uncle Jet shifted and squinted. "I, um, I don't know. What makes you say that?"

"Well, when my mom is mad at my father for one thing, he is also mad at her for some other thing. My father frowns." Nathan demonstrated. "That's how I know he's mad about something."

"No, I think it's more like this, Nathan." Uncle Jet frowned and tilted his head forward. He scrunched his brows.

"He does that, too!" Nathan smiled.

"I bet he does this, too." Uncle Jet stuck his tongue out at Nathan.

Nathan was a bit old for that trick, but it still made him laugh. Nathan did notice that Uncle Jet avoided answering his question. He probably wasn't ready to think about that. So, Nathan didn't push the question further. He stayed with Uncle Jet and told him about Joyce, the girl in his class that he had a crush on.

Uncle Jet grinned. "I think I can help you with that."

Uncle Jet talked about the importance of maintaining a good hair style and about having confidence. One seemed easier than the other.

When Uncle Jet asked him what he was doing with Nali out here, Nathan told him about his science experiment and that something was stealing the seeds. He didn't believe it was a rodent because the holes were narrow and directly atop the seeds themselves. When Uncle Jet found out that Nathan was using the cornfield for his experiment, he agreed to fix the cornfield posts. Uncle Jet even suggested capturing what was stealing the seeds by setting up a steel cage. Nathan grew excited, knowing that soon he could continue with his science project.

Hastą́ą́
SIX

NATHAN WOKE UP IN THE middle of the night with some
brand-new mosquito bites and an immediate need to go to the
bathroom. He found his sandals and his cell phone and worked
up the courage to step outside by himself. He navigated the
dark, silent mobile home, hoping not to disturb Uncle Jet, who
was sleeping on the couch in the living room until the hogan
was cleaned. To his surprise, Uncle Jet wasn't there.

Using the flashlight app on his phone, Nathan walked outside and made his way to the outhouse. The twinkling stars
bathed the entire desert in a glowing silvery sheen. He could
hear the flies before he entered the outhouse. Even at night the
flies were bothersome! They buzzed and zipped and fizzed as
they zigzagged everywhere. He felt them dive-bomb his calves,
his chin, and even the back of his ear! The flies were equally as
unpleasant as the stench. He finished as quickly as he could and

was eager to get back to sleep.

He stuck his hands into the washing bowl and then grabbed the bar of soap at the washing area. He lathered his hands and wondered where Uncle Jet was. Maybe he was in the hogan. To be sure, Nathan decided to quickly peek inside the hogan; then he'd go back to sleep. His cell phone battery was at 4 percent. He felt confident enough to walk in the dark and decided not to use the flashlight app on his phone. The closer he got to the hogan, the more he expected to smell cigarette smoke. But nothing.

Then Nathan saw a small white light shining in the middle of the cornfield. He crept into the cornfield to get a better view. Shocked, he froze in place when he saw the large horned toad standing on its hind legs and holding a glowing quartz crystal. Atop its head was a tiny, horizontally striped turkey feather. A turquoise necklace dangled around its thorny neck and tapped against its smooth, round tummy. A trail of cactus flowers followed it, hovering right about its shoulder area.

Nali was going to be so amazed to hear that there was a standing horned toad walking in her cornfield! Uncle Jet might need some convincing. Nathan needed proof, though. Nathan felt at the rectangular bump in his pocket. His phone had night mode! But he would need to get much closer to get a good picture in this darkness. The horned toad tripped and fell headfirst into the dusty earth. It mumbled to itself and stood back up.

"Oh, more seeds! Come on, hurry up!"

It was speaking English. English? Nathan snuck closer to it, carefully placing his feet and trying not to make noise with his sandals.

The horned toad put its scaly hand above the space where Nathan had planted one of Nali's traditional kernels. Wind circled and drilled into the earth, creating a thin slit. The seed popped out of the hole and into the horned toad's hand.

"This is enough for tonight. Come, before they wake up," it said, and then held the white quartz crystal close to its mouth. It whispered a few words to it and then the crystal glowed even brighter. Nathan squinted and could barely see a tiny white flame inside its clear angular walls. Holding the glowing crystal before it, the horned toad exited the cornfield and entered the vast open desert.

Nathan struggled to maintain enough distance so the horned toad couldn't hear him but so he was close enough to listen in on what it was saying. It entered a cluster of gray sage that must have seemed like a tall forest to the stumpy little thing. Nathan relied on the light of the crystal to figure out where the horned toad was. It stopped and started a conversation, though Nathan was absolutely certain that there was no one else besides the two of them.

"No, please. I really don't want to go anywhere near humans," it said.

He followed it out of the sagebrush clusters and onto a long stretch of sunbaked, cracked sand. Not a bush or shrub in sight for miles in front of them.

"I despise humans, all of them. Well, she'll have to get

another assistant, won't she?"

She, who is this *she*? Were there more like the horned toad? Or were there different beings altogether? Nathan stepped on dried roots jutting out of the ground. They crunched loudly beneath his sandals.

"Who's there?" The horned toad turned quickly around and held the crystal toward Nathan. Immediately, a gust of wind pushed the top layer of sand into the air and into Nathan's eyes. "It's one of the humans!" Before Nathan could rub the sand from his eyes, the horned toad blew onto the crystal and the light disappeared.

"Wait! Can I take a picture of you?" Nathan saw it darting to his right. He quickly reached and grabbed the talking lizard. Despite its appearance and name, the horned toad was squishy.

"Agh, the fat one has me! Wind, aid me!"

"Hey, don't call me fat!" Nathan said.

A strong wind circled Nathan's ankles. The speed increased and turned into a cyclone. Grains of sand pelted against Nathan's exposed skin. The tiny electric stings felt like a sleeping limb waking up. As the winds grew in ferocity and speed, the grains of sand began to sting like bites of mosquitoes and then like splinters. He released the horned toad to shield his eyes and ears. It fled.

A few moments later, the winds calmed, and the grains of sand fell back to the earth. He searched the desert floor to look for more footprints but was unable to even find his own. The winds had erased everything.

Nathan looked around and didn't recognize the landscape. He had been so invested in getting close to the horned toad that he had forgotten to notice which direction he had been walking. He reached into his pocket and realized that his phone had died! Of course, it wouldn't have mattered because he didn't have reception out here.

"Hey! Come back! Where are you?" He shivered, even though it wasn't that cold. His knees wobbled as much as his voice. "Don't leave me. I don't know where to go!" Tears clouded his eyes. He sat down on the earth, overwhelmed by the fact that he had no idea how to get back to Nali's mobile home. "Please," he whimpered. It was so empty and quiet that he could hear his anxious heart thump against his rib cage.

He had no idea how far he had walked. He was thirsty and getting hungry. Should he wait here for the sunrise so he could find his way back? He wanted both his mom and father to be by his side.

He lay down and rested his head against the earth. Small, smooth pebbles pressed into his temple. It was the turquoise necklace of the horned toad. Next to that, he noticed a bright, off-white, tear-shaped seed. His fingers picked it up and felt its smooth belly and sharp pointed tip. It was a pumpkin seed.

"You left these. You should come back for them," Nathan said, hoping the horned toad would return. He slid the necklace and seed into his pants pocket.

He rolled onto his back and stared at the stars. He remembered when Nali had told him that First Coyote interrupted the

Holy Beings during the formation of the stars. The Northern Star, or Sǫ' Náhookǫs, as Nali called it, was the first that the Holy Beings had placed. Nathan stared at that star and his heart bumped more gently and more slowly. He didn't know which direction the horned toad had been walking, but knowing which direction was north was a start. He stood up, decided that west would be his best option, and began to walk. His sandals clacked loudly with each step.

"Nali! Uncle Jet!" Nathan screamed as he approached rows of sand dunes.

Up and down, he walked on the round bellies of sand. His thighs burned from overexertion. He hadn't walked on these before. Or had he? He stopped atop the highest one and looked around, recognizing nothing. He should have stayed where he was. Someone would have found him, eventually.

He changed direction and hoped that he would see some trace of Nali's mobile home. If he kept walking in a new direction, he also might come across a dirt road. Now his back and calves burned. The sandals had blistered the arches of his feet and in between his toes. His stomach growled and his throat ached for water.

He lay again in the cool sand, exhausted. He wanted to be in the mobile home on his hard mattress and feel the gentle weight of the tattered blanket press against his body. More than that, he wanted to be back in Phoenix. To be with his mom and father, all three of them living in their old house again.

The moon was lowering, and a purple radiance grew in the eastern horizon. Nali had said that the Holy Beings pay attention to humans during this time. He closed his eyes and prayed that someone would find him. He didn't care who. After he prayed, he reached into his pocket and rubbed the turquoise necklace. Its smooth texture calmed him a little bit.

Off in the distance, there was a noise. It sounded almost human. Nathan opened his eyes and listened. There it was again. It sounded like crying. He summoned the last of his strength and walked toward the sound.

The closer he got to the sound, the more clearly he heard the pain-filled whimpers. Nathan willed himself forward against the soreness in his feet and the stiffness in his knees. He walked up a dune and fell to his knees at the top. A long tail slid in the dark shadow of the dune before him. The whimpers stopped and were replaced by a low growl.

It wasn't human. It was a beast of some kind. Nathan didn't have enough energy to be scared. He wanted to sit down. The necklace in his pocket poked against his thigh, tickling him. He reached inside to scratch it. The moment his skin touched the smooth stone, the grunts from the creature transformed into the voice of a youthful boy, who sounded about as old as Nathan.

"Leave me alone," the boyish voice said.

Nathan released the turquoise stone and the voice turned back into growls. He touched the stone again. "I can't help you."

"Please, I'm lost," Nathan said.

"What? You understand me?" the boyish voice said.

"I guess so." To make sure, he removed his finger from the stone. The moment his skin lost contact with the turquoise necklace, the creature grunted.

"How is it I can understand you and you can understand me?" the creature in the shadows said in between heavy, labored breaths.

"I think it has something to do with this." Nathan showed the turquoise necklace to the beast in the shadows. "When I touch it, I can understand what you are saying."

A long, thin lizard tongue whipped the necklace and disappeared back into the shadow. "Is that a communication stone?"

The beast limped out of the darkness. Nathan saw the footprints in the sand that he had seen before. He had the head of a Komodo dragon that Nathan had seen in one of his geography books. His iridescent scales sparkled in the starlight. He was the size of a fully grown sheep. He was big. Too big to be able to hide in the desert without being noticed.

The huge creature inspected the turquoise necklace. "It is! That is no ordinary stone. It was made by the Holy Being known as Darkness." The lizard stared into Nathan's eyes. There was a warmth and kindness in his dark pupils that prevented Nathan from feeling fully afraid, though there was a greenish yellowish tinge in the whites of his eyes that didn't look at all healthy. "What would a human be doing with such an item? Did you steal it?"

"No! I'm not a thief! I was following a rude horned toad and it dropped it."

"It would be wise for you to return it, stolen or not. Darkness only creates communication stones for important tasks." The lizard grunted and winced. He lowered his massive body to the ground.

The horizon brightened a little more as the lizard closed his eyes and took in a massive breath. His belly was concave, and his skin pressed against his rib cage. Lighter and darker scales wove geometric designs much like the diamond and mountain designs on the rugs that Nali used to weave. There was something very familiar about this lizard. Nathan had seen drawings of them somewhere. Grains of sand began to cascade down and bury his tail. The lizard seemed to enjoy what was happening because his breathing eased a little and the ends of his mouth curled into a tiny smile. Then Nathan realized what this lizard was.

"You're a water monster! From the Third World!" Nathan snuck his phone out of his pocket, wanting to take a sneaky selfie. Then he remembered his phone had died.

The water monster began to dry heave. His belly rose higher into his spine and he vomited water. The dry earth soaked it up like a hardened sponge. As the water expelled, the water monster shrank in size.

"You're sick," Nathan said.

"Obviously," the water monster said.

Nathan's father rubbed his back whenever Nathan was sick, and that always made him feel a bit better. Nathan reached out and rubbed the water monster's stomach. He didn't flinch or growl at him, so he continued comforting the poor being. Nathan's hand felt a weird, warm sensation. It didn't feel the same as the sun, a fire, or embers. This heat penetrated through his flesh and into his bones.

"Please, don't stop rubbing," the water monster said.

As awesome and amazing as it was to be touching an actual Holy Being from the creation stories, Nathan still had to find a way back to Nali's place. Perhaps this water monster could help him.

"I didn't know that water monsters could get sick."

"I . . . I've been sick for many years now. For humans, it would be about thirty years."

"Thirty years? Hey, wait, that's how long the drought has been going on."

"I've been trying so very hard to bring the rain so that everyone can come back. But I no longer have the endurance for the songs."

"Why would you need endurance to sing a song?"

"One rain song requires a whole day to sing. I must sing sixteen of them day after day with little food or water for myself. The dizziness and nausea make me mix up the words or repeat phrases. When I mess up, I have to start all over from the beginning." The water monster coughed hoarsely, like there was phlegm at the back of his throat.

Would a water monster have phlegm like Nathan did when he had a cold? There were so many questions that Nathan wanted to ask. But he needed to get back to Nali's, and the sun was beginning to break over the horizon.

He squeezed the turquoise necklace. "Water monster, I am lost and am trying to get back to my paternal grandmother's mobile home. If you help me get back, I'll do whatever I can to heal you." Nathan meant to say "feel better" instead of "heal." But he didn't know if the water monster would agree to help him if he was only going to help him feel better.

"I hope you understand that my recovery won't be a simple assignment."

"Oh, trust me, I've had tough assignments. I once wrote a ten-page paper on background radiation. I can do it."

"I accept your offer. For now, it would be best if you held on to the communication stone. I will talk with Darkness about getting you your own so that this turquoise necklace can be returned to its owner." The water monster rolled back onto his hind legs and raised his head toward the rising sun. "With your help, I can bring rain back to this valley, and all the animals will return!"

"Cool, but can you help me get back to my paternal grandma's mobile home?"

"Yes. Here, hold this to my nose." The water monster nudged his nose into the edge of a nearby shadow. Like a blanket, the shadow folded and revealed a braid of sweetgrass. Nali had mentioned that the first beings could fold shadows in the First World! Nathan excitedly began recalling more of the stories that Nali had taught him. The Warrior Twins had used arrows made of lightning and sun rays to kill the monstrous

Enemies that ate humans. They had also used a rainbow to travel across the land. Would the water monster use a rainbow to bring him to Nali's mobile home? He really wanted to travel like that!

Nathan picked up the sweetgrass and held it in front of the water monster's nose. The water monster blew upon it and small embers ignited. Soon, a sweet smoke wafted through the air and into its nostrils. Some of the smoke entered Nathan's nose, and in an instant, he was no longer tired. He was alert, like he had awakened from a night of great sleep, though he was still hungry and thirsty.

"Get onto my back." The smoke must have had the same energizing effect on the water monster, who stood firmly on his legs. When Nathan hoisted himself onto him, he even felt the sinews and muscles. Nathan squeezed his knees together and wrapped his arms around his neck. Despite being a lizard, the water monster had warm blood, and his heartbeat bumped against his forearms.

Slowly at first, the water monster lurched forward. After Nathan figured out how to shift his weight so that he didn't roll off it, the water monster picked up his pace and was outright running. Behind them, there was a string of cactus petals carried by a wind that erased the lizard's footprints.

"Please try not to look back. You may fall off."

"Sorry. I'm not used to riding water monsters."

The wind blew against his cheeks and through his short black hair. Steven and Weslee would never believe this. Heck, not even his parents would believe it. Nali would, and boy, was she in for a surprise!

"Actually, hey! Do you know where my grandma lives?"

"I assume your grandmother is the woman who prays every morning with corn pollen."

"That's her."

"That is where I am taking you. She's not far from here. The Holy Beings hear her prayers and the troubles she endures with her son. When she goes out to pray this morning, say to her 'Enemy Way.'"

"Enemy Way?"

"She will know exactly what that means. We're here."

The mobile home was right in front of him. The outhouse was next to it. It was the most beautiful outhouse in the world! He had made it out of the desert! Nathan was so happy, he could cry.

Nathan dismounted and hugged the water monster. "Can I show you to Nali—I mean, my grandmother? She'll be so excited."

"She will not see me, human youth."

"Call me Nathan. 'Human youth' sounds weird."

"All right, Nathan. Adults, having gone through puberty, never see Holy Beings."

"Will my grandma be able to see you if I take a picture of you?"

"I'd rather you didn't. Even if you did, she won't see me in it," the water monster said. "I must be on my way. The effects of sweetgrass are only temporary, and I must return to my pond. Don't forget our agreement. I saved your life; now you must save mine."

"You can count on me," Nathan said, puffing out his chest. He placed his knuckles on the sides of his hips, hoping that he looked strong and manly. How hard could it be to heal a water monster? Nali had Pepto-Bismol somewhere around here.

Nathan watched the water monster crawl into the desert. Wind erased his footprints.

Nali, then, stepped out of the mobile home. "Nathan? Awake already?"

"Yeah." Nathan smiled awkwardly.

"Want to pray with me?"

A small yellow petal drifted into Nathan's vision and landed below the mobile home. "Before I forget, I have to tell you something."

"What is it?"

"Enemy Way."

Her face dropped. "What? Nathan, where did you hear that? Who told you that?"

"A water monster told me, Nali," Nathan said. He ran to her prayer spot. He had so many thanks to give!

Tsosts'id
SEVEN

NATHAN SAT AT THE KITCHEN table with a peanut butter jam sandwich and two bottles of water before him. Although the sweetgrass smoke took away his weariness, it hadn't taken away his hunger and thirst. He opened a bottle of water and drank. His throat soaked in the lukewarm water like a dry sponge. The chalky peanut butter was the right amount of salty and crunchy. The runny jam was extra sweet. The bland bread was fluffy, tender, and dissolved on his tongue like cotton candy.

"Shinálí, slow down; otherwise you're going to choke," Nali said. She sipped coffee across from him. Uncle Jet gently snored on the couch in the living room. He wore his black Marine leather jacket like a blanket. There was a layer of fresh dust on it.

"Hágoshį́į́," Nathan replied, automatically. The communication stone! It pressed against his thigh in his pocket. How much Navajo could he speak now that he had the turquoise necklace? Although, he already knew how to say "hágoshį́į," which meant "okay, in agreement."

Nathan leaned back in the chair and sighed. His full stomach pushed against his shirt. He never knew something could taste so good. "I'm going to make another sandwich, Nali."

"All right," she said. "We're going to visit your clan uncle after breakfast. So, when you're done, get dressed and then we'll leave."

Nali went to her bedroom, while Nathan made another sandwich.

Nathan devoured his sandwich in the truck. He might have eaten too much. But having survived the desert, Nathan didn't care that his tummy pushed against his waistband.

"Shinálí, what did you mean that a water monster told you to tell me 'Enemy Way'?" she asked, driving the truck on the undulating dirt road.

"About that." Nathan struggled with what he was going to tell Nali. She would get upset if he told her he got lost in the desert. So maybe he shouldn't mention that. At least not yet. "Don't get mad. Last night I went outside to the outhouse. Then I—" He avoided looking at Nali. He really didn't want to worry her. "Then I ran into this water monster. He told me that the Holy Beings hear your prayers. And he told me to tell you 'Enemy Way.'" Not quite a lie, but he still felt uncomfortable leaving out what he had.

Nali didn't respond. The silence between them grew awkward and uncomfortable. The truck bumped as it traveled on the rough road that snaked between the pine trees around them and jerked his body around. Nali sighed and parked the truck on the side of the dirt road.

Nathan tensed up. She was going to yell at him. He thought her facial expression grew angry. Then she reached for and held his hand. She smiled warmly at him, and his beating heart slowed down. Had he imagined her anger? She said, "I believe you."

"You do?" Nathan said, relieved.

"I do." She squeezed his knee. "When you said 'Enemy Way' this morning, I was thinking about your uncle." She was choking on her words. "He's . . . An Enemy Way will fix him." She was on the verge of tears.

Nathan unbuckled himself and slid over. He rested his head on her shoulder and quietly sat with her for a few minutes. When she pulled tissues out of her purse to blow her nose, Nathan said, "Uncle Jet's going to be okay, Nali."

"I believe that, too, with all of my heart." She pulled another tissue out and wiped tears off her cheeks. "Okay. Your clan uncle is a hataałii, a medicine man. He'll know what we need to do."

"Okay," Nathan said and held her hand. She reached over and rubbed his knuckles with her rough palm.

"Now, buckle up, shinálí," she said.

Nathan slid back to the passenger side and buckled himself in, even though there was a 99 percent chance they wouldn't see any other vehicles.

◊ ◊ ◊

It was close to noon when they arrived at the hataałii's place. Up in the Lukachukai Mountains, the heat wasn't as oppressive. A thick, dark green forest of oak and pine crowned pink-orange sand-rock plateaus that extended north and south beyond Nathan's vision.

The hataałii's mobile home was more modern than Nali's. A solar panel gleamed like shadowy obsidian atop a tall metal pipe that reached beyond the canopy of broad leaves. There was also a sheep corral with reflective aluminum panels as fencing, unlike the barbed wire of Nali's. And like all traditional Navajo home sites, there was a hogan.

The hataałii waved at them from inside the sheep corral. He wasn't as old as Nathan had thought he'd be. Short black-and-gray hair poked out from under his brown cowboy hat. Dust covered both his faded jeans and plaid button-down shirt. He shook apart bales of hay to feed his flock. Naughty lambs galloped and jumped beside their round, wooly mothers.

Nali parked the truck next to the corral. "Yá'át'ééh, shiyáázh!"

"'Aoo', 'aoo'. Yá'át'ééh, shimá!" He approached the truck.

"Nathan, go help him with the sheep," Nali said.

"Huh? Sure." He got out of the truck feeling a little tired from the long drive. He hopped into the sheep corral. The flock dispersed away from him.

"Extra pair of hands, huh?" the hataałii asked.

"Yeah." Nathan hadn't been around many hataałii and wasn't

sure how to act. He estimated that he was somewhere between his father's and Nali's age. His face had a few wrinkles, mainly smile lines.

"Here." The hataałii handed him a square chunk of oddly delicious-smelling hay.

"Okay," Nathan said.

The hataałii hummed an old nineties pop song that his mom liked to listen to while they fed the sheep. Done, he led Nathan back to the truck, closing the corral gate behind them.

Nali and the hataałii began to speak in rushed and excited Navajo. Remembering the turquoise necklace, Nathan reached into his pocket and touched it.

"Háájí Jet?" the hataałii said.

"Shighandí 'ałwosh," Nali responded. "Na'ahyílá."

The necklace wasn't working. Had it broken? He released the necklace and touched it again. They still spoke Navajo that Nathan couldn't understand.

The hataałii asked Nali a question and looked at Nathan. His eyes made him shiver like a chilly breeze had blown on exposed skin.

"Díí shinálí 'ashkii, Nathan," Nali said.

"Oh, okay. Nathan, is it?" the hataałii said to Nathan.

"Uh-huh," Nathan responded.

"So you are my nephew, huh? Nice to meet you, shiye'. My name is Devin," the man said. "Your grandma says you live in Phoenix. Bet you're not used to not having running water?"

"It's not hard, but I guess it's kind of cool," Nathan said.

"Cool, is!" Devin laughed. "Come, let's go to the hogan. We can talk about things without the wind pushing our words to unwanted ears."

Devin held the Pendleton blanket that hung above the entrance to his hogan to the side so Nathan and Nali could enter. Nathan stepped inside and onto the soft sandy floor. Each of their steps sent a gentle puff of dust into the air. Directly in the center, an ash pile sat underneath the opening at the very top of the dome.

They moved clockwise toward the western wall and sat down on the blanket that had been placed there. On the western wall hung a large Marine flag. Devin sat underneath it next to Nali. He rolled fresh mountain tobacco in a dried corn husk. Nali had told him that this wasn't the commercial tobacco that was bought in stores. For this kind, medicine folk would have to sing certain songs while they harvested the tobacco plants in the mountains.

"Do you mind if we speak English?" Nali asked Devin. "Nathan doesn't get exposed to his culture in Phoenix."

"Okeydoke. Jet has returned, huh?" Devin said. He wet the edges of the corn husk with his tongue to seal it.

"He has lost another job and was kicked out of his apartment by his landlord," Nali said. "I want N'dáá for him."

Devin lit the tobacco with a lighter and puffed on it. "What makes you say this?" Devin asked, exhaling a plume of sweet-smelling smoke. The smell brought back memories of last night for Nathan.

"'Abínídą́ą́," Nali started. "This morning, as I was heading out to pray, I was thinking of how to help him. I didn't have an answer, and then shinálí 'ashkii said he met a Holy Being. That Holy Being told him to tell me 'Enemy Way' and then I remembered, Jet has never had N'dáá after his tour of duty."

"Hm, we'll return to Diyin Dine'é, or Holy Being," Devin said, looking at Nathan. There was comfort in his eyes and a feeling of mutual respect. He handed the tobacco to her and she puffed. "Okeydoke, tell me a little more about Jet."

Nali gathered puffs of smoke and patted them against her chest and her head. "He stayed in the Marines after his tour, trying to pursue a career. His drinking started very slowly. Like a river carving a canyon, the alcohol began to erode his heart. Just like his father, James. I kept trying to tell him he needed help. Nothing. He didn't listen to me. A few years ago, the Marines discharged him. Then James passed." Nali pressed her thumbs into her eyes as she handed the mountain tobacco back to Devin.

"Does he talk with a therapist?" Devin asked.

"He doesn't like it," Nali said.

"Especially with the passing of his father, he should be with a therapist," Devin said.

"'Éí dooda. Listen. His behavior has gotten worse recently, yes. But he was having trouble before. N'dáá will cure him."

"K'adí. 'Ałtso tsídé tsą́ą́," Devin said. "N'dáá is not a

miracle cure-all, shimá. I don't want you thinking that after the ceremony he is going to be hugs and high fives. Yes, it's an important first step to his wellness. But he needs help from a therapist as well. As Navajo, we live in two worlds, and those two worlds have different ways of healing. Shitsilí Jet has to walk both paths to wellness." Devin pressed the little nub of tobacco into the sand floor. The embers sizzled and dimmed. "I can perform the diagnosis meeting. If he's diagnosed, who do you want to perform his N'dáá?"

"Who? You, of course."

"Earliest I can do one is next year."

"Next year? He could leave by then!"

"I can ask other hataałii if they are able to do a last-minute N'dáá. But I think the earliest any of us can do one is going to be next year."

"Hágoshįį," Nali said. "It'll be my job to make sure that Jet is around."

"I'll put you first in my schedule for next year," Devin said.

"'Ahéhee'," Nali said.

"Now, Nathan," Devin said, turning to him. "Tell me more of this Holy Being that told you about N'dáá, the Enemy Way Ceremony."

"Well, last night I met a water monster and he told me to tell Nali 'Enemy Way.' And long story short, here I am." Nathan squirmed, feeling a little shy. He wasn't entirely comfortable talking with an adult he had just met about almost dying in the desert and being saved by a Holy Being.

Devin stared at him for a few moments. It was hard to read his expression. He nodded. "You are very lucky. It's not every day Holy Beings present themselves to humans, especially in this day and age."

Devin believed him! Nathan relaxed a little. "You don't think it's a fantasy?"

"Doo 'ájínída'! Don't call your culture a fantasy," Nali firmly said.

"Sorry. Do you think meeting a Holy Being is, you know, an everyday thing?"

"When I was about your age," Devin started, "maybe a little bit younger, I saw a being, same shape as you and me. Well, maybe more my shape now. Taller. Grown. But its skin was a glowing rainbow. Nááts'íílid Dine'é, Rainbow Being. It told me that I was going to become a hataałii after I went through many hardships. And, well, long story short, here I am."

Nathan chuckled when Devin repeated his words. With both Nali and Devin easily accepting Holy Beings as real, Nathan was ready to get down to business. "The water monster is sick. He gets dizzy spells and nausea. Is there anything you can think of that can affect water monsters?"

"Sick? You didn't mention that," Nali said.

"Sorry, I forgot to mention it," Nathan said. He squeezed his thumb tightly and felt his forehead grow hot from hiding information from Nali.

"Well," Devin said, "there are four forms of sickness: emotional, spiritual, internal physical, and external physical.

Figuring out the type of sickness is a good start. When I start working with new patients, I look at the symptoms and try to diagnose them. But be very careful to make sure that you yourself don't get sick from what's affecting them. Healing is a delicate process. I'm not able to think of anything in particular that might directly affect a water monster, or any Holy Being for that matter. Like their ways affect us, our ways affect them."

"Thank you, sir," Nathan said.

"Sir?" Devin said.

"Devin's your uncle by clan," Nali said.

Nathan struggled to think of the Navajo word for paternal uncle. Unsure, he guessed, "Shizhé'é yázhí?"

"'Aoo', shiye'!" Devin said. "Do you have any other questions for me?"

Nathan thought long and hard. "No, I've asked all I wanted."

"If there is anything I can do or offer," Devin said, "please let me know. I've healed many people but never a water monster."

Nali stood up and dusted her jeans off. "I'll talk with Jet and convince him. We'll have a diagnosis meeting soon."

"Yo, Nathan. Help me with this," Uncle Jet said later that afternoon. Nathan walked inside the hogan and helped Uncle Jet carry a large, heavy mattress outside. Nathan held on with all his strength. When he stepped outside, the broiling sun dug into the back of his neck.

"Here, lean it against that wall."

"Got it, Uncle Jet."

"All right. Just hit the mattress with this baseball bat to dust it off, sweep the floor inside, and bing-badda-boom, I got my own darn room," Uncle Jet said, swaying his upper body from side to side. He massaged his lower back with his knuckles. "Once we're done, I'll check out the cornfield and see about fixing some of those posts."

"Okay," Nathan said. Uncle Jet went back into the hogan while Nathan stared at the cornfield. He realized that he had to re-sow! After the excitement of getting lost, running into the water monster, and seeing Devin, Nathan had completely forgotten about the horned toad that stole his seeds and very rudely called him fat. Fixing the fence wasn't going to stop it.

"Heads up, buddy," Uncle Jet said from inside the hogan, tossing out a large trash bag. It slammed into Nathan's stomach and pushed him back, knocking both the wind out of his lungs and his glasses to the ground.

"Gotta pay attention, kid. If you were in the field, that could have been fire from the enemy," Uncle Jet said. He puffed up his chest and widened his shoulders.

Nathan searched on the blurry ground for his glasses. All the plants and rocks blended together into a blobby shape. Suddenly, he felt the painful sting of possibly billions of little mouths in his palm. Whatever it was sunk its teeth deeper and deeper into his flesh. An image of the spider he had seen yesterday flashed into his mind.

"Uncle Jet. Uncle Jet, help!"

His breathing became loud and fast. A rush of cold sweat

flowed over his entire body. Was this thing poisonous? Was the poison rushing into his veins? Would they have to take him to the hospital?

"What's wrong? Nathan? What? Dude, it's only a jumping cactus."

"What do I do? What do I do?"

"Come on, man. Don't be such a little sissy." Uncle Jet yanked the tiny cactus out of his palm. The sharp jolts of pain remained. Nathan sniffled. His eyes pooled with tears.

"Stop crying, man," Uncle Jet said.

"But it hurts," Nathan said.

Uncle Jet handed Nathan his glasses. "All right, dude. Man up. Some little cactus going to make you cry? Then you'll be a little sissy your entire life. When you're getting shot at, that's when you have a reason to cry." When Nathan wasn't able to stop sobbing, Uncle Jet sighed. "Here's my trick. Don't think about it. Keep moving." He patted Nathan's back and went back into the hogan, leaving Nathan to suffer through the residual pangs of pain.

Nathan did everything in his power to not think about the words "stinging" and "sharp." He wanted to touch something cool and smooth. Then he remembered that he still had the turquoise necklace in his pocket. He pulled it out and pressed its bumpy, cold exterior to the place that hurt. Even if he still didn't fully understand how it worked, it soothed him.

Nathan grabbed one of the black trash bags Jet had thrown

outside and tried to lift it up. The plastic tore open. A few elaborate handwoven rugs fell onto the dirt. Some had very intricate and detailed geometrical shapes. One had depictions of what looked like Nali's mobile home with a cornfield, plants, sheep, cows, and a family on it. Another rug caught Nathan's attention. It had a depiction of Holy Beings holding bundles in their hands, and a Rainbow Holy Being bordered its edges.

"So, this is where your Nali's been stashing her rug collection," Uncle Jet said. "These can go for huge bucks." His eyes never left the Rainbow Holy Being rug.

Nathan's palm swelled again, so he reached into his pocket to hold the necklace.

"What you got there?" Uncle Jet said. He pried it from Nathan. "Is this a ring?"

Nathan yanked it back. "No, it's a necklace."

"A necklace? That's a little too small for you, don't you think?"

"It's for the horned toad that walks and talks." Nathan put his hand over his mouth. He didn't mean to mention that last part because then Uncle Jet would ask . . .

"What?"

"Nothing. It's nothing."

"You serious? There's a talking horned toad?" Uncle Jet asked, chuckling. A smirk crept to his lips. "What did it say?"

"Stupid thing called me fat. But that's not important. It's been stealing the kernels."

Uncle Jet lifted an eyebrow. "Serious?"

"Yes. I am," Nathan said. "I also saw a Holy Being out in the desert—"

"Come on," Uncle Jet said, interrupting him. "You actually believe in that nonsense?"

"But the hataałii says—"

"Psh! Medicine men!" Uncle Jet leaned against the doorway. "They ain't nothing but phonies out to make a quick buck. They'll 'prescribe'"—Uncle Jet raised two fingers in air quotes—"ceremonies and charge a pretty penny for them. Those ceremonies never helped anyone. Nothing but a bunch of old geezers agreeing with each other." Uncle Jet was huffing and puffing. Nathan didn't know that Uncle Jet would get this angry about Holy Beings. "Don't let them scam you, Nathan."

"Okay, Uncle Jet." Nathan slowly slid the turquoise necklace back into his pocket. Devin didn't seem like a phony. Nathan realized how hard it was going to be to convince Uncle Jet to participate in a diagnosis meeting, much less an N'dáá.

Tseebíí

EIGHT

TWO NIGHTS LATER, NATHAN LAY on his stiff mattress, not wanting to miss his parents as much as he did. Even though Uncle Jet was sleeping in the living room, his snores traveled down the hallways and shook his bedroom walls, keeping Nathan up. He heard a mosquito buzz in his ear. He quickly clapped at it, hoping he killed it. He looked out the window to the star-filled sky. A half-moon rose. He had been here only six days, not even a full week. He wondered if he could last two months out here.

Suddenly, he heard a whimper from outside his window. He was wondering when he'd see the water monster again. Nathan grabbed the turquoise necklace. The moment his skin touched the stone, he heard, "Nathan, are you there?" The stone was working again. Tonight, he needed to ask the water monster how the communication stone worked.

"Yeah!" he whispered, maybe a little louder than he intended. He pushed the window open and then looked outside, seeing nothing. "Where are you? I can't see you."

"Oh, I'm sorry! I forgot I still have this on," the water monster said. The shadow beneath Nathan's window rippled like disturbed water. A tongue slipped out from under the darkness and into the light of the moon. Then the water monster's snout poked out, and his forehead. Soon, Nathan could see the entire water monster in the moonlight.

"How did you do that?" Nathan asked. It was the coolest thing he had ever seen. He wanted to know if he himself could learn to do that, too.

The water monster arched his scaly back and placed his arms onto the side of the mobile home to raise his head up to the window. "The Holy Being known as Darkness lent me a shadow blanket so that I can travel without humans seeing me. Speaking of Darkness, I have arranged a meeting between you two so that you might get your own communication stone!"

"Seriously? I'm getting my own stone? Thanks!" Nathan quickly put on his jeans and sneakers. He wasn't eager to walk in the desert in sandals again. His toenails still had sand underneath them from two nights ago.

Nathan crawled out of his window and hugged the water monster, who backed away.

"Why did you do that?" the water monster asked.

"I'm sorry. I tripped," Nathan said, embarrassed. Hopefully, the water monster believed him. It felt weird to not hug him, especially after he had saved Nathan's life.

"Sorry, another dizzy spell is coming. Nathan, grab a braid of sweetgrass from my pouch near my left leg." The water monster lay down and tilted onto his side, moaning.

The water monster's pouch was similar to the one in which Nali kept tádídíín. Nathan reached into it, expecting the tips of his fingers to feel the other end. Instead, his whole hand slid in. Only when his elbow grazed against the opening of the pouch did Nathan finally touch the other end. He could feel many things: some were hard, smooth, and round like pebbles; some were flat, hard, and angular like crystals; and there were even mounds of fine sand that were cool to the touch like chilled water. Then he felt the strands of braided grass.

Nathan pulled them out of the pouch and his arm felt tingly, like it had fallen asleep. He brought them to the water monster's mouth, remembering how two nights ago he had blown on the sweetgrass to ignite it. Nathan said, "Here you go."

"I can't ignite it without sunlight. I need you to light it for me," the water monster said. "Oh! I am about to vomit. Please hurry."

Nathan remembered Nali always kept a lighter at the firepit. He jogged over and found it next to the pile of ash. He hurried back to the water monster.

He flicked the lighter, but it struggled to light. Meanwhile, Nathan had to ask, "Are you working with that little talking horned toad?"

"What?" the water monster asked.

"Small horned toad. Rude as it is spiky. It's stealing my seeds for my science experiment. I figured you're a Holy Being, it's a Holy Being. Maybe you know each other?"

"Horned toads are usually messengers for the Holy Beings," the water monster said. "On rare occasions will one be an assistant. One must travel to Changing Woman and explain why an assistant is necessary. No, I do not have one."

The lighter finally held a flame. Nathan held the burning tips of the sweetgrass braid under his nose. The water monster stood up. His limbs weren't shaking. Even some of his dark greenish color returned.

"Thank you. Here, smell the smoke. We have a long way to ride and you'll need your energy," the water monster said, nudging the braid toward Nathan. The sweet smell entered his nose and Nathan felt his entire body awaken. He was ready for an adventure!

"Jump onto my back," the water monster said. Nathan mounted, excited to meet the Holy Being known as Darkness.

They zoomed through the cornfield. Nathan still hadn't replanted the traditional kernels. He wanted to deal with the horned toad first. It didn't make sense to plant if the kernels were going to be stolen. The water monster jumped over a large sagebrush. When they descended, Nathan's stomach and lungs dropped like he was on a roller coaster.

Nathan laughed. The wind entered his mouth and dried the back of his throat. The air was cool and tasted like flowers. Far ahead, there were mounds of dunes that rose and fell like frozen ocean waves. The light of the half-moon and stars tinged the sands blue, purple, and silver instead of the daylight colors of orange, red, and white. Nathan leaned forward and wrapped as much of his arms as he could around the water monster's broad neck.

They arrived at the dunes in a matter of minutes. For as fast as the water monster ran, Nathan was surprised at how quiet he was; his feet made almost no sound whatsoever. The water monster ran on the spine of a large sand dune. Sands trickled down one of the sides, causing it to vibrate and hum. It was a very soothing sound, like a father humming a toddler to sleep. Nathan thought of his own father and missed him a little.

"Hold tighter. Your grip is loosening," the water monster said.

Nathan held tighter. He looked back at the sand dunes and then noticed that the water monster wasn't leaving any footprints. In fact, there was a string of cactus petals flowing behind them, erasing them from the ground.

"Does that always happen to your footprints?" Nathan asked.

"Yes," said the water monster. "The Holy Being known as Wind gives each of us water monsters a weave of wind. We then tie it to our ankles so that we can hide our footprints from beings that would wish harm upon us. More often than not, humans are the harmers." The water monster shot a quick look at him. Nathan felt weirdly guilty, even though he hadn't done anything, good or bad, to the water monster. Then the water monster smiled and said, "Not all humans. Throughout the eras, some have aided us."

He realized that the horned toad must also have a weave of wind! That must be how it got around without leaving a trace. Something had to be done about that rude horned toad.

It felt like an hour had passed since they had left the mobile home when the water monster came to a stop. Nathan jumped down and walked around to regain feeling in his feet. His cheeks itched and tingled from being windblown for so long. They were at the base of the sandstone mesa, which was now dark purple. They stood in the middle of smooth, soft sands that sparkled and shone like tiny stars.

"Is this where we are going to meet Darkness?" Nathan asked.

"Yes. It should be here soon," the water monster said.

Excitement bubbled up in Nathan's chest. He would have his very own stone! In middle school, he would have to learn another language, like Spanish or French. Having his own language stone would mean that he was sure to get an A-plus in that class!

"But first, you must pass a test," the water monster said.

"Ugh, a test!" Nathan said. "Well, what kind of test?"

"A test of worthiness," said a deep, loud voice that caused the sparkling sands to shiver. The shadow of a nearby dune bent and then morphed into the shape of a human that was nearly three times Nathan's height. It didn't have any depth and was simply flat, like a two-dimensional figure.

The shadowy body approached Nathan. Its body was darker than any of the other shadows around them. It towered over him. Nathan felt like a spider about to be stepped on.

"Are you Darkness?" Nathan asked.

"Correct, human youth," Darkness said. "Come, water monster youth." They walked a few steps away from Nathan. The way Darkness moved wasn't really walking or floating. The base of its body reattached itself to different shadows and detached from previous ones, like fire moving from kindling to kindling.

The water monster limped forward. Were the effects of the sweetgrass braid wearing off? No, Nathan was still energized and ready for the test. Did this mean that the water monster's pain had grown? The water monster sprawled across the sands and breathed deep and slow.

"Water monster youth, what makes you worthy of salvation?" Darkness said.

"I'm the only being on this earth that knows the Shooting Star songs. If I were to perish, they will be lost forever," said the water monster.

"You remember those songs!" said Darkness, its deep, low voice excited.

The water monster shivered. He said, "I can teach those songs to others so that they won't be forgotten."

"It would bring me great pleasure to hear those songs yet again. I find their melodies to be the prettiest of all," said Darkness. "I will aid in your recovery. Human youth, I understand that you have something that belongs to me?" It moved to

Nathan, attaching to different shadows along the way.

"I, uh," Nathan said. He was having trouble finding words. Nathan couldn't figure out if Darkness was good or evil. Its name was Darkness, so did that mean it was evil? But it was helping Nathan and the water monster, so was it good? It definitely was intimidating. Nathan showed Darkness the turquoise necklace.

"Yes, this certainly is my craft," Darkness said. "Did you steal it?" Darkness's voice boomed, shaking nearby plants. Tiny animals scattered in every direction.

"No! I didn't steal it!" Nathan stood his ground and looked at what he assumed to be the face of Darkness. "A little horned toad dropped it in the desert along with a pumpkin seed!"

"Is this the truth?" Darkness asked.

"I swear!" Nathan said.

"Human youth, why should I not find a different assistant to aid in this water monster's recovery? One who I know and trust? What makes you special, human youth?"

Nathan automatically responded, "I promised him."

"That he did," the water monster said.

"Human promises are fickle," Darkness said. "Well, we shall find out how much weight your promises carry, won't we? When you are ready, human youth, I will assess you."

"I'm ready," Nathan squeaked out, even though he wasn't. What was going to happen? What was he supposed to do?

The very next second, Darkness's body surrounded his feet. The black shadow glided up onto his shoes. Like warm liquid, it submerged his shins, knees, and waist. Nathan tried to shout, but no sounds left his mouth. A deep fear froze his heart as the shadow rose to his neck. He tried to scream, "Stop!" He closed his eyes and held his breath.

There was a muffled argument between a man and a woman who were very far away. The argument grew louder and clearer. It was his mom and father, arguing about who was going to have primary custody of Nathan. There was a second argument behind him that was getting louder, between Nali and Uncle Jet, about Uncle Jet losing his job in Albuquerque. Then he heard his mom crying. After the divorce, his mom cried every single night. He tried his best to cheer her up, but for months nothing helped. Nathan never fully forgave his father for putting his mom through that pain. Last, there was a group of kids laughing and chanting, "Butterball."

The arguments and teasing circled him, growing louder and louder. He tried to cover his ears, but he didn't know where his ears and hands were. His body was gone. He was a disembodied consciousness.

Nathan had to stop the voices. He forced himself to sing a lullaby that his mom sang to him when he was sick. He hummed the tune first and then sang the words. The loud voices began to lose their volume and clarity. In his mind, he recalled his mom's smile, and his father sitting next to her, his hand on her shoulder, looking down at him as well. Then he remembered when all three of them were together at last year's science fair. They didn't argue and even smiled at each other. It felt like the three of them were a family again. The other voices slowed and eventually stopped.

"Nathan," the water monster said. "Stand. It's over."

Nathan opened his eyes. Darkness and the water monster were looking at him.

"You have much kindness, human youth," Darkness said. "And much greatness ahead of you."

"What do you mean 'greatness'?" Nathan asked, reacquainting himself with having limbs and a face. He poked his cheeks and forehead with his fingers.

"Look below you," Darkness said.

Beneath his feet was an enormous sand painting. Different colored sands painted a boy with glasses holding a feather in one hand and a book in the other in the center of a giant circular mural. Nathan recognized Nali, Uncle Jet, and the water monster at either side of the boy. Different Holy Beings were at the edges of the circle. Zigzags and complex geometric shapes filled in the spaces between the figures.

"When I engulfed you, your heart spoke out and caused the sands around you to move and shift. This sand painting reveals your inner being. Now I can assess."

"What do you see, great Holy Being?" the water monster asked.

"Yes, what do you see?" Nathan really wanted to know what this all meant.

"I see much struggle, much hardship," Darkness said. All excitement left Nathan. That was the last thing he wanted to hear. Darkness continued. "And also plentiful hope and kindness. There" — Darkness pointed to one of the Holy Beings — "is the sign of the medicine folk. Next to it are the signs of intelligence, and a little bravery. Human youth, your participation would be greatly advantageous for success."

Nathan had the mark of the medicine folk! Did that mean he could one day become a hataałii? Nathan grinned, thinking of knowing all the traditional songs and helping others. Which Holy Being indicated it again? What about the other marks? Did they indicate what he was going to be when he grew up? Was he going to be rich? Was he going to have a girlfriend?

"Thank you, Darkness," the water monster said.

Darkness turned to Nathan and extended its long arm. "Return the turquoise to me."

Nathan pulled the turquoise out of his pocket and then held it over the palm area of Darkness's hand. He let go of the necklace and it disappeared. Darkness then pointed a finger at Nathan's forehead. Nathan raised his hand to touch his forehead. There was a rugged yet smooth turquoise nugget. He pulled at it and it popped out of his forehead.

"This communication stone is still malleable. It will take the shape of any jewelry you wish it to be. Once you find a piece of jewelry that suits you, place this stone into it and it will solidify."

Nathan squeezed the stone, figuring out exactly how much he could shape it. First, he rubbed the turquoise stone until it became warm and was as soft as a piece of clay. He left it alone and it became hard as stone again. He left it that shape for the time being.

"How do I use it?" Nathan asked.

"It will allow you to speak to any and all beings. Because this is my craft, it will only work when there is more darkness than light."

Nathan looked at the two of them. "What's next?"

"The next direction shall be of your deciding," Darkness said to the water monster.

"Nathan?" Water Monster said, looking at Nathan. "Do you have any idea?"

Nathan rubbed the back of his head, thinking. "I, uh— We should— Maybe we could— I don't know." What was it that Devin said that day? "That's right! We should diagnose you first. Once we find out what is making you sick, we can heal you."

"So, we should have a diagnosis meeting for me?" the water monster said, turning to Darkness.

"Do you have a preference for who should conduct the meeting?" Darkness asked.

"First Turkey," said the water monster. "First Turkey has a connection to the Third World that no one else has. Her feathers were touched by my mother's water."

"I will arrange a diagnosis meeting for you with her. I know that she is currently undertaking a vastly important task, requiring the aid of an assistant. I've encountered her assistant, who is prone to dropping things. A sash with a pocket woven from the finest weaver should suffice as payment. And with that, I'm off to find First Turkey." Darkness shrank and the shadows from which it had emerged returned to their normal shapes.

"Nathan, did you hear that?" the water monster asked, startling Nathan. "I'm going to get better! Thank you, friend. Now we need to find someone to weave a sash."

"Oh! My nálí! She used to weave!" Nathan said. Though she didn't weave anymore because of the arthritis in her right shoulder. Perhaps the Holy Beings could bless her shoulder so that she could weave again. "She weaves really, really well!"

"I'm sure your grandmother is a great weaver," the water monster said. "For a human. No offense to your grandmother, but what we need are the original weavers."

"What do you mean 'original weavers'?" Nathan asked.

"We need spiders to weave the sash for First Turkey," said the water monster.

"Spiders?" Nathan gulped loudly. He was sure his face had lost all its color. Not "spider," but "spiders" as in plural. More than one.

Náhást'éí
NINE

OUT IN THE CORNFIELD, NATHAN stared at the wood-pile. Of all the creatures in the world that he had to ask for help, it had to be spiders. Nathan shivered, thinking about all those pairs of hairy legs, those long fangs dripping with venom, and all those eyes searching for human flesh upon which to chew.

Nathan rubbed his arms to get rid of his goose bumps even though the late-morning sun was quickly warming the air. He then put on the newer oversized gloves that Uncle Jet had lent him. His fingertips didn't even reach the tips, which kept folding at uncomfortable angles. But this discomfort was worth it because when he gripped the mattock, a digging tool that looked a lot like a spear, his blisters thanked him by not erupting in pain.

Nathan slammed the mattock to the side of the metal fence post until it wiggled like a loose tooth. He went to the next post. Uncle Jet, meanwhile, adjusted the tilt so that the posts were upright and then packed the sands at the base. Once they were done with fixing the posts, they would have to wire them. Nathan estimated that it would take about three and a half more hours to finish. They might need to finish this tomorrow morning.

"If she really wants these posts to last, she needs concrete," Uncle Jet said. "Dig out all the posts, put a concrete base, then stick it right in. Post will last for days, I tell ya." He wiped some sweat off his forehead.

Nathan's father had said that, too. His father wanted to fix up the cornfield fence. But like a lot of things that he had said he wanted to do, he didn't have time because of work.

"This post isn't going to stop the thing that's been stealing the seeds," Nathan said. The horned toad could easily walk under the barbed-wire fence.

"Still think it's some talking walking horned toad?" Uncle Jet said, then laughed. "Is it planting its own little cornfield?"

Uncle Jet was making fun of Nathan. At least Uncle Jet wasn't angry with him. To deflect Uncle Jet's ridicule, Nathan said, "Could be a prairie dog."

"How about that? You might be right. Your dad and I used to hunt them around here when we were young. Mm, you got me thinking of prairie dog stew."

"What do they taste like?"

"What else? Chicken. Real gamey chicken. If that's the case, we don't need to fix the fence; just set up a trap," Uncle Jet said. He dropped the shovel and made his way back to the hogan.

"Uncle Jet, we still have ninety-two posts left to fix," Nathan said. Uncle Jet was really leaving Nathan to finish the work all by himself!

"If you wanna keep working, go for it. Far as I'm concerned, we're only fixing the posts for your science project. And since it's a prairie dog, no need to fix the fence."

"Can you at least help me with a trap, then?" Nathan asked. This was unbelievable. Even if setting a trap solved the horned toad problem, Nali still wanted the fence fixed. Nathan slammed the mattock into the ground. Uncle Jet could be so selfish sometimes!

Nathan loosened as many posts as he could until it was too hot for him to continue. The rest of the morning Uncle Jet isolated himself in the hogan, fixing it up and organizing it.

Nathan washed up and went to the kitchen inside the mobile home, where Nali had made ham-and-cheese sandwiches with some canned vegetables. In the middle of lunch, Nali said to Uncle Jet, "Son, I'm bringing a hataałii over for you."

Uncle Jet sighed and rolled his eyes.

"It's for your own good," Nali said.

"No need," said Uncle Jet. He bit into his sandwich.

"You're hurting, son."

Nathan wanted a reason to leave. Maybe he could sneak away to the outhouse. Even the bothersome flies would be better company than these two at the moment.

Before Nathan could sneak away, Uncle Jet stood up. "I ain't gonna see him!" Nathan froze, afraid to move.

"Please," Nali said.

"It's not going to work. Whatever you think will happen won't. So, just don't."

"Jet, for you, I overlooked many things. Nizhé'é—" She wiped away tears from the corner of her eyes.

"Don't bring him up; don't you dare bring Dad into this." Uncle Jet pointed his finger at Nali.

Nathan tried not to cry. His father used to do the same thing to his mother—point his finger at her when he got upset. And like his mother, Nali was shrinking into her chair.

"He acted the same way you act now," Nali said. "His was Vietnam. I couldn't see the signs because I didn't know the signs. But now I do. Those same habits, those same eyes—you have them, too. In our way, when warriors return, they have to have N'dáá, an Enemy Way Ceremony to get rid of the things that attached to you."

"Don't bother."

"I bother. I bother very much, my son." She stood up and stared into his eyes. Neither moved a muscle. Nathan wanted so badly to disappear.

"I'm fine!" Uncle Jet said after many, many tense seconds. His voice shook. "It's a waste of money." He left the mobile home.

"We need to convince him, shinálí. He needs an N'dáá." Nali wiped away her tears and sat back down.

Even though the emptiness in Nathan's stomach made his tummy growl, a new emptiness had formed in his chest, and it overwhelmed his hunger.

"Okay." Without thinking about it, he said, "I'll help you convince him."

"'Ahéhee', shinálí," Nali said. She pulled him into a hug. "He'll listen to you. Talk to him."

Nathan realized what he had said and committed to. Convincing Uncle Jet to have the ceremony might turn out to be more difficult than helping the water monster.

Before dinner, Uncle Jet set up a cage trap in the middle of the cornfield. Nathan wasn't sure if Uncle Jet set it up for acting so terribly toward them, or if he was so bored that he had nothing better to do. Either way, it was ready.

That evening, Nali and Nathan sat under the shade of the chaha'oh, reading their books. As much as he had missed Uncle Jet, he didn't like how his presence had changed the atmosphere around the place. Both he and Nali were always a misunderstood comment away from yelling at each other. If Uncle Jet wasn't there, Nathan imagined that he and Nali would be talking, laughing, and joking. Nathan looked at the rising half-full moon; shadows were covering the desert, deepening and darkening the colors of the land and mesas. Nali turned on the lamp so they could continue reading.

Uncle Jet walked to the washing area.

"You can't do anything right," a tiny, grating, and unfamiliar voice said.

Nathan looked up and searched around for the new speaker.

But it was only the three of them. "Worthless," that voice said. Nathan looked at Uncle Jet, where the voice seemed to come from. It wasn't Uncle Jet's voice, which was normally deep and raspy. This new voice was grating, like listening to metal scratching metal, or a dying rat.

Uncle Jet noticed Nathan staring at him. He dried his hands with the towel. "What are you looking at?" Uncle Jet said, snapping Nathan out of his trance.

"Sorry, spaced out," Nathan said. Nathan felt his communication stone pressed up against his bare thigh through a hole in the shorts he was wearing. "Thanks for setting up the trap, Uncle Jet."

"Huh?" said Uncle Jet. "Yeah, no problem."

"No one will ever love you because you are worthless," that voice said. Nathan didn't hear that voice again until much later.

That night, Nathan worked up his courage to talk to the spiders. Nathan waited until Uncle Jet started snoring in the living room. He took a deep breath and walked through the hallway toward the front door, telling himself he could do this over and over. The half-moon shone through the window behind the couch, on which Uncle Jet was squirming and shifting in sleep. Nathan was about to open the door when he heard that strange voice from earlier.

"You'll never be anything because you are worthless! Worthless!"

Nathan slowly approached Uncle Jet. With every step the

voice got louder. Uncle Jet moaned. Beads of sweat dotted his forehead, neck, arms, and legs, even though he had no blankets on and a cool breeze was flowing through the open windows.

"They'll never forgive you for what you did! You are worthless!" the voice said.

Whatever this voice was, it was messing with Uncle Jet. Then Nathan saw it: a pair of glaring eyes embedded in Uncle Jet's shadow on the floor. The eyes seethed at Nathan, who stumbled backward. The intense stare had scared him to his bones. Goose bumps erupted on the back of his neck.

"You. You're whispering those things," Nathan said. "What are you?"

"Beyond your power is what I am. Now leave." The eyes looked back at Uncle Jet.

"Leave my uncle alone," Nathan said, standing up. He towered over the eyes.

The pupils rolled. The eyes seemed to grow in size as Nathan could clearly see red veins streaking across their white roundness. "You dare meddle in my affairs? You are such a simple idiot. You are worthless."

Nathan recognized the voice. "You were saying those mean things," Nathan said, squeezing the small piece of turquoise. He lifted his foot and stepped onto the eyes.

"What! How are you doing this?" it yelled at Nathan. "Stop, this instant!"

"No," Nathan said. He slammed his foot down and rubbed his shoe left and right.

"Fat child, you will not be forgiven!" The eyes blinked wildly before disappearing. Nathan looked at Uncle Jet, who now slept soundly.

Nathan reminded himself that he had to talk to some spiders and left.

He approached the dark maw where he first saw the large spider. "Hello? Grandpa Firewood?" Nathan said, staring into the entrance. "My name is Nathan. Is anyone there?"

"Why do you bother us, Nathan?" a voice hissed at Nathan. A pair of hairy front legs crawled into the light of the moon. The rest of the eight legs hoisted his bulbous abdomen out of the shadows. The tiny hairs on the spider reflected the moonlight, creating a silvery glow all over his frightful body.

"Hi. Uh, I'm trying to help a friend, who is a water monster," Nathan said, doing his best to not squash the spider even though he desperately wanted to. "He is sick. He mentioned First Turkey is coming over to diagnose. And First Turkey's assistant needs a sash with a pocket or something."

"Water monster? Bah, spiders and water don't mix! My family and I prefer dry conditions. Yes, the creatures we eat need water, but oh, the rain! How it destroyed our beautiful webs, hours upon hours of work! Wasted," Grandpa Firewood said.

"Please, he needs your help," Nathan said.

"Yah! There shall be no helping any water monsters tonight! Or any other night for that matter! Be gone!" He turned around and crawled back into the maw.

"Wait!" Nathan shouted into the spider den.

"I know that voice!" another voice spoke. Another spider, about the size of a golf ball, crawled into the moonlight. "I know you! Grandpa, please listen to him," this spider spoke. Her voice was soft, like his mother's. "He was about to kill me but instead showed me mercy!"

"You!" Nathan said, remembering how he had almost killed her a few days ago, even though he did call her Cheii Chizh.

"Grandpa, consider his plea," she said.

"And what will we get with rain?" Grandpa Firewood said, reemerging from the maw. "We'll be flooded out of the wood-pile. You are too young to remember, my grandchild. Once rain was so frequent, there was a pond not very far from here. Oh, such woeful times! Every day a spider drowned, and every day we had to reweave our webs. Miserable, I tell you." Grandpa Firewood shook his legs at the younger spider.

"Grandpa, do we not face troubles today?" the younger spider said. "We have little success hunting bugs. Every day I lose a brother or a sister from hunger. The plants that interrupted the path of the wind have dried up and been blown away. We maintain the webs daily because the winds have such strength. It might be good for the rains to return, even if that means we have to move to a new location."

"Blasphemy!" Grandpa Firewood said. "We've lived here for generations! We can't just up and leave. Wherever would we live? No. End of discussion."

"Hey, I think I know of a place," Nathan said. They both turned and faced Nathan. "It has a lot, and I mean *a lot*, of flies and it is indoors. You won't have to deal with rain or wind."

"Speak more!" Grandpa Firewood said, stomping his tiny front legs on the wood beneath him. "I demand to know where this magical place is."

"It's the outhouse. It's not magical," Nathan said.

"Outhouse?" said the young spider, her body swaying back and forth as if she were dancing. "That sounds like a lovely place. Everybody, listen!" She turned and faced the maw. "There is a wonderful and splendid place called the outhouse!"

A plethora of tiny voices yelled, "Outhouse? What is that?" Soon, a parade of spiders crawled out of the maw and stood on top of the pile.

"It's a place of bugs aplenty! It is sheltered from rains and winds," the younger spider said.

"I love the outhouse!" one of the hundreds of spiders said. "Yay for outhouses!" said another.

"You guys are way too excited for the outhouse," Nathan said.

"Outhouse, outhouse, outhouse!" all the spiders chanted, waving their front legs back and forth.

"It seems my family has taken to your description of said wondrous outhouse," Grandpa Firewood said. "Heed my warning, Nathan. If you lie to us and this outhouse is short of miraculous, we will move into your sleeping quarters and bite you every time you sleep."

"Are you talking about Phoenix? Because that's pretty far away."

"No matter the distance!" Grandpa Firewood said, growling. "Do not cross me or my family."

"I won't. I'm already scared enough looking at how many of you there are," Nathan said.

"And you should be scared! All right, family!" Grandpa Firewood said to the multitude of spiders. "Who wants to live in the outhouse?" he asked.

In unison, they screamed, "ME!"

"All right, Nathan," said Grandpa Firewood. "If you lead us to this most spectacular outhouse, my family and I promise to weave your sash."

"Pinkie promise?" Nathan was about to extend his pinkie but then decided not to. "Never mind—um, follow me."

Nathan walked slowly to the outhouse, making sure that all the spiders were able to keep pace. All the while, he heard their excited chats about their potential new home. Once they got there, Nathan opened the door and immediately several juicy, fat flies flew into the open air.

Grandpa Firewood raised a hairy leg. All the tiny spiders stopped chatting to watch him closely. Grandpa Firewood darted across the walls, ceiling, and floor, mumbling to himself, tapping here and there, and even biting a corner. "In all my life, I've never imagined." On the ceiling, he rappelled down and hung in front of Nathan's face. "Yes. Yes. This is quite nice," Grandpa Firewood said in a voice that sounded happy. He dangled and rubbed his front legs together. "Family, tomorrow, we begin weaving for Nathan!"

"Nathan! Nathan!" the tiny spiders chanted.

"Nathan," said the young female spider. The rest of the tiny spiders crawled into the mouth of the hole, disappearing into its darkness. "Thank you."

"Please don't bite us when we're in here doing our business," Nathan said.

Grandpa Firewood said, "Family, we shall not bite humans whilst they attend to their business! Nathan, we shall have your sash ready in half of a moon cycle." Grandpa Firewood crawled into the hole.

Nathan nodded, not really sure how long half of a moon cycle was, and said, "Thanks."

"Honorable Nathan," the young female spider said, "I have an unusual request. You are not obliged to say yes, you can say no."

"What?" Nathan said.

"Well, you see, I am almost of adult age. That means I will have to venture out into the world to find my own home. Please don't be mad at me, but I must admit I had ulterior motives for moving my family to the outhouse. With the majority of them here, I could move back to the woodpile. But the adventure I had tonight ignited a fire in my heart. I want to see more of the world. Would it be possible to be your companion? I promise to not interfere with your quest or business."

Nathan thought about this. On the one hand, she was a spider. On the other hand, there were mosquitoes that bit Nathan during the night. Then again, she was a spider, with her eight hairy legs, millions of freaky eyes, and two of the scariest fangs of any animal. But he said, "Sure."

"Yes!" She jumped.

"There are mosquitoes that bite my skin at night."

"Mosquitoes are my favorite!" The young spider jumped onto Nathan's leg. It took all Nathan's nerve and many deep breaths to calm his instincts to squish the spider that was crawling up his leg. When he blocked the image of a spider crawling on him, her tiny feet actually tickled a little.

"Um, what should I call you?" Nathan asked.

"Spider works fine," she said, crawling onto his shorts and on top of his shirt to his shoulder.

"Okay, Spider, let's go," Nathan said.

"Oh! Yes! Let's!" Spider said, yelping with glee.

Back in his room, Nathan raised his hand to Spider. When she jumped into his palm, he reached as high as he could to the ceiling. She placed her feet onto the wall and crawled the rest of the way to the top of the ceiling. She darted everywhere, almost as if she were a puppy running in a park.

"This place is the best place in the world!" she said. "Everything's perfect. I will watch over you as you sleep and ensure the safety of your legs from mosquitoes."

"Cool. Good night, Spider."

"Good night, Nathan!" She waved her front legs at him and then zoomed into one of the corners.

Nathan placed the turquoise stone onto his side shelf. No

longer able to hear the spider or any other being, he slept easily. In his dreams, there was a voice saying, "No one will ever love you because you're worthless." But when he woke, he didn't remember.

Neeznáá

TEN

THREE DAYS LATER, NATHAN EXAMINED the green tips of the modern kernels, which were pushing out of the topsoil in the cornfield. Meanwhile, the cage trap sat empty where the traditional group should have been growing. Nathan didn't dare to re-sow the traditional kernels, at least not until the horned toad had been dealt with. Nathan couldn't figure out why it hadn't fallen for the trap. His science project was on the line and it was starting to feel like all the effort he had put in was, well, worthless.

Nathan couldn't tell if he hadn't slept well last night, but he felt slower and heavier. Not physically heavy, but like something was pulling his heart downward. Even though today he was going with Nali to Gallup for more food, he wanted to be left alone to read his book.

"Nathan, let's go!" Nali said from the truck.

Nathan slumped his way over to Nali and jumped into the passenger side. Nathan really wanted to stay with Uncle Jet, who had now finally moved into the hogan. But Nali annoyingly insisted Nathan come so he could call his father, who was the last person in the world Nathan wanted to talk to.

"How are you feeling?" Nali asked.

"Fine," Nathan said.

Nali grinned and drove. "Thank you for coming with me. I appreciate—"

"Sure," Nathan interrupted her.

"How's your water monster friend?" Nali asked.

"Fine," Nathan said.

Nali seemed to sense that Nathan didn't want to talk and thankfully was quiet the entire drive to Gallup.

On the highway, Nathan's phone shook to life while it charged. It dinged fifteen times in a row.

"Call your dad, shináli. I'm sure he wants to hear from you," Nali said.

Nathan called and hoped it would go to voice mail. He wasn't going to leave a message.

"Nathan, how are you?" his father asked, laughing.

Nathan could hear Leandra in the background giggling. His father must be driving back from Las Vegas to Phoenix.

"I'm here," Nathan said.

"Are you enjoying your time with your nálí?" Nathan could hear his father suppressing laughter.

Nathan really wanted to say, "Better than I would be with you," but he held his tongue. Why was everyone so annoying?

"It's okay," Nathan said.

"I was thinking of making a detour on my way back to spend the night with you guys. What do you think?" his father said.

"Don't worry about it."

"I want to see you."

"Just go back to Phoenix. I need to focus on my science project." Nathan hung up before his father could say another word. He switched his phone to vibrate.

"What happened?" Nali asked.

"He has another case that he has to work on, so he has to go back to Phoenix," Nathan said.

"Yaadilá," Nali said. "I'll talk with him."

"Don't worry. He's busy," Nathan said. With Leandra, he thought.

Nathan's phone vibrated. He let it ring until it went to voice mail.

When they returned to the mobile home in the early afternoon, Uncle Jet had finished stabilizing the last metal post of the cornfield. He grinned and waved at them.

Uncle Jet walked to them and saw the Chinese food they had brought back for a late lunch. "Thanks, Mama. Smells good."

"You're cheerful," Nali said. She stepped out of the truck with a loud grunt. "What's going on?"

"Been sleeping really good. I should have cleaned out the

hogan much earlier," Uncle Jet said, pulling several bags of groceries from the back of the truck. He noticed Nali staring into his eyes. "You wanna check out my pupils?"

"No." She held her purse under her arm. Then she said, "Son, I want you to see hataałii. He says that you need a diagnosis before you can have N'dáá."

Nathan winced. This was for certain going to start an argument.

"Fine," Uncle Jet said, much to Nathan's surprise and probably Nali's too because she coughed.

"You certain?" She hugged Uncle Jet, who almost toppled over with all the grocery bags.

"Beats doing nothing out here. Let's be clear, though. I'm not committing to the Enemy Way Ceremony. But I'll hear him out at this diagnosis thing."

"I'll call today and get it arranged. Nathan, you want to join me?"

"No," he said.

"Yo, Nathan," Uncle Jet said. "You didn't set any bait for your trap. You're not going to catch a thing."

Nathan was surprised he hadn't thought of that. Then again, his head was cloudy, and he wasn't thinking as clearly as he had been. "Yeah. Okay," he said. One more annoying thing to do before he could be alone in his room. His science experiment was looking more and more worthless with each day that passed.

◊ ◊ ◊

It must have been late at night when Nathan smelled the sweet-grass smoke because the air was chilly and the moon shone brightly through his window. The smoke lifted the heaviness inside him and replaced it with energy. The water monster scratched the wall beneath his window. Nathan put on his glasses and reached for his communication stone.

"Nathan!" the water monster whispered.

Nathan stuck his head out the window. "Yeah?"

The water monster stood on his hind legs, leaning against the wall. His head was level with Nathan's. "I apologize for not coming these past few nights. I had a dreadful bout of nausea and couldn't leave my den. I hope I didn't cause you to worry."

"Do you feel better?"

"Yes, I feel much better. Were you able to enlist the help of the spiders?"

"Yes, they said they'll need a moon something before they are done."

"Moon something?" the water monster asked. His head tilted like a confused puppy's.

"Half of a moon cycle!" a tiny female voiced squeaked. Spider walked onto the window. "This is the sick water monster? Oh my, you are quite the sight. My family has agreed to weave, but they need to eat enough flies to have energy to produce the webbing. It should be ready when the moon is full."

"This is wonderful. I'll let Darkness know," the water monster said. He leaned back on the earth but stumbled to the ground.

"Hey, you all right?" Nathan asked, leaning farther out of his window.

"I really could do with some fresh, clean water," the water monster said.

"Clean water, got it." Nathan quickly grabbed his sandals and tiptoed down the hallway. He grabbed four bottles of water from the kitchen and exited the front door.

"Are you able to stand back up?" Nathan approached the water monster.

"I can't," the water monster said.

Nathan opened a bottle and poured water into the water monster's mouth. There was still that weird heat coming from his scaly body. It pulsed like a glow.

"This water, it's different," the water monster said. Like a sponge, his dry tongue started to expand. As Nathan poured two more bottles into his throat, the water monster grew as tall as Nathan. Nathan put the last water bottle into his pocket, where it poked out at an odd angle.

"It's purified water," Nathan said.

"I'm not sure what that means, but thank you nonetheless," the water monster said. He stood up with a firmer stance. He looked less like an old man standing on a boat and more like a stallion ready to gallop.

Nathan still felt energetic from the sweetgrass. He couldn't wait to go with the water monster wherever he was going. Nathan needed an adventure, away from the mobile home.

"Well, I must be off," the water monster said.

"What? You're leaving? After you got me energized with the sweetgrass? Rude." It *was* rude! Nathan was wide awake and wouldn't be able to go to sleep for hours.

"Did I offend you?"

"Next time, ask me first before you use sweetgrass on me. Now I'm going to be up, and everyone is asleep. I can't read with no lights. I'm going to be bored." Nathan sighed. What was he going to do—talk with Spider? Fat chance.

"I apologize. I'll ask for your permission the next time. Actually, I don't have to go right away to Darkness. If you want, I can show you my old pond."

A smile crept across Nathan's face. Last time he rode the water monster was fun and he had been wondering if he could do that again. "That sounds cool. Yeah, let's do that."

"Okay, hop onto my back," the water monster said.

Nathan mounted the water monster and they were off into the desert.

The desert had energy and electricity in the air. Small mammals were scurrying away from the two of them, and a few birds were up chasing after flashing fireflies. The constant pressure of the sun was replaced with a refreshing coolness.

They traveled a while and arrived at a bowl-like land formation. Some bushes and agave stalks were growing at the bottom of its smooth, round depth. The air and the ground were much cooler around here. Nathan hopped off the water monster. The moist ground sank gently with every step he took. The agave stalks swayed in the night breeze.

"This is what remains of my water," the water monster said. His head hung low.

From the bottom of the bowl, Nathan looked around. Had this space been filled with water, Nathan could have swam. On the sides, layers of different colors were stacked on one another like the distant mesas. The smooth sands beneath him were white.

"There are a lot of agave plants," Nathan observed.

"I am known as the Water Monster of the Agave Pond," he said.

"More like Agave Lake," Nathan said.

"My songs were becoming strong. Strong enough to turn this pond into a lake. I needed a few more years. Now I'm afraid all I'll ever be known as is a pond water monster instead of a lake water monster."

"Pond," Nathan said. "Mind if I call you that?"

"I have no issue with it," Pond said. He slumped down onto the ground and it sounded like he was sniffling.

"I don't have to call you that," Nathan said, feeling bad. He might have called Pond a disrespectful name. He was still figuring out how to interact with water monsters.

"It's fine," Pond said. "All the animals that used to drink from my waters, they used to call me that, too. They were my friends. I miss them so much."

Nathan thought about Weslee and Steven and how they would hang out at lunch playing the latest video games on their smartphones. He missed them. He wondered if Pond felt this way about his animal friends. Nathan walked over to him and hugged him.

"I miss my friends, too," Nathan said. "We'll bring the rains back, Pond. You'll see. And soon, your waters will return, and I can call you Lake instead of Pond." He pulled the purified water bottle from his pocket and poured it into the basin. "Look, we're already starting to bring water back."

Pond smiled. Like an overgrown dog, he nuzzled his head underneath Nathan's armpit. Nathan felt Pond's warmth pulsating through his rib cage and even approach his heart.

"I'm glad our paths crossed those nights ago."

Pond told Nathan of all the animals that used to drink from his waters. He told Nathan of how years and years ago, before the excavation of the nearby mining cave, this land was green, and grass would grow as tall as Nathan's knee. Nathan wanted to see how this land looked when the animals and plants returned. He wanted to bring the rains back to the desert.

The moon hung low on the western horizon when Nathan and Pond made their way back. Pond charged up a mound, and at the crest Nathan could see a huge amount of the desert. In front of them about a football field away, he saw a tall metal fence with looping razors at its top. Pond sprinted forward, forcing Nathan to squeeze his legs against Pond's rib cage to hold on. They passed a sign that said "Church Rock Mine."

Many minutes later, they arrived at the mobile home.

"Thank you for coming with me, Nathan," Pond said. "I'll tell Darkness to have the diagnosis meeting during the full moon. You know, full moons are special for water monsters. They make us stronger and our songs more potent."

"Full moon. Got it," Nathan said. Nathan hugged Pond.

"Have a good night, my friend," Pond said. He walked to a nearby dark shadow that was cast from the brightening horizon. He nudged his nose and pushed the shadow back like a blanket and crawled underneath it.

Before Nathan could climb back up into his room, he heard a voice yelling from the cornfield. It was the horned toad! He ran into the cornfield and saw the lizard trapped in the cage that Jet had set up.

"Help! The sun is rising!" the horned toad said. It was banging its tiny arms against the cage. "Someone! Help!"

Nathan approached it and it stared at him. "You! Why do you keep stealing my seeds?" Nathan said, pointing his finger at it.

"You're the one who trapped me! What are you going to do, you pudgy human?"

Nathan didn't like being called that. This horned toad was really getting on his last nerve. He firmly said, "Don't call me pudgy. Please." He added "please" because this was still a Holy Being he was dealing with.

"Are you going to let the sun strike me? How evil of you!" It looked at the horizon and crumpled over. "This is the end of me. Woe! Woe to the world! I never completed my task!"

"Calm down."

"Leave me be so that I may perish alone without your cruel eyes watching!"

"I don't want you to die," Nathan said. It looked up at him.

"Then why? Why do you hold me here while the sun is about to rise?"

"I want you to stop stealing the seeds I'm planting. I need them for my experiment!" Nathan said.

"That is something I cannot do! I have been given a most sacred task. And you would prevent me from completing it. I knew you were cruel! From the very moment I discovered you sneaking up on me. Like a wolf sneaks up on a most productive lamb!"

"How can a lamb be productive?"

"None of your mockery! Release me. I have to complete my task lest . . . lest . . ."

"No. I'm not going to let you out." Nathan sat down. "Unless you promise to stop stealing the seeds for my science project."

"Bah! May your kind perish!" the horned toad said. Nathan wasn't sure how much power this thing had. It obviously wasn't like Pond, as it couldn't change its shape.

"Fine by me," Nathan said. He noticed that it was looking at the horizon and shaking.

"So be it! I will leave alone any seeds you plant in this corn-field. You must let me out this very moment! I need to make myself scarce. The sun rises!"

Nathan unlatched the lock and the horned toad sprinted away to a nearby ditch. It disappeared and soon its tiny footprints did, too. Nathan went back to his bed and fell asleep for a few hours.

When Nali woke him, she told him that the diagnosis meeting for Uncle Jet was going to be in six days, this coming Saturday evening. Nathan then went to the cornfield and re-sowed the traditional group, glad he was able to finally begin his science experiment.

Ła' Ts'áadah

ELEVEN

IT WAS SATURDAY AFTERNOON, THE day of both Uncle Jet's and Pond's diagnosis meetings, and near the end of June. Nathan lay on his mattress staring at the ceiling. An emotional heaviness pinned his limbs down into the hard mattress, immobilizing him. It pushed the air right out of his lungs. Like a wave, it rushed down to his feet, then up to his head, then back down, passing through his heart each time. Each time it did, he wanted his parents to be by his side.

He wanted to be with his father. But his father clearly didn't want to spend time with Nathan because otherwise he wouldn't have invited Leandra on their Las Vegas vacation. Nathan missed how when he was sick his father would massage his head with care. He missed how when he was very young, his father would take him to Tempe Town Lake and they would feed the duck families. He couldn't control his memories, and more arose, one right after another. He missed when his father did this. He missed when his mom did that. His chest felt so bloated with heartbreak that his lungs struggled to inhale. The memories flowed at increasingly dizzy speeds. It was useless to resist. It was useless because he was worthless.

Nathan knew that this sadness, this feeling of worthlessness, wasn't natural. He tried to remember when it started. The past six days, since he last saw Pond, had been uneventful. Uncle Jet finished rewiring the fence and started repairing Nali's second truck. Nali was busy with getting things ready for Uncle Jet's diagnosis meeting. Each day, though, the weight had grown. His mood soured. He felt worthless all the time, and nothing he nor Nali nor Uncle Jet said or did helped. To make things worse, he was having trouble finishing thoughts and thinking up solutions. All he wanted to do was to be left alone to endure whatever was pushing his body to the ground.

Nathan heard Uncle Jet walk down the hallway. Uncle Jet entered, standing in the warm orange afternoon sunlight that came in from his bedroom window. Nathan turned himself around to face the wall. Hopefully, Uncle Jet would get the hint and leave him alone.

"Everything all right?" asked Uncle Jet. Nathan felt the mattress buckle under Uncle Jet's weight. Nathan desperately wanted his head to be massaged but couldn't muster up enough energy to ask.

"What do you think?"

"Don't you talk to me like that. Man, chill out."

Nathan didn't really care. Whatever would make Uncle Jet leave more quickly.

"What's going on with you? Did I say something?" Uncle Jet sighed really loud. Uncle Jet's warm palm pressed against Nathan's spine. Nathan shrugged and squirmed closer to the wall. "I was going to say that *if* you were feeling better, you could wear this at my diagnosis meeting."

A reflection of light in a rectangular shape slid across the wall. Curiosity got the better of him, so Nathan rolled over. Uncle Jet was holding a bow guard. It was a thin strap of charcoal-tanned leather that held a rectangular plate of sterling silver. Men wore them on their wrist. Tiny dents in the silver created intricate and delicate patterns where turquoise and red coral were imbedded. There was, however, one empty spot. It was the perfect size for the communication stone.

"Your grandpa James told me men wear bow guards on the left wrist because that's how our ancestors held bows when hunting. He told me that you always shoot your prey with your back to the north and you shoot southward so that the sun doesn't get in your eyes. Be it an animal, or someone . . ." Uncle Jet inhaled deeply and took a moment to regain his composure. "Be it an animal or something else, you always shoot from the north to the south. Because, you know, north represents death. You could wear it, but whatever. Stay in here and mope."

"I could wear that?" Nathan regretted being so grumpy toward Uncle Jet. This bow guard was really, really cool.

"It would mean a lot to me if you came in with me," Uncle Jet said and stood.

"I don't know," Nathan said. He had already committed to going to Pond's diagnosis meeting. It wasn't like Nathan could ask First Turkey to reschedule it. But he also really wanted to go to Uncle Jet's diagnosis meeting in Nali's hogan.

"You're coming in, man." Uncle Jet left the bow guard next to Nathan. "You're the reason I'm doing this in the first place." Uncle Jet left.

Nathan's emotions swelled up and pinned him back down onto the mattress. It would be easier to not go to either diagnosis meeting. He put the bow guard under his pillow. He lay on his side and stared at the orange rectangle of afternoon sunlight that shone in through the window. For the next three hours, pinned under the terrifying weight of massive heartache, he watched the color of the rectangle change from orange to red to purple. It was worthless to resist.

Nathan awoke to Nali rubbing his back. He noticed that the emotional heaviness had transformed into bland lifelessness.

"Sha'awe'. Hazhóó'ógo," Nali said. Her voice soothed him. Nathan turned over and saw that Nali was wearing a velvet maroon skirt and a solid white silk blouse. She had on her deep red coral multistrand necklace and matching earrings that she wore to his fifth-grade graduation ceremony. "Do you think you can come inside the hogan?"

Nathan sat up and lay his head on her shoulder. He didn't know what was wrong! If he couldn't tell Nali what was happening to him, how could she or anyone help? It was worthless to resist, because he was weak. He wanted to go in with Nali and be with Uncle Jet. But Pond . . .

"I'm not going, Nali," Nathan said.

"Okay," Nali said. "You are bigger than your heartache."

"My heartache?" Nathan wondered if Nali knew what he was feeling.

"You must miss your parents so much. You must be so homesick," Nali said.

So, Nali didn't know. Yes, Nathan did feel those things. But the intensity of his feelings wasn't normal. There was something else to his heartache that Nathan couldn't identify.

"Yeah, that must be it," Nathan said.

"How about we go to Gallup Monday and do a video call with your mom? You can ask her when she's going to be back in Phoenix." Nali stood up and stopped at the door. Before she left, she said, "You are a strong young man, shinálí. You are going to get through this mood. But you don't have to go through this alone."

Hearing that from Nali, Nathan was able to stand up and get ready for Pond's meeting. He tried imagining meeting other Holy Beings, from the Warrior Twins era, from the Changing Woman era, from the First Coyote era. Perhaps Changing Woman could help get rid of this bland lifelessness that was now taking the shade of a gray cloud. He grabbed Uncle Jet's bow guard from under his pillow and the communication stone that he kept in his duffel bag.

"Nathan!" yelled Spider. "Nathan!"

"What?"

"I've been calling your name for hours!"

"You know I can't hear you unless I hold this." He carefully inserted the stone into the empty cavity of the bow guard where a stone had fallen out. As he pressed it in with his thumb, there was a clicking sound as it slipped beneath the metal tines that cradled it and solidly held it in place.

Would he have to constantly touch the turquoise or would touching the bow guard be enough? He held on to the strap of leather and said, "Spider?"

"Yes?" she responded.

Nathan could still hear Spider. The bow guard now had the same effect as the communication stone. "Are you ready?"

"Yes, the sash for First Turkey's assistant should be ready."

She rappelled down and landed on his shoulder. Normally, the mere thought of a spider, with its fangs, its hairy legs, and all eight of its eyes, would repel Nathan and would make him shudder. Now, however, he didn't care one way or another. It was one more thing that was worthless to resist.

On his way to the outhouse, Nathan changed direction and instead walked to the front entrance of Nali's hogan. There was a blanket draped over the open door, and light from the fireplace was piercing the evening night. He overheard Devin speaking. "You're going to have to be truthful. You have to talk with us."

A small part of him, through the grayness, wanted Uncle Jet to feel better and hoped that he would talk.

"I'm sorry, Uncle Jet," he whispered. Nathan forced himself to the outhouse.

Nathan was expecting a flurry of flies to harass his face but was surprised when he opened the door to the outhouse. He used his fully charged phone to light the inside. Silky strands of webbing stretched along the upper corners. They strummed as a captured fly tried to wiggle free.

"Hello? Grandpa Firewood?" Nathan called.

"It's Grandpa Outhouse these days, young human!" The large old spider crawled out from the hole. "This is indeed the greatest place in the world! There are bugs aplenty and wind does not tear down our webs!"

Spider jumped from his shoulder onto the bench.

"Have you found your own place, my child?" Grandpa Outhouse asked her.

"I have! It's warm and dark, and there are plenty of mosquitoes for me to eat! Is the sash ready? I'm going to carry it for Nathan."

"Yes, go and fetch it."

Spider disappeared into the hole, leaving Nathan and Grandpa Outhouse to awkwardly stare at each other. Nathan thought about turning off the phone light to save the battery. He had no idea how long he was going to be gone, and he might need every bit. On the other hand, he wanted to know where

Grandpa Outhouse was at all times.

"So, about this outhouse? You enjoy it?"

"'Enjoy' is too small an expression!" Grandpa Outhouse raised his front legs in the air and waved them excitedly. It was kind of cute. Nathan chuckled softly.

When Spider finally returned from the hole, the size of her abdomen had doubled to the size of a golf ball. She jumped onto Nathan's leg and crawled up to his shoulder.

"Okay! Let's be on our way!" Spider yelled.

"You're right by my ear." Nathan shifted his shoulder, forcing Spider to regain her balance. "Where's the sash?"

"It's in my abdomen. It'll be safe," Spider said.

"Off you go! I wish you much success!" Grandpa Outhouse declared with a tiny, grand voice and then disappeared back into the hole.

"Do you know where to go?" Nathan asked Spider as they stared at the vast desert before them.

"I thought you did."

Nathan scratched his head. "Nope." He walked along the cornfield and surveyed the nearby desert. The full moon shone on miles and miles of glistening blue sands. It would be useless to randomly choose a direction. Nathan would get lost in the desert again.

Nathan told himself that if no one showed up to help in five minutes, he could call it quits and would go into Nali's hogan. He could explain to the Holy Beings that he had no idea where to go and, if they didn't help, he couldn't help.

"I know the way," an airy voice whispered into Nathan's ear. Nathan sighed in disappointment.

A gust of wind blew against his calves and then began to circle in front of him, picking up grains of the dark blue sands. Yellow petals floated between and around Nathan's legs into the circling winds before him. The gust quickly spun into a cyclone that was growing taller than Nathan. Limbs began to form from the spinning sands, which were becoming more and more humanlike in form.

The being spoke. "I am the Holy Being known as Wind. The Water Monster of the Agave Pond asked that I retrieve you, as he is currently enduring a bout of nausea. Step lightly and my body will carry you to the meeting place."

Just another Holy Being, Nathan thought, unable to feel any excitement.

"Don't be afraid, human youth. Several of your ancestors have used my back as a means of travel before. I know how to make your journey safe and prompt." Wind Being raised its arm and pointed into the heart of the desert. Wind Being's human form unraveled and disappeared. Before Nathan, there was a trail of petals on the soft desert sands.

What did Wind Being mean by travel on its back? He felt Spider crawl underneath his shirt at the base of his neck. Then he walked forward, not sure what was going to happen. With each step, he felt a gentle yet firm push underneath his shoe. As he approached the last petal, the wind behind him picked up the row of petals and carried them ahead of Nathan, continuing the path. He jogged a little and the wind lifted him higher into the air and pushed him forward. He saw a sage bush far ahead in the distance, and in a few moments zoomed right by it. The sadness he had been feeling diminished. The racing winds in front of him pulled his lips into a wide smile.

"Woo!" he yelled. And then a small bug splatted on his cheek. "Ow!" If the bug had been an inch to the right, Nathan would have definitely swallowed it.

"What happened?" Spider asked from his back.

"A bug hit my face," Nathan said.

"Ooo! Save it for me! I'm hungry," Spider said.

Far ahead was a grand hogan, much bigger than Nali's. There was something different and special about it. The closer Nathan got to it, the more details he was able to distinguish. Instead of wooden beams, the walls were made of the four sacred stones— white shell stone, turquoise, abalone, and jet-black stone. The roof was made of black thundering clouds that swirled in a clockwise fashion. Tiny little thunderbolts emitted sparks of light. The entrance glowed with strands of woven blue-silver strings. They sparkled like the stars in the sky.

The wind beneath his feet slowed when they arrived at the entrance. Sands began to swirl in front of him, and then Wind Being took its human form. Though Nathan's legs stopped running, his heart was still sprinting.

When his adrenaline wore off and the excitement ended, the sadness regained control. It transformed from a grayness to a dense feeling in his heart, like he had lost something important and would never get it back.

Wind Being's hand beckoned him and pushed aside the blue-silver strings, moving them like fabric. It said, "Mind the starlight blanket. The last human to touch one became a ball of fire."

Nathan thought that bursting into flame wouldn't be such a bad thing. He wouldn't have to try anymore. Best of all, the sadness would end.

That thought was wrong! There was definitely something wrong. This sadness. This weight. This okayness with dying. This wasn't normal! He became scared of his thoughts. Whatever was affecting his mood, Nathan was smaller than it, and it was winning. He needed help. Nathan stepped inside the hogan, forcing himself to be terrified of the starlight fabric.

Directly opposite the entrance, Pond sat to the left of an enormous turkey. Pond wagged his tail slightly when he saw Nathan. Like all hogans, there was a fire in the middle of the red sand floor with an opening to the night directly above. Beings of many forms and sizes sat against the stone walls. There were four pairs of boy and girl twins, each made of one of the sacred stones: white shell, abalone, turquoise, and jet stone. There was a female being comprised primarily of dim silver light; her skin had the same glow and splotchy texture as the moon. Sitting next to the moon-skinned female was Darkness, who nodded its shadowy head when it saw Nathan. There was a broad-shouldered being made up of water that smelled salty and fishy like the ocean. Last, Yellow Corn Pollen Boy and White Corn Pollen Girl sat on opposite sides of the entrance. They all watched Nathan as he walked to sit beside Pond.

"I want to thank everyone for attending," Darkness began. "Please, let's welcome Nathan."

"I know that human!" a tiny, familiar voice yelled. "He's not to be trusted!" The Holy Beings whispered among themselves. Nathan searched for the voice. Then the horned toad jumped out from behind First Turkey and pointed at Nathan with its finger.

"He tried to kill me!"

All at once, the whispering stopped, and the Holy Beings stared at Nathan.

"Kick him out of this sacred hogan at once!" the horned toad screamed.

Naaki Ts'áadah

TWELVE

FIRST TURKEY RUFFLED HER MOSS-GREEN feathers. As she moved, her great wings glistened like velvet. The white speckles that dotted her feathers, which rose to the ceiling, made her plumage look like a snow-covered pine tree forest. She then loudly gobbled over the discussions that had erupted. All Holy Beings quieted and looked in her direction.

"Please," First Turkey started. "No aggressive behavior in this holy hogan. If you would sit down, my friend," she said. Slowly, First Turkey turned her head to look at Nathan. "It appears that you already know my assistant, Seed Collector. Explain yourself."

"Uh, I am Nathan," Nathan started.

"No! His name is Killer; he tried to end me!" Seed Collector jumped from First Turkey's side, pointing an accusatory finger at Nathan.

"Seed Collector, be patient. We will resolve this issue with peace and understanding," First Turkey said.

Nathan felt everyone's eyes staring at him. He resisted the urge to turn to the wall and hide his face. "I, well— Okay." His mind went to Nali's teachings, and he felt the words leaving his mouth out of habit. "I am Red Running Into Water Clan. Born for Tangle People Clan. My maternal grandfather's clan is Walks Around the Hogan. My paternal grandfather's clan is Towering Rock People." After he said his clans, the Holy Beings relaxed their postures and their gazes. Nathan felt a little more sure of himself. He sat back and looked at the glowing red embers at the base of the fire.

Seed Collector said, "He caught me in a trap and then held on to me as the sun was rising. He was going to let the morning rays strike me!"

"Oh, please, I wouldn't have done that!" Nathan said, even though right now he kind of wished he had.

"I have suffered such disgrace and indignity!" Seed Collector said. "Who would do such an evil act to a noble Holy Being? Him, I tell you! Him!"

"Is this true, Nathan?" asked First Turkey.

"Yes. I trapped him," Nathan said. His cheeks tingled and turned red.

"Did you intend to hold him until the sun fully rose?" First Turkey asked.

"Not really," Nathan said.

"Liar!" Seed Collector said.

"I have a science project that I'm working on and he kept stealing my seeds, First Turkey. I'm sorry but I didn't know what else to do."

First Turkey slowly turned her head toward Darkness and said, "Darkness, you have tested young Nathan. Would you weigh in on Nathan's credibility?"

Darkness nodded and spoke to everyone in the hogan. "I have tested Nathan and can say he has vast amounts of kindness as well as the grandest of courage. He has within him the dormant abilities of a talented medicine man."

Even with the huge amount of sadness he felt, Darkness's compliments made Nathan momentarily smile. But as quick as an exhale, Nathan's happiness evaporated.

"Why are you vouching for this evil five-fingered?" Seed Collector asked.

"Your fickle hands, much like your tiny brain, have trouble grasping things," Darkness said to Seed Collector. Its deep voice caused the entire stone hogan to vibrate.

"Calmly, calmly," First Turkey cooed. "We are all friends here. It is settled."

"Nathan. Give the sash now," Darkness whispered.

"Huh, sure," Nathan said. He sighed. Whatever made this go faster. He stared at First Turkey's feathers.

"The sash," Darkness said.

"Oh, right," Nathan said. "Hey, Spider?" Spider crawled out from underneath his shirt and onto Nathan's shoulder. He said to her, "Give them the sash."

Spider pulled from her abdomen a folded white sash that was two inches thick. She held it in the air with her tiny, hairy arms. "I present this gift to First Turkey. On behalf of the Water Monster of the Agave Pond, through Nathan, made by my family, a sash."

"Pity, that is too small for First Turkey," joked Moon. "It may make a fashionable anklet." She giggled.

"It wasn't specifically for First Turkey, Moon," Darkness explained. "It's for her assistant, the Seed Collector. The spiders of this desert weave pockets onto their sashes. That is how they preserve their bugs for later meals. I think the Seed Collector will find it quite helpful considering you don't have opposable thumbs."

"I'm perfect without thumbs!" Seed Collector grumbled. Seed Collector took the sash from Spider's arm and wrapped it around its body. "It fits. Okay, I'll wear it on my seed searching. But I'm not going to enjoy it!"

First Turkey smiled as Seed Collector tightened the silk sash. In her sweet and slow voice, she said, "This is a wonderful and useful gift. We are very, very thankful. With it, we are sure to save many plants."

Spider crawled back onto Nathan's shoulder. Nathan wondered what First Turkey meant by saving plants.

"Now, let's get to the business of the Water Monster of the Agave Pond," First Turkey said.

All in the room nodded and as one said, "Ha-ho."

First Turkey shook her evergreen feathers. They reflected the crackling fire in the middle of the hogan and looked like a forest stirred awake by strong winds.

After a nasty fit of coughing, Pond lifted his head. His forked tongue slashed at the air. "These past few years, my health has been getting worse and worse. It started as small fevers and dizziness. I often became so dizzy that I could not sing. Then I began vomiting yellow chunks, small at first. I thought little of it, but soon I began throwing up entire meals. Now I have trouble eating without vomiting. I've lost half my body size."

Pond was half his original size? Nathan couldn't imagine how enormous Pond had been. Pond must have been the size of a truck. Nathan noticed the yellow-greenish tinge to his scales again. He had seen that color before. He couldn't place it. That dense blah, gray feeling was interfering with his thought processes.

Pond continued talking. "I have used all the medicine in my pouch to keep the sickness at bay. I have only a few days left of sweetgrass that was blessed by my mother's waters. I fear that when I run out completely this sickness will overpower me."

First Turkey raised a wing to massage her head. "When did these symptoms begin?"

"Maybe thirty-five winters ago?" Pond said. "It's hard to say when. But the dizzy spells became disruptive to my work about twenty-nine winters ago." Pond rested his chin on the soft red sands on the floor of the hogan.

First Turkey asked, "Is there any event in particular that you can summon to memory that might shed more light upon this illness?"

"None," Water Monster said weakly.

Nathan had a half-formed hypothesis. He recognized the symptoms. He had seen them somewhere before. The more he tried to form a hypothesis, the more his headache grew.

"All right, we'll begin the diagnosis," First Turkey gobbled. Then she motioned at Pond to approach the fireplace in the middle of the hogan.

"Help me, please," Pond said, looking at Nathan. Nathan rushed over to Pond's side and wrapped his arms around Pond's massive chest. Each step was strenuous and cumbersome, but they made it to the fireplace.

The Turquoise Twins approached Pond and began their diagnosis. Nathan had to look away. It was too much for him to see Pond crying and moaning while dry heaving.

Once the Turquoise Twins finished, they said, "There is no single spot for the illness. This sickness is in his entire body. This is not the work of ill will or the use of malicious medicine. Of that we are certain."

Nathan heard another pair of twins approach the center, but he didn't dare look. His head was pounding, and the slightest light gave him a headache. Nathan knew Pond's symptoms. The sickness was on the tip of his tongue. Though, there was the possibility that after Pond was healed, they would no longer be friends. Because why would anyone, much less a Holy Being, want Nathan as a friend? Nathan wasn't cool. He wasn't smart. Nathan was worthless. Worthless.

Suddenly, as if they heard his thoughts, one of the twins said, "Young Nathan, come near the fireplace."

Nathan saw White Shell Boy and White Shell Girl extending their hands to him.

"I'm sorry." He had messed something up. He knew it. Nathan tried not to think of all the eyes watching him as he walked to the fireplace, closer to Pond, who hocked up a thick clump of mucus. "I'm sorry."

"Be quiet. There's something at play with you. Be brave. This may be painful." They both walked behind him.

Nathan felt fingers reaching into his neck—not into it, but through it. The fingers grabbed at something that felt like a nerve; it electrified Nathan's entire head. Nathan screamed loudly as the electric sensation turned into burning, raging, fiery pain.

"Breathe, Nathan. Breathe, you'll be okay soon," White Shell Girl said.

White Shell Boy pulled and pulled. A loud scream that wasn't his own emerged through Nathan's own screaming. The White Shell Twins pulled until a head emerged from the back of Nathan's skull.

Immediately, Nathan's heart and lungs expanded. It was as if he had been breathing through a straw and was finally able to use his whole airway to inhale again. His thoughts cleared. The sadness, the grayness, the denseness, had miraculously disappeared. Nathan turned around and stared at the gray being, the size of Seed Collector, that had been extracted from the back of his skull.

Covered in ash, the thing that had been pulled from the back of his neck tried to run into a nearby shadow. Darkness pulled the shadows away like fabric. With no shadows to dash to, the Ash Being backed up against a wall and searched the room for an exit. White Shell Girl walked toward it. "Worthless, all of you!" it screamed. Nathan instantly recognized the voice. It was the being that was in Uncle Jet's shadow. Somehow it had attached to Nathan. Was it the reason Nathan had been so depressed these past days? "Worthless," it said again.

"What business have you with Nathan?" White Shell Boy interrogated.

"Curse all of you. May your pitiful water monster never regain its former health!" it yelled and made a mad dash for the fire. White Shell Girl leaped and tried to wrap her fingers around its neck. The Ash Being dodged and dove right into the embers. A plume of flames wrapped around the being. Its eyes looked toward Nathan. Then the flames died down, leaving no trace of the mysterious Ash Being.

"What is that?" Nathan demanded to know.

"That," began White Shell Boy and White Shell Girl, "is an Ash Being. It was created by the spirit of a recently deceased human. That spirit's desire for revenge was so great that an Ash Being was created and attached itself to the person that killed him."

"Uncle Jet!" The Ash Being was the reason for Uncle Jet's behavior and also must have been why Nathan had been so downtrodden these past few days.

"Nathan, did you interact with it?" First Turkey asked.

"Yes. I stepped on its stupid eyes because it was messing with my uncle."

"When you physically touched it, you dislodged it from your uncle and it attached to you," First Turkey explained. "From then on, it warped your thoughts and your emotions. You must have been feeling so much turmoil."

"We only severed its connection to you," White Shell Boy and White Shell Girl said. "It will return to your uncle. An Enemy Way Ceremony is the only option for conquering it."

Nathan rubbed the back of his neck. He could think clearly again. He looked at Pond and suddenly everything added up. "I know what's affecting Pond—sorry, the Water Monster of the Agave Pond," Nathan said to everyone.

All the Holy Beings murmured. First Turkey leaned forward and asked, "Well, what is it?"

The greenish-yellow hue. The unnatural warmth that reverberated through his skin to his bone. The nausea. He had seen all these when he was researching his science project last year. "He has been poisoned by radiation." Nathan knew the consequences of prolonged radiation poisoning. Nathan looked into Pond's eyes. "And if we don't heal him, it will kill him."

Táá Ts'áadah

THIRTEEN

THE ENTIRE ROOM HAD GONE silent. Pond stared into the fireplace, his face frozen in fear. Slowly, Pond looked at the others in the hogan. All at once, the Holy Beings started talking.

"This cannot be!" Moon said, louder than all the others. She stood and stomped her foot on the ground. "Does this mean *all* Holy Beings are at risk for radiation poisoning?"

"We don't know what it fully means, Moon," Darkness said in a smooth and soothing voice. Nathan looked at Darkness and was unable to discern any facial features.

"Then what does it mean? For all of us?" asked the Ocean Being.

"It means we must first find a method of curing the Water Monster of the Agave Pond so that we can heal any other Holy Beings should the need arise," First Turkey gobbled. She rubbed under her chin with a large wing. "How did he become poisoned?"

"There is an old uranium mine near here. Church Rock Mine," Nathan said, recalling his research for his science project. "There was a spill thirty years ago. The contamination must have affected Pond's water."

"Is there anything we can do, Nathan?" Pond asked, looking at Nathan.

"I don't know. I mean, there is medicine for humans, but I'm not sure if it'll work for water monsters," Nathan said. How would Nathan even get radiation poison medicine? He might need to ask Nali to help him. Would human medicines even work on a Holy Being?

Moon was pacing in a small circle. "Human youth," she said, pointing at Nathan. "Is it contagious? Does his sitting in this hogan mean that all of us are at risk of the same poisoning?"

"I'm contagious?" Pond said.

"No!" Nathan said. "I mean, to be poisoned by uranium, you have to be exposed to radiation for a long time, depending on how strong the contamination area is. There is an old uranium mine nearby, close to Pond's pond. Pond must have been exposed for decades by the time his first symptom showed. I don't think that by being in this hogan with Pond means we'll all be sick." Nathan was surprised how easily he remembered his science project research. "I think we should try testing some human medicine on Pond to see if it'll make him feel better."

"Never before has the way of the five-fingered affected us

so," Nathan heard Darkness whisper to itself. Then Darkness said to him, "Nathan, we've tried human medicine on our own before with other helpers. And each time, we've had no success."

Something didn't add up for Nathan. He said, "I'm confused. If the human medicine didn't work, then how did the uranium affect Pond? Isn't uranium a human product?"

"The rocks that humans named uranium," Darkness said, "are actually the petrified blood of the Enemies felled by the Hero Twins. Even in death, the Enemies of old manage to disrupt the harmony we have created in the Fourth World." Darkness shook its head.

With a loud yet gentle voice, First Turkey said, "Water Monster of the Agave Pond, you must attain medicine from your mother to buy us more time." The entire room nodded in agreement.

"My mother?" Pond said, quivering as if from fear. "I'm unable to travel back to the Third World in my current condition. I barely made the journey to this holy hogan, and I have used almost all the medicine in my pouch."

First Turkey curved her yellow beak into a smile and turned to Nathan. Her plumage bloomed as she inhaled deeply and said, "And this is where young Nathan comes into play. He will return to the Third World to gather sacred medicine in your stead."

"What?" Nathan wasn't sure if he had heard them correctly.

"Nathan, will you venture to the Third World on behalf of

the Water Monster of the Agave Pond?" First Turkey asked him.

Nathan felt the eyes of every Holy Being staring at him. His cheeks flushed, his forehead flashed hot, and he got dizzy from holding his breath. Were they really asking him, of all people, to go the Third World? "Yes?"

"Thank you, my friend," Pond said.

First Turkey gobbled, then said, "In return for your efforts, we will gift you wonderful material possessions, such as fine silver jewelry, holy pelts, sacred stones, and . . ."

While First Turkey was talking about what he'd be receiving, Nathan rubbed the bow guard that Uncle Jet had given Nathan. That evil spirit made life unbearable. Nathan had experienced it for a few days, whereas Uncle Jet had been living with it for years. Nathan interrupted First Turkey, "Um, please excuse me. But instead of giving me stuff, can you help my uncle?"

"Help your uncle?" First Turkey said, her plumage deflated.

"My grandma wants to have an Enemy Way Ceremony for him. She says it's a lot of work and many conditions must be met. Anything you can do for him, I'd like that instead of material possessions," Nathan said.

When the Holy Beings didn't respond, Nathan grew nervous. He worried that he had offended them. Slowly, the Holy Beings glanced at one another and nodded.

"Consider it done," Wind Being said. "We, Holy Beings, will aid the medicine man through the process of healing your uncle."

"We must hurry," White Shell Boy and White Shell Girl said.

"We only severed the connection the spirit had upon Nathan. Right now, it is finding its way back to his uncle. It will be very angry."

"Nathan has demonstrated the strength of kindness," Darkness said. "This is why I believe in him. However, I think he should not go alone. There are many ancient beings and the four obstacles that he will not know how to overcome. I wish to accompany him."

"You would make a mighty companion, Darkness," First Turkey said. "Unfortunately, you have many duties in this world to mind. We cannot have a world bathed in complete brightness. Life would wither in the heat of the sun. You must remain here in this world to maintain harmony."

"I will go," Wind Being said. "I will create massive gusts that will continue to move through the atmosphere while I'm gone."

"I will send my assistant, Seed Collector, as well," First Turkey said. Immediately, the horned toad jumped out from her side and took a big angry breath, inflating its round tummy.

"You told me that my only duty would be to collect seeds!" Seed Collector said.

"And it will continue to be," First Turkey said, bowing her long neck so that her eyes were level with Seed Collector's. "I dropped a few seeds when we ascended the tall reed to this world. It is possible that they might have taken root and made more seeds that you can gather. Those seeds would be untainted by the ways of this world."

"Fine," said Seed Collector. It exhaled and sat back against the corner, looking unhappy.

"Can I go, too?" Spider peeped out from Nathan's shoulder. "I promise to be helpful!"

"What can a spider do?" Moon chuckled. "Your webs are much too small to be much use."

"We'll need a way back," Wind Being said. "With her webbing, she will leave a trail that will guide us back to the Fourth World."

"Yes! I'll do that," Spider said. "I'll begin eating as many bugs as I can so that I can produce as much webbing as you'll need."

"Water Monster of the Agave Pond," First Turkey said, turning to look at Pond. "You will teach Nathan some of your songs. When we left the Third World, Mother Water Monster set up several barriers to prevent our return. With those songs, Nathan, you will be able to pass them in safety. Nathan, he will train you, immediately, and when your training is complete, you will venture to the Third World."

"What of gravity?" Moon said, smirking. "Do you want him to collapse inside of himself?"

"I did not consider that," First Turkey said.

"Gravity?" Nathan said.

"Gravity's influence is greater in the Third World than this world," Darkness said. "It's so strong that time in the Third World is slower than it is up here."

"Like a black hole in space," Nathan said.

"Exactly," Moon said. "There is a way to overcome those influences. If Darkness is willing to perform a blessing, that is."

"Of course I am," Darkness said.

"Very well," Moon said. "I will offer my sands and support. In return, if I ever need assistance from either the water monster or the human, I shall expect them to help me."

Pond said to Moon, "Thank you. Anything at all, I will be glad to assist."

"Pray listen, young Nathan," First Turkey said. "This task is proving to be most important and daunting. Once you have been blessed with moon sand, and after learning some of the Water Monster's songs, you will journey to the Third World to meet Mother Water Monster. We will aim for the next full moon, as water monster songs have much more influence at that time. In return for your services, we will aid your uncle. If there is no more to contribute, I declare this diagnosis meeting a success."

"Ha-ho," all the Holy Beings said. With that, the Ocean Being extended his arm and let fall fat drops of water onto the fireplace and the fire was extinguished. Embers flew into the air and dimmed out of existence.

Nathan stood outside the holy hogan with First Turkey, Seed Collector, Darkness, Moon, Wind Being, Pond, and Spider, who slept behind Nathan's ear.

"Young Nathan," First Turkey said in between gobbles. "It has been a pleasure meeting you. I don't have a very positive opinion of your beings, but you stand out as top quality. Not every human would so willingly volunteer to venture to the Third World. And I'm not surprised. I have no desire to meet Mother Water Monster again. She was absolutely terrifying."

Nathan felt his knees become wobbly. Human beings were banned from the Third World because First Woman had kidnapped an infant water monster. Mother Water Monster was sure to still be angry with humans after all these years.

"Don't be scared, Nathan," First Turkey said. "Once she learns that you are representing her child, she will listen and aid you."

"Are you sure about that?" Nathan asked, wanting more reassurance.

"I'm not," First Turkey said. She chuckled and smiled. "But as I've said, you defy expectations. The mere fact that I can touch you and physically interact with you"—First Turkey wrapped her large wing around him, and he felt an amazing warmth emanating from her bosom—"shows how special you are."

"I'm not that special. I mean, there must be others who can do this, too," Nathan said, hoping someone else could go in his place to the Third World.

"If you ever choose the path of medicine folk, I will gladly reunite with you. Remember that in your adult years, Nathan." She pulled him into a hug. "With that, my assistant and I must be off. Seed Collector will continue to gather seeds until Darkness says you are ready to go to the Third World. You will not encounter Seed Collector until then."

"Thank goodness." Seed Collector tilted its pointy chin upward.

"Goodbye, Nathan," First Turkey said. She and Seed Collector left.

"Nathan, are you ready to return?" Wind Being asked.

"Yeah," Nathan said, yawning. He didn't even realize that he was getting tired. So much had happened that he needed time to think.

"We will meet tomorrow night," Darkness said. "And we will begin your training. With the sands of the moon, you will be able to learn the songs with no danger to your being."

Nathan wondered what Darkness meant about danger to his being. Was there something dangerous about the songs?

"Thank you, Nathan, for everything you have done for me," said Pond through raspy coughs and body-shaking dry heaves.

Nathan went over and gave him a hug. Pond smiled and then left with Darkness and Moon.

"Wind, I'm ready when you are," Nathan said. He yawned again. His entire body felt as though he had worked for hours in the sun. All this excitement must have worn him down more than he realized.

"Yes," Wind Being said. And off Nathan and Spider went through the desert back to Nali's mobile home.

Back in his bedroom, Nathan lifted his hand to a corner of the ceiling. Spider's tiny feet tapped against his forearm. As soon as Spider was safely off his arm, he scratched where she had traveled.

"I'm so excited to go to the Third World!" Spider said. "I will hunt extra hard so that I can produce miles and miles of web for you!" She crawled into a crack and disappeared, still talking in her upbeat voice.

Nathan took off the bow guard and sprawled across the mattress. He closed his eyes. But his fear of meeting Mother Water Monster kept him awake.

Later that morning, when Nathan heard Nali walking around in the kitchen, he went out to her.

"How are you feeling, shinálí?" Nali said.

He glanced over at Uncle Jet on the couch; Jet looked like he wasn't having bad dreams. "Why isn't Uncle Jet sleeping in the hogan?"

"The hogan is still set up for his diagnosis. Not fit for sleeping in."

"Oh, okay. Nali, can I join you this morning for your prayer?"

She smiled. "Come get your sandals on and we'll go together."

In a few minutes, Nathan was ready and met Nali on the front porch. They walked toward the morning horizon. The rising sun set the eastern horizon on fire with golden rays.

"What are you going to pray for?" Nali asked.

"I'm—I think I'm gonna pray for Pond, the water monster," Nathan said.

"Oh, so she has a name?"

"He. I call *him* Pond, because an agave pond belongs to him."

"I remember that place. How did you know about that?" Nali asked.

Nathan blushed. He forgot that she didn't know that he had been sneaking out at night to help Pond. "Pond told me," Nathan said quickly.

"There certainly have been a lot of different things happening around here. Just please tell me if any of this becomes too much for you to handle. I need to know that you're safe and not putting yourself in danger," Nali said.

Nathan imagined facing Mother Water Monster and remembered that she was set on drowning his ancestors. He didn't want to go. Maybe he could find someone else. Nathan looked at Nali. But he didn't think Nali was the right person to go in his place. Even if he did tell Nali, she might try to protect him and prevent him from going to the Third World. "I'll tell you, Nali."

"Nizhoní. Nathan, I want you to pray for your uncle," Nali said as they reached the eastern edge of the cornfield. "Devin has officially recommended an N'dáá. I'm not sure how long your uncle's good mood will last this time. At times he'll be a gentleman and then later will go on a drinking spree. He needs to have this ceremony, shinálí."

"Nali, I think there's something attached to Uncle Jet," Nathan said. Nali had to know what was happening with him. "It's like a thing with a pair of eyes that whispers mean things to him."

"You've seen it."

"Yes," Nathan said.

"I know that something is messing with your uncle," Nali said. "N'dáá helps the patient confront the Enemy to get rid of it. 'Éí biniinaa, that's why it's called Enemy Way. That thing that is attached to him, it will be gone once your uncle has the ceremony."

So, Nali had already known that something was attached to Uncle Jet.

Nali sniffled and tears flowed down her cheeks. She said, "It's difficult seeing your uncle hurt so much."

Nathan leaned against her shoulder. He could hear her heartbeat. "It's okay, Nali. Everything will be all right."

"I believe so, shinálí. We have to get him through the ceremony, and then he will be healed. Everything will be better after the N'dáá. We can do it."

Nathan remembered what Devin had said: that the ceremony was only part of Uncle Jet's path to wellness. But Nali was talking about the ceremony like it was the one and only thing that was going to cure Uncle Jet.

In the back of his mind, Nathan felt a gnawing fear that made his knees weak and his spine ache. He needed to find someone to replace him; otherwise he would have to talk to Mother Water Monster, who was certainly still very angry with all humans.

Dį́į́' Ts'áadah
FOURTEEN

NATHAN SCOOPED OATMEAL AND RAISINS and held them on his spoon. He wasn't hungry even though the previous spoonful was sweetly delicious. Nathan worried about how he was going to tell Pond and Darkness that they should find someone else—another Holy Being, and not a flawed chubby human—to go in his place.

"You okay?" Nali asked and sat down next to him. She stared at Nathan the same way his mom would while searching for a pimple on his face.

"Huh? I am. Just a little tired. Sorry," Nathan said. He forced himself to yawn, even though he was still energized from Pond's sweetgrass.

"Let's go to Gallup today," Nali said. "You can call your parents, huh?"

"Sounds like a plan." Nathan ate the oatmeal. He scratched

the back of his neck and could still feel the phantom tingles of having the Ash Being pulled out of himself. He was so very thankful to not have that constant heaviness in his heart and the forever emptiness at the back of his throat. That Ash Being was going to go back to Uncle Jet. Nathan did not want Uncle Jet to feel that way again—that if he didn't wake up the next morning, it wouldn't be that bad.

And at that moment, Uncle Jet entered the mobile home rubbing his stomach. "See you guys didn't wait for me."

Nathan wanted to warn Uncle Jet about the voice that was going to return to him. But Uncle Jet would probably make fun of Nathan for believing in the Holy Beings.

Nali said to Uncle Jet, "Son, Nathan and I are going to Gallup today. Do you want to come with us?"

"Nah, gonna hang back and finish fixing the truck." Uncle Jet pulled a bowl out from the cupboard. "Actually, can you pick up some motor oil? I think it takes 5W-20. I'll have to check. What are you going to Gallup for anyway?"

"I need to start raising money for the ceremony," Nali said.

"Hold on, Mama. I'm still not one hundred percent sold on the ceremony," Uncle Jet said. He put his plate of food down and leaned toward Nali.

As their voices became louder, Nathan felt an increasing need to disappear. They weren't arguing yet, but it sounded like that's where they were heading.

"How much is it going to cost you?" Uncle Jet asked.

"Don't you worry about it," Nali answered.

"How much?" Uncle Jet said. His voice became deeper.

"It's not going to be cheap," Nali said. "The ceremony lasts seven days. All throughout, there will be guests who will give material donations, and some will sing the songs with the hataałii. They all must be fed. And we have to put a down payment on the ceremony."

"Jeez, Ma! Listen to that! A down payment? Doesn't that sound the slightest bit suspicious? And how are we going to get all that money, huh? I don't have a job, remember?"

"I'm going to pawn my jewelry and my mom's rugs. I think it's time I sell my rugs," she said. She pressed her knuckles to her lips and squeezed her eyes closed.

"You don't have to do that," Uncle Jet said.

"They're just material possessions, my son," Nali said, her voice quivering.

"This ceremony really means that much to you?" Uncle Jet asked.

"If it means bringing back your smile"—she looked at Uncle Jet—"I would sell the very hair on my head."

Uncle Jet had to have the N'dáá. Nathan said, "It's going to help. It will."

"The two of you," Uncle Jet said. "Fine. But if this ceremony doesn't work, don't say I didn't warn you."

"Yes!" Nali said, jumping up and running toward Uncle Jet. She wrapped him in a hug that made Uncle Jet roll his eyes.

Nathan felt the back of his head tingle, where the Ash Being had been pulled out. He only hoped that the Holy Beings could arrange that the ceremony happen before the Ash Being returned.

After he quickly washed up, Nathan immediately noticed that Nali had put four large plastic trash bags in the middle seat of the front of the truck. As Nali drove over uneven surfaces or cattle guards, something in the bags would jingle brightly. He noticed it in between thinking of who could possibly replace him. Wind said it wasn't able to. Darkness wanted to, but First Turkey said no. He could ask the Holy Beings if someone else would take his place. Nali drove over the last cattle guard and onto smooth pavement. One of the bags jingled.

"You can look if you want," Nali said. "Go on."

Nathan untied the knot at the top of the bag and saw elaborate pieces of shiny jewelry. There were bracelets, rings, and necklaces of dazzling sterling silver that had beautiful decorations, and each held pieces of turquoise, yellow abalone, white shell pieces, and dark jet stone. They weighed heavy in his hand as he held each one. Even the rings were heavy. Nathan pulled out a bracelet and it reflected the sun like clear water.

"That bracelet is called a cuff," Nali said, pulling onto the highway. "It used to be your nálí hastiin's. He always wore this on special occasions. I think he liked it most out of all his sterling silvers."

Nathan put the large silver cuff bracelet on his wrist. It was cold to the touch and it slid down to his elbow. He pulled the silver cuff off and held it at a different angle to let its polished exterior shine. He couldn't wait until his wrist was big enough to wear it. He was too entranced by its design to fully pay attention to what Nali said next.

"Your nálí hastiin wanted me to give it to you when you graduate from high school. And I have a bow guard that'll be yours when you graduate from college. It's missing a turquoise. I didn't bring that one; I don't know where it is. You uncle better not have pawned it."

Nathan put the cuff back with the other sterling silver jewelry and untied another trash bag. He said, "It's your rug."

"Yes, for now."

"What do you mean 'for now'?" Nathan asked.

"I'm pawning some rugs and jewelry for the down payment on the N'dáá," Nali said with a loud sigh.

"What's that mean?"

"It's like a loan. I'll give a pawnbroker my stuff. That person will then say, 'I can give you this amount of money for them.' Over time, I repay the pawnbroker the amount the person gave me, with interest, and I can get my jewelry back. If I don't pay back the money within a certain time, then the pawnbroker owns the jewelry," Nali said.

"Oh. Will it cover the N'dáá?" Nathan asked.

"I hope it will. But realistically, no. I'm going to have to sell the rugs I wove. I'd pawn them, but I only have four. I can't find my Rainbow Being rug. I think your uncle has been selling my rugs for beer money." She wiped a small tear off her cheek.

"Don't be sad, Nali. You can always make more," Nathan said.

"No, I can't, shináli. Shiwos neezgai. My shoulder has arthritis. My weaving days are done. No more talking of selling and weaving, please," Nali said.

"Okay." At that moment, his phone vibrated and his screen filled with one notification right after another.

In one of the pawnshops in Gallup, Nathan stared at the rows and rows of bracelets, rings, bow guards, and stones displayed in glass cases. Price tags with large numbers sat next to each piece of jewelry. There was even a case with old video game consoles and smartphones that were years older than his. Nali waited in front of the pawnbroker, who was examining all the jewelry she had brought. Nathan came to the end of the glass case and saw a sign that read "Dead Pawn."

He wondered if he could ask Devin to go to the Third World. After all, Devin did say he would help Nathan and Pond in any way he could. Okay, Devin was a good option. Also, Devin was a hataałii and knew many songs for the ceremonies, so learning the water monster songs would be easy for him! All he had to do was ask Devin. Nathan felt a little better now that he had a decent replacement. His fear of standing in front of the massive and angry Mother Water Monster vanished.

The white pawnbroker said something to Nali that Nathan couldn't make out. Nali then said, "Yes." The pawnbroker gave Nali some large bills and took the bag of jewelry.

"Please take care of them," Nali said to the pawnbroker. She stared at the bag of jewelry until it was tucked underneath the counter.

Then the pawnbroker looked at the four rugs, carefully inspecting the designs and weaving. "Four hundred apiece."

"Four hundred? I spent a year on each one. I'm selling them to you, not pawning them," Nali said, her voice loud enough that other people in the pawnshop looked over.

"You're free to go to other places. Offer will last until five. But you'll find that I give the best price. I'm not trying to sell you short."

"I've seen your other store in Phoenix. You sell these same rugs that we Navajo weave for thousands of dollars. You're ripping us off," Nali said. Nathan had never heard Nali speak in such a way. Not even to Uncle Jet.

"If you think you can sell it for a higher price on your own, be my guest. It's going to take a long time," the pawnbroker said to Nali.

Nali folded her fingers together and covered her mouth. She squeezed her eyes closed. "I'll take your offer." Nathan heard her whispering, "It's for Jet. It's for Jet."

Back in the truck, Nali sat behind the steering wheel without turning on the truck. She was staring at the doors of the pawnshop. In her lap was the envelope containing all the money that the pawnbroker had given her. She picked it up and held it against her chest.

"Nali?" Nathan said. She didn't respond. Nathan tugged at her shirtsleeve. "Nali?"

"Huh? What?" She shook her head and gave a smile that didn't seem genuine to Nathan.

"It's for Uncle Jet," Nathan said.

Nali smiled. "Thanks for reminding me."

"Like you said, you'll repay the pawn guy and then he'll give you back the jewelry," Nathan said.

"You're right. Your uncle won't be able to steal them and sell them for his beer money," she said. "Let's go to the bank. After that, we'll pick something up for dinner. How does pizza sound?"

Nathan nearly jumped out of his seat. "Yes!"

On the drive back, Nathan called his mom. He held the phone to his ear, anxious to hear her voice. After a few seconds, his call went to voice mail. He hung up, frustrated.

Seconds later, his mom called him back. Nathan immediately answered and pushed the phone against his ear.

"Mom?" Nathan said.

"Nathan. Oh, honey, I miss you so much," his mom said.

"I miss you, too, Mom. How much longer are you going to be out there?"

"It's looking like this protest is going to last for a while. I'll be back as soon as I can. If you want to go back to Phoenix, I'm sure your dad would love to have you at his place until I get back. All you have to do is call him."

"I'm fine," Nathan said. "I need to finish a few things out here."

"How's your project coming along?"

Nathan couldn't think where to begin. So much had passed in the two weeks since he had come to Nali's home. "It's coming along." He didn't think his mom would believe him if he told her about the Holy Beings. She had this whole mantra of "facts and nothing but the facts." And anything that she herself couldn't verify wasn't a fact. "Something was stealing some of my kernels, so I had to deal with that first."

"Take pictures; I want to see your crops!" she said. Suddenly, protestors in the background chanted, "Water is life." "Honey, something is happening and I need to document it. I love you and tell your nálí 'adząą that I said hi."

"Love you, Mom," Nathan said. He hung up after she said the same thing. Hearing his mom's voice filled an absence in his heart.

"Feel better?" Nali asked.

"Yeah," Nathan said. He looked out at the desert.

"I'm sorry that you were feeling so down these past days, shinálí," she said.

"Yeah," Nathan said. Nali still assumed he was homesick and had been missing his mom. Yes, he did feel sad and wanted to be home. But the mood that he endured under the influence of the Ash Being was very different. That mood was as physical as it was emotional. Also, there was a difference in its depth; his current sadness was as deep as a pool that went up to his neck.

Whereas the sadness caused by the Ash Being was like he was desperately trying to keep his head above water in an ocean that was constantly tossing him around and pushing him downward with massive waves.

Either way, he felt better now that he had talked to his mom. And tonight, he would tell Darkness, Wind, and Pond that Devin would be a good replacement. He breathed a sigh of relief and felt ready to face the three of them.

'Ashdla' Ts'áadah

FIFTEEN

WHILE HE WAS BEING CARRIED on Wind Being's back to meet with Pond and Darkness, Nathan had practiced many different ways of saying that he wasn't going to the Third World. The best reason he thought up was this: if Mother Water Monster had banned humans from entering her domain, then Nathan should respect that. He'd then suggest getting an assistant like Seed Collector, and if that wasn't enough, he would recommend Devin. Nathan tried his best to ignore the fact that Devin was an adult and also a human. He hoped his suggestions were enough to get him out of meeting Mother Water Monster.

As Wind Being began to slow down, he saw the outline of Darkness, tall and black, moving up ahead. Then, a few seconds later, he saw Pond, whose head was drooping. He didn't have to stop helping them. He could introduce them to Devin, who would have an easier time learning the water monster songs.

Wind Being slowed and Nathan stepped onto the sands.

"Pond, are you all right?" Nathan asked.

"I will be in a little bit. Isn't that true, Darkness?" Pond said, looking at Darkness.

"Moon has given us some of her sands," Darkness said. "On occasion, her heavenly body passes through the dust tails of comets. Much like the pollen from corn, her sands contain holy attributes that will: one, help you learn the water monster songs; two, protect you from the immensity of gravity; and three, be a most appropriate gift to Mother Water Monster."

Nathan shivered at her name. It was now or never. "Umm, hey, guys. I was wondering if maybe . . ."

Nathan tried to force the words out of his mouth. Pond was looking right at him. It was like looking at Steven or Weslee. He couldn't break Pond's heart.

"Yes, Nathan?" Pond said.

Nathan grew dizzy. He had to sit down.

"Are you sick, too?" Pond asked.

"No, I'm dizzy. You know, from riding Wind Being's back for that long time," Nathan said. Nathan made himself believe that that was what was making him nauseous and not that he was scared out of his mind.

After a minute, Darkness loomed over him and said, "What was your question?"

To buy himself time to build up his courage, Nathan said, "I was wondering how many songs I have to learn."

"We all agreed upon four," Darkness said. "A lullaby. And

three water monster songs. We think that we should spend half of a moon phase with each song."

Nathan's guilt pushed and prodded his heart. Darkness towered over him, making him feel as small as the turquoise in his bow guard. He distracted himself. Half a moon phase, he thought. From full moon to full moon took about four weeks. So roughly a week learning each song.

"That's all?" Nathan said, forcing his voice not to quiver.

"That is all, Nathan," Darkness said. His body moved to Wind Being. He said, "Would you be so kind as to spread the moon sand and stardust? We'll start with the water monster lullaby."

"Of course," Wind Being said as its flower petals fell to the ground.

Darkness lifted up a pouch the size of Nathan's backpack and turned it upside down. The silver sands glowed like the surface of the moon against the dark of night. Winds rushed from behind Nathan and toward the glittering sand and caught the tiny specks in midair.

The sands began to move around Nathan and Pond, floating in circles and hovering above the desert floor. It only took a few minutes for Wind Being to construct a complex sand painting around Nathan and Pond. When done, the sand painting glowed, making it easier to separate Darkness from the night shadows. Nathan completely forgot about what he had to tell them.

The sand painting was intricate and beautiful. It circled all around them, and at the edges of the sand painting was the elongated body of a Rainbow Being. At the center of the sand painting, Nathan saw a human with a square face and what looked like glasses. It must be him. Next to him was what looked like a square and angular version of Pond. Below the two of them was a depiction of the Hero Twins fighting a large bird, a large pig, a large rock, and a large human. Underneath the Hero Twins was a picture of Mother Water Monster and waves underneath her feet. Next to her were a cluster of egg-shaped ovals and smaller water monsters. Wind Being returned to its human form made of swirling winds and dancing flower petals.

Nathan looked at Pond. Tiny beads of sweat covered his scales. Even standing probably two feet away from Pond, Nathan was able to feel that unnatural heat. The radiation poisoning was becoming stronger and starting to spread further.

"Thank you," Darkness said, gesturing to the sand painting. Darkness tilted its head up, bringing it closer to Nathan's eyes. "I am going to bless you, Nathan, with these sands. After this, you'll be able to hear and sing water monster songs without the threat of the water inside your body responding to them. Through all of this, Nathan, you must remain positive. Hold on to your happy memories and what you want to achieve in your heart. If you slip into a negative memory, the blessing will be ruined." Darkness turned to Pond. "Same for you. You'll have to be hopeful."

The sand painting suddenly glowed brighter. Nathan had to cover his eyes. He had to stop the blessing before it was too late for him to back out! He tried to speak but was unable to push the words out of his mouth.

"Everything all right, Nathan?" Pond said.

Nathan was so scared to tell everyone that he couldn't breathe. It felt like the world around him was falling apart and it was all his fault. They were going to be mad at him. But he couldn't talk to Mother Water Monster. He took a big breath and said, "I can't."

"What? I didn't hear you," Pond said.

Nathan stared at the ground, then the stars, anywhere but at Pond's disappointed eyes. "I can't go, Pond."

"Nathan? You said you would help me," Pond said. He tilted his head and it looked like he was shrinking.

"Don't you think that since your mom doesn't want humans in her home, sending a human is a bad idea?"

"No, no, no, no. I saved you, Nathan! In the desert. And you promised. You promised me!" Pond said. Now it looked like he was growing, and his scales were pushing outward, making his shape look sharp and dangerous. "Why, Nathan?"

"I'm scared, Pond," Nathan answered. "What if your mom gets mad and hurts me?"

"She won't, Nathan," Pond said. "If you sing the lullaby, she will know that you are helping one of her children."

"I can't. I'm sorry, Pond," Nathan said.

"This is what I get for trusting a human," Pond said. "I should have listened to my older sister."

"Wind can go without me. I'd just be weight. You can teach it the songs." Nathan pointed at Wind Being.

"I am forbidden to sing water monster songs," Wind Being said. "If I were to sing, my voice would create a tornado from only one verse. It can't be me, Nathan."

"How about Devin? He's a medicine man."

"Is this Devin an adult?" Darkness asked, in a disappointed tone.

"Yeah, why?" Nathan said.

"Having gone through puberty, adults are very unlikely to see Holy Beings," Darkness said.

"Only youths can interact with Holy Beings," Wind Being said. "Once you go through puberty, you will no longer be able to see us or interact with us in this fashion. Devin is also a human, like you."

"What?" Nathan said. It never occurred to Nathan that his role in the realm of Holy Beings was temporary. He thought he was going to be able to see and talk to them way into his adult years. He thought that he was going to be friends with Pond throughout his entire life. "Does this mean once I hit puberty, I won't be able to hang out with Pond?"

"No, you won't," Pond said, snorting and turning to face Nathan. He scowled at Nathan, and the corners of his lips were formed in a grimace like he was clenching his jaws. Pond lowered himself to the ground.

"How about getting a horned toad like the Seed Collector for Pond?" Nathan asked.

Darkness said, "Finding an assistant, such as First Turkey's Seed Collector, takes two moon cycles. And someone would have to go to Changing Woman herself."

"Nathan, you made a promise and you can't back out of that!" Pond said, still lying on the ground. His voice was so loud that Nathan's knees wobbled.

"I'm sorry, everyone," Nathan said. He stared at his feet.

"We are short on time, Nathan," Darkness said. "And you need to learn the songs *immediately*."

The ground beneath Nathan tilted and shifted his balance, while everyone else stood firmly. He was getting dizzy.

"Tell us, Nathan. What can we do to convince you to go?" Wind Being asked.

"I can't go!" Nathan said.

"There is the girl in the mountains," Wind Being said, turning to Darkness.

"She does have aptitude to communicate with us, but she doesn't always see and connect with us," Darkness said. "She is already losing her ability to see us."

Nathan didn't hear the rest of their conversation. He was looking at Pond, who had closed his eyelids and was forcing himself to breathe. He didn't think and leaned down to rub Pond's back. The penetrating warmth was still there. Nathan knelt down when Pond didn't reject the comfort. Wind and Darkness were still talking.

"Nathan, why don't you want to go?" Pond asked, looking directly into his eyes. "Is it really that you're scared? She won't harm you if you learn the lullaby."

"You've said that many times, Pond," Nathan said.

"We water monsters are forbidden from sharing our songs with humans," Pond said. "The only exception being when we are in grave danger and need help. Once she hears you singing my songs, she'll know that I'm in danger and won't harm you."

"But how do you know that?" Nathan asked.

"Do you trust me?" Pond asked.

"I'm so scared," Nathan said, folding to the ground and hugging his knees.

"I wouldn't send my friend into danger," Pond said, crawling next to him.

Nathan's heart swelled when he heard Pond call him his friend. Nathan looked into his greenish-yellow eyes. Nathan hugged Pond's neck and whispered into his ear, "I trust you, friend."

Nathan was finally able to breathe. "Wind Being, Darkness? I'll do it."

"Yes?" Darkness said. Both of the Holy Beings turned toward them.

"I'm still scared to my bones. But I will do it," Nathan said.

In its loud, deep voice, Darkness started to pray. Almost immediately, anxious feelings hastened Nathan's heartbeat. He started breathing heavily, and a panicky feeling made him want to stop the blessing immediately. The moon sand painting glowed.

Then Nathan thought about his mom's smile. Her white teeth that she brushed in the morning and in the evening. He thought about the way she looked when she was fully concentrating and typing a report on her laptop. Then he thought of his father. He remembered the first time his dad brought him out here to Nali's mobile home. He had fallen asleep against his father's shoulder. He remembered his father rubbing his back one time when he had gotten sick. Nathan then realized that he missed his father, and he started to feel bad for being so rude to him this summer.

Then Leandra and her annoying laugh came into his mind. He remembered the tears his mother cried when she found out about her. It surprised Nathan that she cried because they had been divorced for a year. But there were other times he had seen his mom cry. Each time, he wondered how his father could do this to his mom. He hated his father for it, and at the same time he still loved him. Those two feelings were always in him, fighting each other—like the way his mom and father were constantly fighting with each other. He remembered trying to keep his grades up so that they wouldn't argue over his academics when they were all living together. He remembered trying to hide things, like picking up after his father because his mom hated how he left things lying around the house. It was always like that, like he was desperately tiptoeing through a field of buried explosives.

"Nathan?" Darkness said. "Breathe. Inhale and exhale. Focus on the love your parents have for you."

Nathan forced himself to remember how his father used to hold his hand as they walked through the Fashion Square mall. His father always remembered which burger chain was his favorite, even after the divorce. And sometimes his father would be player two in his video games. Even though he wasn't any good, he kept playing the games that Nathan wanted. His breathing had become even; the panicky feeling began to lessen. He pictured the wrinkles that appeared in Nali's cheeks whenever she smiled at Nathan. He thought of Uncle Jet, in the far future, after the ceremony, healed and happy. He thought of Pond, fully healed, no longer dry heaving or coughing. He imagined dark clouds over the mobile home and fat raindrops pelting the corn-field, where his corn had grown five feet high.

"That's it, young Nathan," Darkness said. "Hold those images in your mind and repeat this sacred prayer after me. 'Mother Earth; Father Universe; sacred mountain of the white east, Sis Naajiní; sacred mountain of the blue south, Tsoodził; sacred mountain of the yellow west, Dook'o'osłííd; sacred mountain of the black north, Dibé Nitsaa; mother of all that is good and holy, Changing Woman: watch Nathan as he ventures to the Third World. Bless him from the tips of his toes to the tips of his hairs atop his head. Bless him in a good, positive, holy way so that he will be successful and bring back medicine for this ailing water monster. There is beauty around me, there is beauty around me, there is beauty around me, there is beauty around me.'"

Nathan finished repeating the last phrase and opened his eyes. The giant moon sand painting was moving! Both he and Pond were dancing. The Hero Twins were shooting arrows at the Enemies. Mother Water Monster was creating massive waves! He felt Pond nuzzle his nostril against Nathan's thighs. Nathan looked down at first, but then had to look upward to see Pond's face. Pond was no longer wobbly and looked like he was ready to run across the desert.

"I've heard of the effect of moon sand, but never would I have imagined it to be such!" Pond said, smiling.

"Ah, water monsters have a special relationship with the moon. In due time, you will need to return Moon's favor," Darkness said. "With that, are you ready, young Nathan?"

"I am." He was ready for the challenge.

Hastą́ą́ Ts'áadah
SIXTEEN

"FIRST," POND SAID, "SINGING IS a form of ceremony. When you sing these songs, you are considered holy and must act in such a way. Your thoughts and actions have to be positive. You cannot have any negative thoughts. All right, I want you to listen to the song first, friend, and then we'll learn the verses. This is the water monster lullaby, and all water monsters learn it when we first hatch."

Pond cleared his throat and sat on his hind legs. He closed his eyes and threw his head back. He looked like a massive wolf howling at the moon. Pond began to sing. And then he kept singing and singing and singing. Nathan's limbs started to fall asleep, and if it weren't for the sweetgrass from earlier, Nathan was certain that he too would have fallen asleep. The song itself was pretty simple and kept repeating phrases. There were three different times when Pond stopped singing. Nathan assumed that Pond had finished one song and started on another. The moon had traveled across the entire skyline when Pond finally stopped singing.

"Was that all the songs?" Nathan said, stretching his limbs. He stood up and his vision became blurry and his feet tingled back to life. He was thankful that Pond was finally done.

"That was the lullaby," Pond said.

"What? That took like four hours!" Nathan said. This whole entire time, Pond had sung only one song! "I don't think I'm going to have enough time to learn all the songs. May I record the songs on my phone so I can learn them faster?"

All three said, "No."

"There are things you need to know and remember," Pond started. "When any song mentions a Holy Being, that Holy Being will be present the moment you sing its name. When these songs are recorded and replicated, the Holy Being has to be present at many places at many times. It will weaken the Holy Beings' abilities. That is why these songs, even the very names of certain Holy Beings, can never be written down or recorded and must be committed to memory. When these songs are passed to a new singer, it can't be through artificial means.

"Second, you must not sing these songs around other humans," Pond said, "as they affect water in the sky, in the earth, in the plants, and inside bodies as well. Should a human ever sing these songs, she or he will manipulate the water inside their body, causing great harm to their internal organs. The moon sands protect you from that effect. So, do not sing aloud these words outside the protection of these sands."

"How about practicing?" Nathan asked.

"Only in your mind. Don't hum the melody or whisper the verse. You and those around you will live longer," Wind Being said.

"Will I have enough time to learn the songs?" Nathan asked.

"We are nervous as well," Darkness said. "Do your best."

"Are you ready to return, Nathan?" Wind Being asked.

"Yeah."

"Actually, I was wondering if you wanted me to take you back," Pond said. Nathan wasn't sure how to respond. Pond still looked mad at him.

"Are you well enough to carry him?" Darkness asked.

"Yes. I feel much better than I have felt in a very long time," Pond said. He approached Nathan and whispered, "I want to talk with you."

Nathan nodded and then mounted Pond. What could he want to talk about?

"Very well, I will meet you two out here tomorrow night." Darkness bent over, reached underneath a shadow, and lifted it up like he was pulling off a sticker. Darkness slid underneath it and let the shadow fall back down. After a few water-like ripples, the shadow returned to normal and Darkness was nowhere to be seen. Wind Being waved goodbye, and its human form disintegrated into strings of wind carrying cactus flower petals and sand.

Pond took them up a hill and jumped, sending them into a

short free fall. Nathan missed riding on Pond. He felt safer, and trusted Pond more than Wind. Pond ran, quicker than he had previously, for a good distance before Nathan realized that he wasn't taking him to Nali's mobile home. He could think of only one other place where Pond would take him: his pond.

Nathan had guessed correctly. Pond stopped when they arrived at the dry waterbed. Nathan dismounted and could feel the smooth rocks underneath the thin soles of his sneakers.

Before Nathan could say anything, Pond said, "I need to know that you are going to follow through with what you said."

"I said I would." Nathan kicked one of the smooth rocks and it flew into the air.

"That's what you said earlier, too. How do I know you won't back out at the last minute?" Pond pressed.

Nathan wasn't even considering going back on what he said. "I guess you're going to have to trust me."

"I did and I got hurt."

"I'm sorry, Pond. I'll pinkie promise if you want me to!" Nathan held out his pinkie and then realized that water monsters couldn't pinkie promise. What else could Nathan do to prove to Pond that he wasn't going to want out again? "I'm sorry that I hurt you, Pond. But those were my feelings before. I hope that, as my friend, you can understand them."

"Know that trusting you isn't going to be as easy as before." Pond walked up to him and rested his chin on Nathan's shoulder. "But I'll try."

Nathan wrapped his arms around Pond's scaly neck.

"Can you feel the water?" Pond said, untangling himself from Nathan's hug.

Nathan stuck out his arm and could feel that there was something in the air. It was cold and heavy. Nathan looked at the ground and saw solitary blades of grass poking upward.

"There's groundwater very, very far below us," Pond said. "I bet I can sing it up."

"Do you think you have enough strength?" Nathan said.

"I want to try. When you're ready, cover your ears."

Nathan covered his ears. Pond's mouth opened and closed. After a few minutes, the earth beneath his feet started to sink in like a sponge. It turned dark brown and grew muddy. Water was seeping through the tiny spaces all around them. Water kept rising and rising until the entire pond bed was filled with a thin layer of water. It took Nathan a moment to realize that he wasn't standing in water. Instead, the water avoided his feet. He lifted his foot and placed it in another spot. The water moved and his foot touched the earth.

"Cool!" Nathan said.

"I haven't done this in a while, so it won't be perfect," Pond said as he stretched. His claws protruded out of his fingertips as he reached and reached above his head and kicked his leg back. He twisted and turned his neck, like a waking cat. Then he raised his tail and slammed it down. The water evaporated into a mist. When Nathan inhaled, some of the water touched his tongue and it was sweet. The mist rose and rose and then became a hovering gray cloud above both their heads. It kept rising and rising.

Pond gently pawed Nathan's fingers away from his ears. "What's your favorite kind of rain?" Pond said.

Nathan didn't like the monsoon rains in Phoenix that flooded the streets. Now that he thought about it, he didn't like rain all that much. But he did like snow. "How about snow?"

"Close your ears, or else you might turn into a human ice cube," Pond said, a smile curving his lips. After Nathan covered his ears, snow began to fall around him. He opened his mouth and caught a snowflake that tingled his tongue as it dissolved.

"This is so . . ." Nathan said but trailed off. He only got to see snow when his mom would take him to his grandparents on her side of the family, who lived in Sawmill, Arizona. Certain that Pond had stopped singing, Nathan reached out to grab a falling flake.

"Cool?" Pond said.

"Yes!" Nathan said.

"When you finish learning the songs, you, too, will be able to control water a little. Not exactly like this, as this takes many winters of practice. Some of my older siblings only think the songs and the water responds."

Nathan leaned against Pond and watched the rest of the cloud fall down as snow. If he came back to Nali's next summer, would Pond be able to teach him more songs so that he, too, could make it snow? Next summer, Nathan thought, he was going to be twelve, and then thirteen. His time with Pond wasn't going to last forever.

The eastern horizon was glowing a deep red when the last snowflake fell.

"Okay, this is the best way to travel!" Pond inhaled and forced out a great warm gust. The snow melted and surrounded Nathan's ankles but didn't touch them. "Hop on, Nathan!"

Nathan jumped onto Pond. Some water entered his eardrums and froze, blocking out sound. Pond then hummed and swayed his long body back and forth. The water began to circle around them and froth as if heated. Pond lifted his foot to step onto the water. Pond pressed his foot onto the gushing water, and they were propelled forward so quickly that Nathan almost fell off. He squeezed Pond's rib cage with his thighs and wrapped his hands around Pond's neck. Specks of water splashed Nathan's exposed arms and face. The water drops dripped back down into the gushing stream below them.

The water pushed them into a dry streambed. They rounded narrow corners and passages wide enough to allow them through. It sounded and felt like being on a water slide.

"Woo!" Nathan said. Up ahead, he saw a flat wall of sand before them. They were approaching it very fast. "Pond, a wall! There's a wall!"

Nathan couldn't hear if Pond said anything. Water from behind them streamed ahead and curved upward to make a wall of water. The two of them were launched into the air so high that Nathan could see Nali's mobile home in the far distance.

All around him beads of water sparkled as blades of sunlight struck through them. Nathan's stomach upended as he fell back to the earth.

The water collected into a giant spire beneath Pond and Nathan. They both splashed into it and it spread out into a stream again. His clothes and hair were soaked, but Nathan was having too much fun to care. The waters carried them across waves of sands and rock, and in no time, they had arrived at Nali's. The water in his ears melted and Nathan could hear again.

"Let's return this water back to the earth," Pond said, a little too loudly.

"Shh!" Nathan said. "Nali and Uncle Jet are still asleep."

"Sorry," Pond said. The water spread evenly in a circle around the mobile home and seeped into the ground. The ground was dark brown for a minute and then became its usual dry color. It looked normal, but there was a sweet floral scent that wasn't there before, the smell of earth after rain.

"Be sure to practice and rehearse the lullaby in your head," Pond said. "No humming. No singing."

"I remember. I like the water in my body the way it is," Nathan said. He hugged Pond and went to the front door. Before entering he turned and waved at Pond.

Pond smiled and turned toward the desert. A weave of wind behind his tail was blowing his footprints away. There was something wrong with the way he was walking. It wasn't in a straight line. He was swaying back and forth. Nathan had to learn the songs quickly so he could save Pond.

Tsosts'id Ts'áadah
SEVENTEEN

AN HOUR LATER, NATHAN LUGGED a bucket to the cornfield to water his science project. He walked through the area where Pond had spread the water. Tiny green plants pushed out of the ground. Blades of grass and bright colorful flowers the size of fingernails had emerged. It was as if the plants had been waiting for any amount of moisture.

Nali stepped out of the mobile home behind him. She walked over to the washing area, her silver hair let down. She said, "Look at all this greenery! Did it rain last night?"

Nathan yelled, "Pond stopped by this morning and brought some water for us."

"Hash 'akót'é?" Nali said, wiping some sweat off her brow. "Be sure and tell him 'ahéhee'."

Nathan entered the cornfield with the heavy bucket of sloshing water. Nathan factored into his data collection the fact that the modern corn in the square shape had two more weeks to grow than the traditional corn in the circular shape. The modern cornstalks already were as tall as his knees while the traditional ones were barely seedlings. He watered all the plants, including the squash and beans that Nali had planted. Then he measured both corn groups. He jotted how many days each had grown and how tall they were as well as how many ears of corn there were. Nathan planned on comparing the measurements and number of ears by the days they had grown instead of directly comparing them.

Nathan barely heard Nali say, "Who's that?" He pushed his glasses higher on his nose and then squinted. A familiar truck drove on the dirt road toward them.

"Is that Devin? 'Aoo' it is!" Nali said.

The truck stopped next to Nali, who was busy rinsing the soap off her face and drying off. Nathan walked over as Devin rolled his window down. They spoke Navajo to each other.

Nali and Devin shook hands and smiled. After a few minutes, Nali grabbed on to Devin's truck and put her other hand over her mouth. When she removed her hand, a large smile spread from cheek to cheek.

"What's going on, Nali?" Nathan asked.

"Such great news! There's been a change of plans. We're going to have Uncle Jet's N'dáá *this* summer."

"What? Are you serious?" Nathan asked. Excitement bubbled up in his chest.

"I had another N'dáá scheduled for July, but the male patient had a job offer that he had been wanting," Devin said.

There was much that Nathan still didn't know about the Enemy Way, and this talk of a male patient only confused Nathan.

"And he'll need to be doing some job training out of state," Devin continued. "So that means that, if the female patient agrees, Jet can be a part of *this* N'dáá."

"What do you mean by male and female patient?"

Both Nali and Devin looked at Nathan. Nali smiled and said, "Hataałii, I think you would be the person to answer questions about N'dáá."

"Okeydoke. A lot of the ceremonies require both man and woman to participate. Because when 'Adzą́ą́ Nadleehí created the four major clans, she used various parts of her body to create one man and one woman. She grabbed flesh off her body from here, here, here, and here." His hand patted his shoulder, chest, forehead, and thighs. "With those four pieces, she created four pairs of man and woman. She said, in that way, man and woman balance each other. In N'dáá, a woman from a clan different from the male patient needs to participate."

"Not sure I get it, but I trust you," Nathan said. He could ask Nali for more information later.

"The woman still wants to have the ceremony for herself, and there is a need for a man to participate, so I thought of your uncle. The clans work."

"We'll need to go visit the family right now," Nali said.

"Is Jet around?" Devin asked. "I think it would be good for him to tag along."

Nali said, "Nathan, go get your uncle. He is still asleep in the hogan."

"Can I make a sandwich after?" Nathan said.

Nali patted her hair and realized it wasn't in a bun. "Yes. But be quick."

Nathan hurried over and knocked on the door to the hogan. Uncle Jet didn't answer, and after a long moment, Nathan knocked again. When he again didn't answer, Nathan pushed the door open. Uncle Jet was still on his bed, not moving.

"Uncle Jet?" Nathan said. He held his breath and walked slowly toward Uncle Jet's sleeping body. There was something off about this that Nathan couldn't put into words. Then the stench of alcohol crept up Nathan's nostrils. He tapped Uncle Jet's shoulder.

"Leave me alone," Uncle Jet said, with a snappy, unpleasant tone. Uncle Jet pushed his upper torso off the bed and shot an angry expression at Nathan. Nathan stepped back, terrified of what Uncle Jet might do. It was like looking at a raging bull. Uncle Jet then pulled the blanket over his head. "Let me sleep." He fell promptly back asleep. Nathan searched Uncle Jet's shadow for the Ash Being before leaving the hogan. Had it already reattached to Uncle Jet? Nathan didn't find or hear any trace of the Ash Being.

Devin had already left. Nathan found Nali in the mobile home hastily putting her hair into a bun. When Nathan told her about Uncle Jet, she didn't speak for a while and stared into space.

"He's hungover," Nali said finally.

"I figured," Nathan said. He didn't see the Ash Being, so it may have not reattached itself yet. Nathan remembered Devin saying that the N'dáá wasn't going to miraculously cure Uncle Jet and that he would need therapy as well. Nathan rubbed the back of his neck. When the Ash Being was attached to him, it made all the bad feelings that he already had worse. Uncle Jet's drinking wasn't a result of the Ash Being. Rather, the Ash Being made Uncle Jet's drinking worse. Like Devin said, the N'dáá was the first step toward his wellness. And hopefully, Uncle Jet could have one this summer!

Nali said that the family of the female patient was north of Chinle, Arizona, a two-hour drive away. Nathan brought his cell phone and car charger in the truck. When they got to pavement, Nathan's cell phone vibrated. He sent some updates to his mom and his friends. He even told his dad that he was doing okay.

Nathan had also brought the second book of the series that he had borrowed from the library. He had gotten used to reading in the truck without getting as carsick. He liked that there was a new protagonist in the same world and that the previous protagonist was now the antagonist. They drove through Chinle and kept on driving through the outskirts of town and onto dirt roads. By the time they reached the house of the female patient, it was mid-afternoon and the sun was at its hottest.

The house was very nice. It was an actual house, not a mobile home. Big panes of glass lined the walls. The roof had rows of solar panels. Several kids were playing basketball on a cement court that was nestled next to a canyon wall. *These guys must have money*, Nathan thought.

Nali parked behind Devin's truck, and all three of them waited for someone from the house to walk outside. Finally, a woman about Uncle Jet's age walked out and went to Devin first. She had a great big smile. Devin then stepped out and motioned to Nali.

"Hágoshı́ı́, let's meet the family," Nali said.

"Are we going to tell them about Uncle Jet?" Nathan asked.

"Let me handle that," Nali said.

Nathan, Nali, and Devin followed the young woman into the house. The moment they stepped in, Nathan noticed that there was air-conditioning! And it was blowing on top of his head. How he missed the artificial arctic air! The carpet he walked on was so plush that his feet sank half an inch into the floor with every step. There was a television! And below that were all three recent video game systems!

The woman stepped into the kitchen and did the most wonderful thing ever: she filled two cups with water from the sink and put ice cubes into them from the freezer. When she handed Nathan one, it was cold to the touch. Before he drank, he had another pressing concern.

"Um, miss? Where's your bathroom?" Nathan asked.

She smiled at him with bright white teeth. She tucked her silky black hair behind her ear, revealing large squash blossom earrings. "It's the second door to the left down that hallway."

She pointed with her lips.

Nathan almost skipped on his way to the bathroom. When he washed his hands, he laughed because the water was warm. No fire necessary to heat this water up! The clean towel that hung to the side of the sink smelled citrusy orange. He shoved his face into it and sniffed until his lungs were at maximum capacity.

When he stepped out of the bathroom, there was a girl slightly taller than him standing and staring at him. She had a few pimples dotting the sides of her cheeks near her ears.

"Who are you? What are you doing here?" she asked.

"I, uh, uh?" Nathan stammered. He backed up to create some space between them.

"I said," the girl pressed, "who are you? What are you doing in my house?"

"I'm Nathan," Nathan forced out of his mouth. He never found it easy to talk with girls. Especially if the girl was older than him.

"Okay, what are you doing in my house?" she asked.

"I'm with shinálí 'adzą́ą́, and she's talking with that lady with the earrings."

"What does she want with my mom?"

"They're talking about the N'dáá," Nathan said.

"Oh yeah, that."

Nathan exhaled and was able to finally look at her. She was wearing a shirt with a video game logo that Nathan immediately recognized.

"Hey, that's *Angelic Ring*." He pointed to her shirt.

"Duh," she said.

"Have you beat the fifth one?" Nathan asked. Even though she was a girl, and kind of pretty at that, Nathan now felt more at ease talking with her.

"Yeah. Do you think they'll make a sixth one?" she asked. Her voice had become lighter and her body language friendlier.

"I hope so," Nathan said. "Maybe they'll announce something at the next E3 convention."

"Yeah, maybe," she said. "Do you want to play *Angelic Ring 4*?"

"Yeah! The fourth one has the best maps." Nathan couldn't hide his excitement. He used to play *Angelic Ring* with Steven and Weslee.

"I'm Andrea." She held her hand out to him.

"Nathan." He shook her hand. He was ashamed to admit that she had a stronger grip.

He followed her to the living room, where Nali was talking with Andrea's mom. Andrea handed him headphones and turned on the television.

An hour flew by before Nathan felt Nali tap his shoulder. Andrea paused the game and they took their headphones off.

"Come on, Nathan, we're heading back," Nali said.

"Okay. Andrea, can you add me to your friend list?" Nathan asked. He would love to keep playing with her. She was a very decent player. He wanted to introduce her to Steven and Weslee. He was certain they would love to have another online player.

"No can do," Andrea said. All his hopes crashed down. Did

she not want to add him because she didn't like him?

"Oh," Nathan said. His emotions deflated.

"The internet doesn't reach out here, so. Yeah," Andrea said. The way she said that, it seemed like she was embarrassed.

"Come on, you both can talk later," Nali said. She started walking toward the door, with a very different energy than this morning. Her chin was raised, and her eyes sparkled. She was happy.

"Do you guys want water for the road?" Andrea's mom asked.

"We'll be fine, thank you very much!" Nali said.

"No, thank *you*! If it weren't for your family, we'd be stuck in a bind." She pulled Nali into a hug. Nali, her face first surprised, then relaxed, patted the woman's shoulder.

"Ni'dó 'ahéhee'," Nali said.

"Hágoshįį. Hágoónee'," Andrea's mom said.

Driving back to the mobile home, Nali was humming, actually humming, along with the radio. She leaned over and through a wide smile said to Nathan, "Your uncle is going to have the N'dáá in three weeks. Hastóí lą'í, their family has lots of nephews and uncles who are all willing to help with building a chaha'oh for N'dáá and gather chizh for the fires. We got very lucky, Nathan. This doesn't just happen. It's like the Diyin Dine'é are helping us out."

"They are, Nali," Nathan said, hiding as best he could a smile.

Tseebíí Ts'áadah

EIGHTEEN

THAT SATURDAY, FIVE DAYS LATER, Nathan tied the bow guard onto his wrist as the sunlight diminished. He was getting confident enough to sing the water monster lullaby on his own. Tonight, after he sang the song without Pond's help, they would start on the second song.

"Nathan!" Spider said. "Can you hear me? Nathan!"

Nathan pulled the bow guard up his forearm so that it wouldn't slide up and down. "I'm here. What's up?"

"I'm vexed. There are enough mosquitoes and other bugs for me to live comfortably but not enough for webbing for our expedition."

"So you need more bugs," Nathan said.

"Yes."

"Do you eat anything else? Like have you tried chips?"

Nathan said. He could leave her a bag so that she could eat it. Simple enough.

"Spiders don't eat human food. But it does attract what we do eat," Spider said.

"How does this sound? I'll start leaving some food for you to use to attract more food for you to eat," Nathan said.

"Thank you, Nathan!" Spider said and then crawled back into the ceiling.

Nathan tiptoed through the living room. He closed the front door and then looked at the moon, which was three-fourths full and waning. During the next full moon, he would be going to the Third World. He took a deep breath to calm his nerves. He reminded himself that the songs would protect him from Mother Water Monster's anger.

He stood by the cornfield. He was about to call out to Wind Being when the hogan door suddenly slammed against the outside wall. Nathan turned around quickly and saw Uncle Jet emerge from the dark interior. Uncle Jet cursed, grabbed the door, and slowly closed it as if he didn't want the hinges to creak.

Nathan panicked and looked everywhere for a place to hide. Even though the cornstalks had grown, they were too thin and not tall enough to hide him. Then Nathan saw the truck that Uncle Jet had been working on. He dashed over and climbed into the back before Uncle Jet could see him.

He held his breath and listened for Uncle Jet's footsteps. Uncle Jet was probably going to the outhouse. As soon as he heard the door to the outhouse close, Nathan planned to sprint through the cornfield and call for Wind Being. This was merely a short delay, nothing more.

Uncle Jet's footsteps grew louder and were actually getting closer to Nathan! Had he seen Nathan jump into the truck? Nathan quickly started thinking of reasons for being out so late and in the back of the truck. Then Uncle Jet grunted as he pushed the front of the truck. It was moving!

Coming to a downward slope, Uncle Jet jumped into the driver's side and steered the slow-moving truck for a few minutes. Then he turned the truck on. The truck wasn't supposed to turn on! Nathan was so surprised that he couldn't move. The truck drove backward and then turned around. Nathan slowly lifted his head and saw Nali's mobile home grow smaller and smaller, then blend into the dark landscape.

Nathan stared at the stars above as Uncle Jet drove, and he was rocked and jolted around in the back of the truck. He shivered while thinking his way through this. As soon as Uncle Jet parked the truck, he would sneak out and run into the desert and call for Wind Being or Darkness, who were probably wondering where he was right now. Then either would help him meet up with Pond. He simply had to be patient.

The truck slowed to a stop and the engine turned off. Loud hip-hop music blasted through speakers from inside a house. Greenish light from a lonely light post shone on him. Nathan curled up against the corner of the truck bed in the shadows and held his breath. All he had to do was wait until Uncle Jet left. The truck door slammed, and Nathan heard footsteps walk away.

Nathan poked his head up and saw a hogan that was falling apart. The outer logs that made up the eight walls had holes in them. There was a massive gash-like opening that was shaped like a frown on the roof. Light from the inside streamed out of these cracks, making the hogan look like a sad jack-o'-lantern. There was a man walking toward it, but he was much heavier than Uncle Jet. Then Nathan noticed that there was a truck to the side of him. It was too late before he realized that Uncle Jet was still standing by the truck.

"What the . . . ! Nathan?" Uncle Jet said, his voice loud and angry. "Dude, seriously, what are you doing back there?"

"I, uh, I—" Nathan said, but nothing came to mind.

"You know what? I don't care. Don't tell your grandma about none of this, and I won't tell on you. We have an agreement?"

Nathan nodded, too startled to speak.

"Seriously, what am I going to do with you?"

"Jet!" a woman by the entrance of the hogan yelled.

"Whatever," Uncle Jet said to Nathan. "Get in the front of the truck and go to sleep. Okay?"

Nathan quickly untied the bow guard before Uncle Jet could see it and put it in his back pocket. "Yeah, okay. I'm pretty tired." Nathan pulled himself out and jumped to the ground.

Uncle Jet said, "What in the world were you doing back there?"

"I like to look at the stars," Nathan said. The words flowed out of his mouth. "I go out at night when I can't sleep and then I stare at the stars and I like to lie down in the truck and it's comfortable."

Uncle Jet didn't say anything and stared at Nathan. Then he said, "Were you back there last night?"

"Yeah. I'm not going to be able to see the stars when I go back to Phoenix," Nathan said. Uncle Jet's faced dropped. His eyebrows scrunched together.

"Jet!" the woman said again.

"Stay in the truck and don't leave."

Nathan lay inside the front of the truck and Uncle Jet locked the doors. He waited a little bit before he sat up. Uncle Jet was completely distracted with talking to the woman by the hogan. Now was the time to sneak away. Nathan jiggled the handle and opened the door.

Suddenly, the truck honked so loudly that everyone looked over at Nathan. The headlights flashed on and off. All his blood drained to the tips of his toes. Uncle Jet ran to him.

"Nathan!" Uncle Jet yelled.

"I'm scared of the dark." He couldn't think of anything better to say.

Uncle Jet's dark eyes glared into Nathan's. The light post created menacing shadows on his face. "Get out of the truck. You're coming with me."

"No, I'll be fine. I'm sleepy and—"

"Out of the truck. Now!"

Nathan was so scared of the loudness and firmness in Uncle Jet's voice that he wasted no time slipping out of the truck. Uncle Jet turned the alarm off and locked the truck. Then Nathan walked as quietly and as invisibly as possible behind Uncle Jet. He hoped that Pond would understand why he was so late.

The two of them approached the woman. She wore a lot of makeup and many pieces of cheap jewelry. She held a dark brown bottle of beer in her hand.

The woman smiled and then said, "Is this your son, Jet? He looks just like you." Her body swayed back and forth. "No, I'm being serious. He's very cute." She grabbed Nathan's shoulders. "If you lost a little bit of weight, I'm sure all the girls would line up for you."

Nathan tugged his shirt down. Somehow, this woman managed to make Nathan feel both confident and self-conscious at the same time.

"Let's go inside," Uncle Jet said to the two of them.

Inside the hogan, a crowd passed brown bottles and silver aluminum cans around. They were trying to talk over the loud music blaring out from a large black speaker tucked into one of the corners.

"Hey, everybody!" Uncle Jet shouted. "I heard that this was a BYOB. So I brought my own boy! Everyone, this is my nephew, Nathan!" He pointed at Nathan and laughed. Uncle Jet guided Nathan toward the boxes of beer.

A man wearing a black rock-band T-shirt and blue jeans yelled, "You all right, man? You went a little overboard last night."

"I'm good. Slept it off. Now back for more," Uncle Jet said with a sly smile.

"Well, amen to that!" the woman said. She tilted her head and poured the rest of the beer into her mouth.

"How about Nathan?" she asked. She turned to him and lowered her eyes to the same level as his.

"I, uh, what about me?"

"No. He's too young," Uncle Jet said.

"You were younger when you had your first drink," the woman said, giggling.

"This is different. My first taste was with my dad. I'll not take that away from his dad. That moment is sacred. No beer for him." Uncle Jet chugged his can.

For the next hour, Nathan stood against the wall and watched Uncle Jet drink three more cans. Nathan worried about Uncle Jet's ability to drive back. He was going to have to do something. Perhaps if he pretended to get sleepy, they would leave this party.

Nathan approached Uncle Jet, yawning. "Uncle Jet, can we go back? I'm tired."

The woman he was talking with said, "You can't leave now. You just got here."

"Hold on," Uncle Jet said. "Let's get you back to the truck. You can sleep in there."

"He's a big boy. I think he can make it by himself, don't you?" the woman said.

"Uncle Jet, I want to go to sleep." He forced himself to yawn.

Nathan's eyes watered and he rubbed them. He actually was sleepy. But with Pond's sweetgrass, he could get energized.

Uncle Jet reached into his pocket, pulled out the truck keys, and handed them to Nathan. "Go back to the truck and stay there." Uncle Jet was no longer paying attention to Nathan. He had fallen for it. Now all Nathan had to do was go into the desert.

Nathan walked past the truck. When he was certain that Uncle Jet wasn't watching him, he tied the bow guard back onto his wrist and walked to the edge of the light of the light post. He heard the grunts but was still surprised to see two big men fighting each other in the middle of the cars and trucks. They were cursing and saying many things that would make his mom mad. Their fists and knees and feet slammed into each other's bodies with a loud smack. Nathan kept close to the cars and tried to blend in with the shadows.

Then they both fell to the earth, and a large dust cloud bloomed around them. Some dust flew into Nathan's eyes. As he was rubbing his eyes, Nathan felt the full weight of two massive bodies pushing him up against the car. All the air in his lungs was forced out like he was a half-filled balloon. Nathan fell to the earth. He felt the strings of the bow guard unravel and the bare air blow across his exposed wrist. Last thing he remembered, he heard a loud smack and then a lightning-like flare of pain made his vision blurry, then go dark.

Nathan came to with a stabbing pain on one side of his head. He pressed his fingertips against that area. His finger might as well have been searing embers, as the large bump on his head throbbed against the touch. The men who were fighting weren't around.

He had a tough time pushing himself up. Then he realized that his glasses must have fallen off. He felt against the cold sands and found his glasses. The frames were bent. He carefully pushed them back into their original shape and put them on. Long scratches stretched across the lens. He was going to call out to Wind Being and then he felt the skin on his left wrist. The bow guard was gone! His hands frantically sifted through the dirt. A dust cloud began to thicken around Nathan, his hands were moving so fast on the top layer.

He hugged his knees against his chest. He knew he was alone and that someone had stolen the bow guard from him.

Náhást'éí Ts'áadah
NINETEEN

NATHAN NAVIGATED THE MAZE OF parked cars and trucks. His chin pressed on his chest as he looked for his bow guard. Nathan spotted something round and shiny. His heart deflated when he realized it was an empty beer bottle. He kept searching. He didn't find it under any of the trucks nearby or in the middle of the sage bushes. Then he noticed a very faint trail of adult footprints in the light of the light post.

The prints led Nathan to the end of a row of trucks where there was a group of people about Uncle Jet's age sitting around a fire. They raised silver cans to their lips, slurping loudly. One of the men was holding his bow guard! He tilted the bow guard and watched as the light of the fire reflected off the shining silver.

Nathan snuck as quietly as he could over to them. He held his breath and pressed his feet very softly into the ground.

That man said to the others, "How much do you think I can sell this for?"

"Don't you mean, how much 'we' can sell it for?" one of the other men said.

"What are you saying?" the man said. His voiced deepened. He stood up and towered over everyone else. Nathan's spine shivered in fear, seeing how big this person was.

The other guy stood up, his head only reaching to the tall man's shoulders. "I'm saying that I found it, and I am gonna get half the money."

"You think so?" the taller man said. Nathan crept alongside one of the trucks and lost sight of the people. There was a loud sickening smack of skin slamming against skin. Then almost immediately after, another loud thud.

"Anyone else think they deserve half?" the tall man said, his voice growling like a bear's. "Didn't think so."

Nathan snuck a quick peek. The other man was lying on the earth, a huge purple welt growing on his forehead.

Simply asking the man to give him back the bow guard was a no go. Nathan had to come up with another way to get it back. If only he could ask for help from one of the Holy Beings! But without the bow guard, he couldn't communicate with them.

The man wrapped the bow guard around his wrist and smiled. He was missing a few teeth.

Nathan started formulating plans. If only he had the bow guard, he could talk with Wind Being or Darkness! That was it! Darkness was a being of the First World. It would be able to hear him without the bow guard. And if what the Holy Beings said was true about not recording the songs because calling out their names would summon them, then all Nathan would have to do was to call out Darkness's name.

He whispered, "Darkness." And nothing happened.

This had to work. It had to. Nathan sat down and closed his eyes. He thought of the shape of Darkness, its tall body that was flat like a shadow. He thought of how Darkness bent and moved from shadow to shadow like a fire jumping from tree to tree. He whispered again, "Darkness." Still nothing. Maybe if he spoke Navajo . . .

Nathan tried to remember how the words felt coming out of his mouth when he had the bow guard. He tried to remember the sounds. He had the image of Darkness in his mind and whispered Darkness's Navajo name.

The shadows before him bent and became distorted. It was Darkness! If ever Nathan saw anger in Darkness's form, this was what it looked like. Its hands were on its hips. Sharp pointed edges jutted out from its fingers, shoulders, and ears.

"This is where you have been?" Darkness shouted. "The Water Monster of the Agave Pond has been waiting for you!"

"Yes, it worked!" Nathan said. "Wait, how can I understand you without the bow guard?"

Darkness huffed. "You heart and your mind exist in the darkness of your body. Your thoughts form and your desire to be understood exist in the shadow of your brain and heart. Communication is my creation. Speak any language to me and I will speak it back to you. Now, let's be off. I'll call Wind Being and—"

"I don't have my bow guard, which has the communication stone."

"You lost it? This is very unbecoming of you."

"It was taken from me, by that man." Nathan pointed to the man. "I need your help getting it back."

"Very well," Darkness said. "Isolate him and then I will do the rest."

With Darkness at his side, Nathan's fear disappeared. He stood up and threw a stone at the head of the tall man.

"What the—" the tall man said.

"You stink!" Nathan said, and ran in the desert away from the fire. He didn't stop to see if the man was following, because Nathan could hear him cursing and his large feet slamming against the ground.

Surrounded by shadows, Nathan turned around and looked at the large, bullish man charging toward him.

"Now! Darkness!" Nathan shouted.

Instantly, Darkness wrapped the shadows from the trucks around the man. The man knelt down. His screaming was muffled, as if his head were under a pillow. The man screamed and writhed. It was kind of terrifying, and Nathan hoped that the man wasn't in pain. In seconds, the shadows unraveled, and like black ink slipped off the man, who was sound asleep.

"Let that teach you to steal," Darkness said. "Come, Nathan. To the Water Monster of the Agave Pond."

Nathan walked behind Darkness as they headed away from the party. He wondered if Uncle Jet was going to be okay. His concern grew and grew until he couldn't ignore it. Nathan had to be there for Uncle Jet. He also had the truck keys.

"Darkness, I'm sorry. I can't. My uncle is still here."

"Nathan, we are talking about the very life or death of the Water Monster of the Agave Pond. Your uncle has made his choices. He must deal with the consequences."

"Don't you remember that part of the deal was that you'd help heal my uncle?"

Darkness mumbled to itself. It didn't sound very happy.

"Very well," Darkness said. "We'll have the Water Monster of the Agave Pond rest tonight. Yes. Rest would do him well as he is becoming weaker. I expect your full attention tomorrow night." Without a goodbye, Darkness returned to the shadows and disappeared.

Although he felt bad for having upset Darkness, Nathan knew that he had made the right decision. He walked back to the party, practicing the water monster song in his head.

The dark horizon was softening, and the stars were dimming one by one. The light post was flickering on and off.

He came to the truck, with no idea where to begin his search. In case the bow guard slid off, Nathan took it off and shoved it into his pocket. Then he yelled, "Uncle Jet!"

"Nathan?" Uncle Jet's head popped up from the back of the truck. Dirt covered his face and his hair was sticking up.

"Ah snap! Thas right," Uncle Jet slurred. "Em suppose to get back to you. Yeah, yeah, yeah. Txį' skoden."

Nathan wondered how many beers Uncle Jet had drunk. He had never seen his father drunk like this. His father did drink but never once to this extreme. How would they drive back to the mobile home? The eastern horizon was brightening every single second, and Nali was sure to wake up soon. They had to leave, now.

"Come on, Uncle Jet. We have to go." Nathan reached to grab Uncle Jet, who held his palm against him.

"Hold on. Right there, stay. Let me . . ." Uncle Jet slithered over the side panel. His entire body flopped over, slamming against the floor.

"Uncle Jet! Are you okay?"

Uncle Jet pushed himself up and held a finger to his lips. "Not so loud."

Nathan unlocked the truck and sat down in the passenger seat. This night was almost over. He grew even more worried about Uncle Jet's ability to drive.

Uncle Jet forced himself into the driver's side and looked at himself in the rearview mirror. He reached over to grab the keys from Nathan. His hand that he placed on the seat slipped. He slammed the side of his head against the steering wheel and cursed when the loud horn went off.

"Come on, Uncle Jet. Let's get going! The sun is going to rise soon!" Nathan said. They couldn't delay any more, or Nali would find out.

"I'm pretty faded. You gotta drive." Before Nathan could

respond, Uncle Jet had stepped out of the truck. Nathan had never driven before. Well, he had played his fair share of car-racing video games. But that was completely different! Uncle Jet crossed in front of the truck, leaning against the hood for stability.

Nathan rolled down the window and said, "I don't know how! Uncle Jet, don't make me."

Uncle Jet pulled the door open and pushed Nathan to the driver's side.

"It's all good. It's easy; it's automatic," Uncle Jet said. "You pull the gear there and use the steering wheel. Easy-peasy lemon-squeezy."

Nathan looked at the steering wheel. Beyond it, through the windshield, the sky was brightening even more. Nathan gripped the black circle with his sweaty palm and then reached to turn the keys. The truck jolted to life; his hands shook from fear. He breathed so hard and fast that he got a little dizzy. When he felt the world tilting, Nathan took a few calming breaths. He never thought that this was how his first time driving would be.

Nathan had to tilt his chin up so that he could see through the windshield. He scooched himself to the edge of the seat so that his legs could reach the gas and brake pedals. He pushed the pedal on the right, and the engine roared loudly. With Uncle Jet's instructions, he shifted the truck into drive, and it moved on its own.

"Check you out, bro. You got this," Uncle Jet said.

Nathan pushed his big toe down on the gas pedal and didn't

dare go faster than thirty-five miles per hour. When they got to the main dirt road, Uncle Jet told him to keep going until he saw a big dead tree with a tire around its trunk on the left side and to make that turn. It would take them right back to Nali's. He then fell asleep, snoring very loudly. When Nathan finally felt that he had control of the truck, his adrenaline calmed and his senses came back under control. And that's when he could smell Uncle Jet. Nathan rolled down his window so he wouldn't feel like he was about to throw up from the smell.

He turned off the main road when he saw the tree with the tire around its trunk. He slapped Uncle Jet to wake him up. The sun brimmed over the horizon. And judging from Nathan's appetite, it was breakfast time. Uncle Jet got up and then realized where they were.

Uncle Jet said, "Make sure that your grandma doesn't find out. All right?"

Nathan pushed the brake and shifted the gear to park.

Nali was standing right in front of the mobile home, still in her pajamas, her long hair not yet woven into a bun. He had never seen her this angry. And she was looking directly at Nathan.

Naadiin
TWENTY

NATHAN EXPECTED NALI TO SCREAM her head off, but what she did was even scarier and more unsettling. She quietly walked over to Nathan and opened the door for him. Then she told him in a very cold, emotionless voice to go inside. Even though her body language was serene, Nali's eyes contained a lake of fire, and he didn't dare disobey. He cautiously stepped around Nali and made his way into the mobile home.

Starving, he made himself a peanut butter jam sandwich and holed up in his room. He saw Spider crawling down his wall. There was too much daylight for the communication stone to work. But he remembered he was supposed to give her some bait for bugs. He took a small piece of his sandwich and gave it to her. Her long legs grabbed it and she darted back into the ceiling area. Nathan inhaled the rest of his meal, put the bow guard into his duffel bag, and took a nap.

Later, Nathan awoke and stayed in his room reading the third book in the trilogy. He hated feeling anxious while waiting for Nali to yell at him. It was like waiting for a dentist to stab his gums with a thick, long needle. He knew that he was going to get chewed out—there was no question about that.

He read the black words on the page through his scratched lens. Thankfully, the frames were sturdy and hadn't been bent too out of shape.

Then he heard Nali yelling at the top of her lungs at Uncle Jet. A few seconds later Uncle Jet yelled back, at the top of his lungs, too. An explosive slamming of a door shocked Nathan upright. He ran into the living room, parted the curtains, and peeked outside.

Uncle Jet emerged from the hogan with a stuffed duffel bag. An arm of his black leather Marine jacket flapped out of the opening. He was walking away. Nali followed. She grabbed at the bag and Uncle Jet pulled it away from her. Nali lost her balance and fell down.

Her right hand shot out and took the brunt of the fall. "Ow!" she cried, and rubbed her right shoulder, which had arthritis.

Nathan rushed outside to Nali's side to help her up. But she was already standing when Uncle Jet turned around to say, "You can take your ceremony and . . ." Uncle Jet noticed Nathan. "Your ceremony is a huge waste!"

Nathan placed his hand on Nali's elbow; she yanked it away from his touch and shot him an angry expression.

"Get back here. I'm not done with you!" she said. Uncle Jet

was still walking away from them. She brushed the dirt off her skirt, then held her right elbow with her left hand.

"Is this how you're going to live your life? Just run away from everything?" Nali yelled. "Your father would be ashamed!"

Uncle Jet stopped and dropped the duffel bag. When he turned around, there were tears in his bloodshot eyes. He said, "What do you know about that drunk? What did he ever do to help out around here? He did nothing. He was worthless."

"Go on, then. Get out of here!" Nali said. "Go on! Go!"

"I AM!" Uncle Jet picked up his bag and walked.

Nathan moved to run after Uncle Jet. But Nali grabbed his shoulder. Unable to chase after him, Nathan said, "Uncle Jet! Don't go! Uncle Jet!"

Nali said, "This is how he chooses to deal with problems. Inside, now!"

Not wanting to anger Nali any further, he followed her into the dark mobile home. She found her shoulder brace and wore it.

Throughout the rest of the quiet day, Nathan reverted to his familiar routine of dealing with an angry adult. He moved around Nali in awkward, silent steps. He held his breath whenever they were in the same space. He tilted his head down. Back in the days before the divorce, Nathan had perfected these techniques so that his mom or father wouldn't direct their anger toward him.

When it was dinnertime, Nathan set the plates as inoffensively as possible. He tried to remember exactly how Nali had taught him to do even the tiniest of things.

Nali sat down next to him and dropped a bag of white bread, cheese, and Spam on the table. She smelled of Bengay. Nali stared at the door, like she was waiting for Uncle Jet to enter. Tears were sliding down her face like a cracking dam doing its best to hold an overflowing lake. She didn't bother fixing herself a sandwich. She drank a bottle of water with two pain pills that were specifically for arthritis.

"Nathan," Nali said, completely surprising Nathan. "Did Uncle Jet take you with him? He says that you were already in the bed of the truck."

"I—I—" Nathan said. "Yes."

"Why?"

Nathan took a big breath and then said, "Well, I was heading out to meet Pond when Uncle Jet scared me. I didn't want to get caught, so I jumped in the truck to hide from him and then he drove me away."

"So, when you help Pond, you go out into the desert to meet him? On your own? In the middle of the night?"

"No. I'm not alone. I'm with Pond and Darkness and Wind Being. Sometimes Spider."

"Nathan." She took a long, loud sip, which shredded Nathan's nerves. "I'm uncomfortable with you going out in the desert on your own."

"But I'm not on my own. Wind Being or Pond meet me there," Nathan said, pointing beyond the cornfield to where he usually met a Holy Being. "And then they take me to the desert, where I learn the songs."

"Sing one for me," Nali said.

The words of the lullaby rushed to his mouth, and his lips quivered at the chance to sing the song he had put so much effort into learning. "I can't."

"Why is that?" Nali asked.

"Because the song is dangerous to humans. I'm only allowed to sing it with Pond and Darkness, when I am protected by moon sand." Nathan stood up, intending to walk to the cornfield.

"Where are you going?" she asked.

"The cornfield," Nathan said. "Come on. You can meet and see them. Oh, wait, I forgot you can't see them because you're an adult." Nathan sat back down, defeated.

Nali groaned and massaged her temples. "I had been so caught up with the N'dáá I overlooked what was happening with you. I should have been paying more attention to you when you were feeling down."

"That actually was the Ash Being!" Nathan said. "I stomped on its stupid face because it was whispering mean things to Uncle Jet and it stuck to me. We still need the N'dáá to get—"

"Enough, Nathan," Nali said. "There might not be an N'dáá for your uncle."

"What? But we need to. Uncle Jet needs it!" Nathan said. An idea popped into his head. The bow guard! Maybe it could help Nali hear the Holy Beings! Even if she couldn't see them, she might be able to hear them with the bow guard.

"Wait, Nali. I have an idea. You can use my bow guard!"

"Bow guard?" Nali said.

Nathan sprinted to his room and went straight to his duffel bag to pulled it out. While he was tying the bow guard to his wrist, Nali entered his room. She gasped and stared in horror at the bow guard.

Pointing to it, she said, "Where did . . . ? How did you get this bow guard, Nathan?" She grabbed it from Nathan and cradled it with both hands like it was made of thin glass.

"It's mine. Uncle Jet—" Nathan said.

"This is *not* yours!" she said. Tears were freely flowing down her cheeks. "It's not yours. I thought he had sold it."

Nathan felt woozy and the world was tilting again. He did the only thing he could do. He cried, too. He didn't know how, but he had hurt Nali.

"This belonged to James," Nali said. "Your nálí hastiin."

"Uncle Jet gave it to me."

"It wasn't his to give!" Nali said. "Nathan, I am so very mad right now. You should have told me the moment, the *exact* moment, he showed this to you. If I had pawned this earlier, I wouldn't have had to sell my mom's rug! Shimá. I'm so sorry."

Nathan leaned against the wall for stability, because the rush of emotions took the air out of his lungs.

"I need it to learn the songs," he whimpered. "One of the stones is my communication stone."

Nali left the room, slamming the door behind her. Nathan sat against the wall on the mat. Darkness and Pond were going to be really mad at him.

◊ ◊ ◊

Later, the moonlight shone through his window. Nathan would have to tell Darkness what had happened with the bow guard. He had spent the past hour or so thinking of a way to move forward. And he actually had come up with a good solution: he would ask Darkness to make another communication stone and use the second one to learn the songs. That way he wouldn't have to steal the bow guard from Nali.

"Is this where you have been? We need to continue with your lessons. This. Very. Instant!" Darkness said in an angry tone. The shadows around the moonlight rippled like an ocean wave and Darkness's body formed in front of Nathan.

Darkness was not going to like hearing what he had to say.

"I lost the bow guard again."

"What?"

"I'm sorry. My nálí took it from me when she saw it."

"Then get it back!"

"I can't. She said I'm not allowed to have it back."

"Who is she to decide such matters? It is yours, is it not?"

"I thought so. My uncle stole the bow guard from her and gave it to me."

"Oh my, Nathan. We've already wasted so much time. Fine, I'll repeat what I did to the man who first took your bow guard."

"No, please don't do that to my nálí!" Nathan remembered the man's agonizing scream and how his body writhed.

"Then what are we to do? Pond waits for you in the desert!"

"Could you make me another communication stone?" Nathan asked.

Darkness sighed. "Young healer, when I test a being, I gaze into the being's heart and take a small piece of it. This fraction of your heart is what allows you to communicate with all beings. You have such a tremendous amount of kindness; that allowed me to create the stone. But if I were to take more from your heart, you'd grow into a spiteful, hateful man. It's unwise to create another communication stone."

Nathan had been so sure that this would work. No. Nathan had to come up with something else. There had to be another way. He needed more time to think.

"I'll think of something, Darkness. I'm so sorry, but I can't leave tonight."

"This is not who I thought you were, Nathan." Darkness's body dripped back into the shadows.

Nathan was very aware of how his light his forearm was without the bow guard. He felt like giving up. Pond was going to die. And there was nothing he could do about it.

Naadiin Dóó Bi'ąą T'ááłá'í

TWENTY-ONE

NATHAN'S MODERN CORNSTALKS MEASURED TWO feet tall. Small ears grew on the sides of the stalks. The traditional cornstalks were coming up fast; they were now a foot tall. Nathan looked at the notes on his phone; once he got to reception, he'd upload his measurements to the cloud.

Nathan finished and sat near Nali by the cooking fire. She was no longer sad but was angry instead. She forced the spatula into the pan of potatoes and stabbed the dough next to it. Even though she still had her shoulder brace on, she was using her right arm more today.

Nathan had no idea what to do next about the bow guard. He couldn't have another communication stone created. Maybe Nali would let him borrow the bow guard? But what about Uncle Jet and the N'dáá? Nathan dusted himself off and made himself and Nali a plate. She had been so rough with the potatoes that they were basically mashed potatoes. The tortillas were torn in several places. Nali ignored the plate he made for her and went to the woodpile and began to furiously slam the ax into innocent stumps.

Nathan finished eating and then washed the dishes. Through it all, Nali chopped and chopped and chopped. Every time she split a stump, a loud roar of pain erupted from the poor pieces of wood.

Nathan walked to her after he washed the last fork. Nali's sweaty hair clumped to her cheeks and shoulders. Her shirt stuck to her body. She no longer looked angry, but exhausted.

"Nali?"

"Yes, Nathan?" Her voice was calmer than yesterday. She made small circles with her right arm, then massaged it.

"Are we still going to have the N'dáá for Uncle Jet?"

"Huh, what? No, he has made his choice. I will have to tell the family that he has taken off."

"But we have to help him."

"We can only help those who want to help themselves, Nathan. Some people are stuck in a cycle and they will always be stuck."

"We can help him get unstuck. The N'dáá will help him."

"And then what? What about after the ceremony? He'll go back to his ways, drinking and taking off. K'ad amá 'idiiłjii bí'oh díneshdlį́į́'. T'ááshí ako. I've done everything in my power, and I have to make peace with that." Nali wiped the sweat off her forehead and leaned against the ax. Her right shoulder drooped down.

Nathan reached out and grabbed her hand. She looked into his eyes. Nathan saw something that he never thought he'd see again. Nali wasn't sad. She wasn't angry. She wasn't happy. She just was there. But she also wasn't. It was the same look his father had when they received the news that Nathan's grandfather had passed away. It was like looking into the plain eyes of a toy doll.

"Nali, we have to keep trying."

"Shináli," she said. "Your uncle is going to be like this, always."

Nathan let go of her hand, then did the only thing he could think of and hugged her.

"Please, don't give up on Uncle Jet. We can still help him. We can still heal him."

"Nathan, stop." Nali peeled herself away from his hug and held his shoulders at arm's length.

"Do it for me," Nathan said. "I still believe we can help him."

Nali didn't say anything for a few moments. Nathan stared into her eyes and matched her silence. Slowly he saw the kindness re-form and warm the depths of her eyes.

"For you," she said.

Nathan wrapped his arms around her waist.

Nali drove them to Gallup in the afternoon. She drove off the uneven dirt road that led to the mobile home and onto the smooth pavement. Nathan checked his cell phone. Still no service. He wondered where Uncle Jet was sleeping and if he was eating.

Was Uncle Jet even safe?

And Nathan still hadn't figured out a way to get the bow guard back. If Nali didn't let him borrow it, he needed to know where it was so he could take the communication stone and leave the bow guard. But Nathan would still have to snoop around Nali's room. No matter how he tried to justify it, he could not imagine himself doing that. It was wrong.

When the truck got a little closer to Gallup, Nathan's phone began to vibrate. His father missed him. His mom was finishing up her reporting at the protest. She would be heading back to Phoenix soon. Steven and Weslee had returned from their trips and said they couldn't wait to hang out. He took his time responding to each and even sent a text to his father that said that he missed him, too.

In Gallup, Nali drove to several different bars. Nathan waited inside the truck while Nali went inside to ask about Uncle Jet. At each bar, Nali returned with a sad expression and no information about where Uncle Jet might be.

Nathan opened a video game app that he hadn't played since he had last fully charged his phone. He wondered if he called Uncle Jet's prepaid cell phone, would he answer? Then again, since Uncle Jet hadn't had a job, he probably didn't have minutes for his phone.

Nathan worried that the Ash Being was getting stronger and tormenting Uncle Jet. A tiny shiver crawled down his spine. Nali drove up to the last bar, but Jet wasn't there.

◊ ◊ ◊

That night, after he gave Spider a piece of candy he had gotten at a gas station, Nathan snuck out into the desert through his window. He ran through the cornfield and then he heard an airy voice that was speaking Navajo to him. It was Wind Being.

"I can't understand you," Nathan said. "And I'm not sure if you can understand me, Wind Being, but I'm ready to meet Pond and the others when you are." Nathan sprinted forward, and with the help of Wind Being, Nathan was in front of Pond and Darkness in no time at all. The moon sand had already been spread out and was glowing beautiful and soft blue.

"Yá'át'ééh shik'is, Nathan. Ni dootł'izhii shą́?" Pond said, looking at Nathan. By the tone of inflection, Nathan guessed that Pond was asking him a question. "Dootł'izhii" meant "turquoise."

"My nálí still has my bow guard."

Darkness grunted and then spoke to everyone. Pond looked at Nathan after Darkness had translated. Nathan couldn't tell if he was curious or mad.

"Nathan, I think it may be time to consider putting your grandmother under the same—" Darkness said.

"No. No one's doing anything to my nálí." Suddenly he realized something. Did he really need the bow guard at all? He could hear Pond, Darkness, and Wind fine without it. "Let's get started! Right now, right here! I can hear everyone without the bow guard. I'll learn the songs in Navajo. It'll give me time to get my communication stone back. Until then, I have the other three songs to learn."

Darkness spoke with Pond and Wind Being in Navajo. After a few minutes, Pond nodded and then Darkness turned to Nathan and said, "You found an excellent solution, Nathan. Not the easiest. We'll begin a new song. We think it best that you learn a protection song instead of a water monster song. It'll be easier to memorize."

Pond nuzzled his nose against Nathan's hip and leaned gently against him. Nathan petted Pond's head, feeling that familiar unnatural warmth. They walked to the center of the moon sand painting and Pond began to sing. Nathan listened first to the melody of the chorus. Nathan then listened to the Navajo words, recognizing a few here and there.

It took Pond ten minutes to sing the entire song. Pond rested briefly before singing again. Meanwhile, Nathan hummed the melody as best he could.

The second time that Pond sang, Nathan concentrated on the words. He closed his eyes and focused his entire attention on the song. The third time Pond sang, Nathan hummed the melody and picked up more words here and there.

During the fourth time, Nathan felt brave enough to sing a small portion of the song. Nathan stumbled over the pronunciation of the words. As he grew more confident, the Navajo language flowed from his mouth. Nathan felt the hard, short consonants and the long, lyric vowels weave together. The language created vibrations in the atmosphere around them. The air around his lips went from cool to hot with the threads of sounds. It felt like the Navajo language itself was its own being.

Pond fumbled and lay on his side. Darkness said, "That's enough for tonight. Pond grows weak."

Pond mumbled something in Navajo. Nathan looked at Darkness and waited for the translation. Darkness said, "He wants to nap before returning to his pond."

Nathan petted Pond's head. The warmth radiated through his hand. While the hardest part of the water monster lullaby was how long it was, the hardest part of the protection song was actually singing in Navajo without the aid of the bow guard. "Hang on, Pond," Nathan said. "I'll learn the songs in time."

Naadiin Dóó Bi'ąą Naaki
TWENTY-TWO

THREE DAYS LATER, BOTH NALI and Nathan ate lunch at Earl's restaurant near the main street that ran through Gallup. They sat by the window so they could keep an eye out for Uncle Jet. Long shot, but still a possibility.

Nathan's burger and fries smelled delicious. Like Nali, however, he didn't have much of an appetite. Nali watched people walk past the window. Weariness weighed down the skin under her eyes, creating heavy pools of shadow. Nathan reached out and held her hand.

"We'll find him, Nali," he said.

Her calloused hands squeezed his. "I don't think soon enough, shinálí. We're going to have to cancel the N'dáá. But I promise you, I won't give up on him again."

Their waitress returned with the check. Nali put her debit card on top of it and said to Nathan, "I'm going to wash up.

After that, we'll call Devin and let him know." Nali stood up and left.

In the parking lot, Nathan spotted a police car. Its red and blue lights were brightly spinning. The police officer, who looked Navajo, was putting a young man into the back of the car. Nathan recognized the black leather jacket. It had the Marine seal on the right arm. "Uncle Jet," he yelled. He ran out of the restaurant.

The officer had closed the back door when Nathan finally reached the police car.

"That's my uncle!" Nathan explained, out of breath. But when he looked in the back of the police car, he could see the man wasn't Uncle Jet.

"Is this your uncle, kid?" the Navajo officer asked. Nathan shook his head.

"Nathan! Get back over here!" Nali shouted. Nathan continued to stare at the man. He could have sworn that it was Uncle Jet. Then he looked at the jacket, and Nathan was 100 percent certain it was Uncle Jet's. He had seen it so many times.

"Excuse me, Officer, may I ask the man a question? Please? He might know where my uncle is," Nathan said as politely as he could.

"Hágoshį́į́," the officer said.

"'Ahéhee'," Nathan said. "Sir, where did you get that jacket?"

Nali approached Nathan from behind and looked at the man. "Nathan!"

The man looked at Nathan. Grime covered his entire face.

His knotted, long black hair dangled in front of his face, where scars crossed paths with one another. "Pay my bail, and I'll sing like a little bird for you."

"Eugene?" Nali said. She leaned forward and looked at him. "I'll call your dad. He'll help you with your bail."

"My dad? He don't care about me," Eugene said.

"My late husband used to be his best friend. He hasn't stopped praying for you. I'll tell him where you are, even if you don't help us."

"Please, sir, where did you get that jacket?" Nathan pleaded.

"I traded it," he said. "I had a bottle of pretty strong stuff and he had a jacket. Idiot chugged all of it as soon as he had it in his hands. He got into a fight and got himself arrested."

"He's in jail?" Nali asked. "But I already called all the police stations. They don't have him."

"Did he have identification on his person?" the officer asked. "If he doesn't and won't indicate his name, he'd be listed under John Doe." He tilted his head to speak into his radio. "Officer 44 to base."

"Base to Officer 44, ten-two," a female voice responded.

"Can you do a quick computer check for a John Doe at the adult detention center?" the officer asked.

"Sure." A minute passed before she responded. "We have a John Doe at 451 Boardman."

"Thank you! Thank you!" Nali said. For the first time since Jet left, Nali smiled and squeezed Nathan's hand.

◊ ◊ ◊

Thirty minutes later, they walked into the adult detention center and stood in front of the receptionist. She smiled at them and asked how she could help them, with the sun beaming behind her through large panes of glass.

"I believe you have a John Doe? He may be my son," Nali said.

"Let me get Officer Begay to escort you to the holding room," she said.

A few minutes later, Officer Begay led them down a narrow, windowless hallway with cracked tile floors and harsh lighting. Officer Begay opened the door at the end of the hallway with a key attached to a large loop with hundreds more rings.

They stood at one end of a large room, which was split into two sections by thick metal bars. There was almost no light. There were about eleven different men lying on the floor or propped up against the wall on the other side of the bars. It was hard to figure out who was Uncle Jet.

A man lay on a thin mattress and faced the wall in a fetal position. He had the same body shape as Uncle Jet. Then Nathan saw it. The Ash Being's evil eyes stared back at Nathan from the man's shadow. A sudden cold fear wrapped around Nathan's jugular.

"Uncle Jet! Nali, he's right there!" Nathan said, pointing.

"Shiyáázh! Please come over here," Nali said.

"That's your son?" Officer Begay asked Nali.

She nodded. "Don't worry! I'll get you out. Just be patient."

Uncle Jet didn't respond to them.

As they left the holding room to pay the fine, Nathan took one last glance and saw those evil eyes blink and disappear.

Later, the county clerk looked at the computer in front of her as she talked to Nali. "Your son has been charged with simple battery and a petty misdemeanor. His sentence is thirty days in detention or full payment of the fine, which is three hundred dollars."

"Three hundred dollars!" Nali stared at her watch. Nathan noticed that there were pieces of turquoise embedded in the middle of elaborate silver flowers.

"Yes," the county clerk said.

"Okay, thank you, ma'am. I'll see what I can round up." The two of them left the police station. As she drove, Nali kept staring at her watch every time they hit a stop sign or red light. By the time Nathan figured out what she was planning to do, Nali had already parked the car in front of the pawnshop.

Nali's hands fidgeted while the pawnbroker examined the turquoise watch bracelet. She was blinking so much that Nathan wondered if she was trying not to cry.

The pawnbroker said, "One twenty-five."

"Please, I need three hundred to get my son out of jail. I don't have anything else. I've pawned everything!" Nathan had never heard this desperate tone in her voice.

"Two. Take it or leave it," the pawnbroker said, grumbling and standing up.

"I have nothing else," Nali said. "I've pawned and sold

everything for his N'dáá."

They didn't have enough money to pay Uncle Jet's fine. Nathan's eyes blurred from frustration, and everything became fuzzy. He rubbed his eyes. His vision returned and Nathan saw the dead pawns, beautiful rugs and dazzling jewelry. Nathan wondered how many people had been in their same position, pawning everything they had to make ends meet. Farther to the side, he saw televisions, computers, and other electronic devices. Then he saw cell phones, most of them pretty old models, unlike his.

"Nali, give me the truck keys!" Nathan said. He knew how they could make up the last bit of money.

"Huh?"

"I can help."

Nali handed him the keys with a questioning look and he took off to the truck.

Inside the truck, Nathan opened the glove compartment and saw what he needed: his cell phone. Nathan grabbed it along with its charging cord and ran back into the store.

Nali looked at him and then at what he had in his hand. "Nathan, I can't let you do this."

"I want to help Uncle Jet," Nathan said, then turned to the pawnbroker. "It's the latest model. No scratches anywhere. I took good care of it."

"It work?" the pawnbroker asked.

Nathan turned it on and a second later its familiar waking tone rang out.

The pawnbroker looked at it from various angles, and after a minute of intense inspection said, "I can do one fifty for pawn," the pawnbroker said.

"How about selling?" Nathan said.

"If you want to sell, I can do three fifty."

Before Nali could say anything, Nathan extended his hand to shake the pawnbroker's. "Sold." As the pawnbroker counted the dollar bills, Nathan pushed Nali's watch back to her.

The next two hours felt like two minutes for Nathan. He and Nali were able to get Uncle Jet out of jail. Before they left for the mobile home, they picked up some Chinese food for dinner. Uncle Jet barely moved and barely talked. If he had his bow guard, Nathan knew that he would have heard the Ash Being tormenting Uncle Jet. An uneasy feeling grew in Nathan whenever he looked at Uncle Jet. He didn't exactly know how or why, but Nathan knew that Uncle Jet was about to do something drastic. Possibly something scary.

Naadiin Dóó Bi'ąą Táá'

TWENTY-THREE

NALI PARKED THE TRUCK AND Uncle Jet went straight
into the hogan without saying a thing to them. The door quietly
closed. It didn't even creak or groan. The silence of the door
closing bothered Nathan, because it seemed like Uncle Jet was
hiding something.

Nali approached Nathan and rubbed his shoulder. "Shinálí,
ch'iiyáán 'adeiilnííł, let's warm up the Chinese food, huh?" Her
voice was bright and melodic again. Nathan looked up at her
and saw that her wide smile had returned.

Later, Nali used the fire that he had built and her cast-iron
pan to warm up their food. Its steam rose into the air. Nathan's
stomach rumbled.

Nathan ate his orange chicken while Nali warmed up her
dish. She placed the beef and broccoli she'd bought for Uncle

Jet into a bowl and handed it to Nathan. "Give this to your uncle for me. I don't think he wants to talk to me."

"Okay," Nathan said. He ate a forkful of food and chewed it on his way over. He slyly pocketed a chunk of beef to give to Spider later.

Nathan stepped into the hogan and immediately noticed how thick and stale the air inside was. Dust motes floated through the sunset-red light and disappeared into dark shadows like lost, lonely phantoms. It stank so much that even standing by the door, Nathan could practically taste the alcohol.

Uncle Jet grumbled from the opposite end of the hogan, covered completely in blackness. He opened his eyes and Nathan mistook them for the eyes of the Ash Being.

"Uncle Jet?" Nathan's voice wavered. Something was wrong here. Something terrified him. Nathan had felt this way before, like his life was on the line, when he was lost in the desert and thought that he would never escape. It was hopelessness.

Uncle Jet leaned into the bloodred rays of sunlight. His head dangled downward, and a long teardrop-shaped glop of drool fell to the dry earth. His duffel bag was torn open and its contents were thrown around him. Among them was an empty plastic bottle of booze.

"Uncle Jet? Do you want to eat?" Nathan asked.

Uncle Jet slowly lifted his head up and stared at Nathan with lifeless eyes.

"I don't need to eat, son," Uncle Jet said very slowly.

"You need to eat, Uncle Jet." He extended the bowl of food to him.

"I'm fine, son. It's all good. It'll all be good. Very soon," Uncle Jet said. He leaned back and disappeared into the blackness. But his eyes. Nathan could still see his red eyes watching every move Nathan made. It was like looking into the eyes of wounded prey staring back at a predator. The air inside Nathan's lungs turned cold.

"Come on, Uncle Jet. Let's eat something," Nathan said, pushing his way through the fog-like atmosphere toward Uncle Jet.

"I need to be left alone, son. Now go."

"I can't. You have to eat, Uncle Jet."

"Nathan. I'm not going to eat anything. So get out of here, now." His voice sounded like that of the Ash Being.

Nathan teared up. The eyes and the voice. It brought everything back, that same feeling of sinking in the middle of the ocean. The weight of the ocean pushing down on his heart. The light unable to penetrate the depths that surrounded him. Nathan said, "No."

"Please, Nathan. Just go!"

"No."

"What will it take to get rid of you?!"

"You have to eat, Uncle Jet." Nathan couldn't think of any other words to say. "The ceremony, you have to be strong enough for it."

"There ain't gonna be any ceremony!"

"Please eat some beef and broccoli. For the ceremony."

"Both you and my mom can't stop all this ceremony business. It ain't gonna help. Didn't help Dad. Do you know how many ceremonies she did for him? Huh? And look what good it did him. Nothing, Nathan. Sure ain't gonna help me. Nothing can help me."

"Eat. Eat." Nathan was crying now.

"It's all worthless. Everything is worthless. Even her damn rug and jewelry."

"No." Nathan remembered Nali's sadness when she pawned her jewelry, when she sold her own mom's rug. He remembered how much each had cost. "They weren't worthless. The gray rug cost four hundred. The blue-and-white rug, four hundred. Her necklace was seventy-five. Her bracelet was two hundred. My cell phone was three hundred fifty."

"Your cell phone?"

"I sold it for you."

"You did that for me?"

"All of us are trying to help you get better. Because you're not worthless, Uncle Jet."

"Oh God!" Uncle Jet cried out.

"You're not worthless. You're not worthless."

"Stop saying that. Please."

Nathan kept repeating those words and walked over to Uncle Jet. He wrapped him in a hug and let Uncle Jet's warm drool run down his arm.

"It's not true," Uncle Jet said. His body shook as he sobbed.

"You're not. But you have to try, Uncle Jet. We're all trying to help you. But you have to try, too."

Nathan held Uncle Jet and they swayed like wilting flowers searching for sunlight.

Uncle Jet wiped his nose and said, "I need help." Uncle Jet tugged on his shoulder and Nathan hoisted him up. Uncle Jet's body bumped against the wall behind them. "I need to talk with your nálí. Take me to her."

Nathan carefully led Uncle Jet to Nali, who was eating her leftovers. When she noticed them approaching, she stood up and was prepared to yell. But then she saw their faces.

"What's going on?"

"Mama," Uncle Jet whimpered. "Can I talk to you? Please?"

"Okay," Nali said. "Let's go inside. Nathan. Here, I got him."

Nathan tried to help Uncle Jet into the mobile home, but the two of them told him to let them have an adult conversation. It irked him, but this wasn't the time or place to let being called a child get in the way of helping Uncle Jet.

He went to the fire and spread the neon embers. He sat down and ate his food, which had chilled. He wanted to know what Nali and Uncle Jet were talking about. He looked up at the stars and prayed for Uncle Jet. Nathan couldn't shake the sadness he felt. He knew that was what Uncle Jet was feeling right now.

The next morning, the three of them waited in the reception area of the Gallup Indian Medical Center. After Uncle Jet told Nali what he had been feeling, Nali called around and, with the help of the IHS Zero Suicide Initiative, was able to figure out how best to help Uncle Jet. After they left the mobile home, Nali called Nathan's dad to inform him of what was going on. But he must have been too busy to pick up the phone, so she left a message.

Uncle Jet and Nali were filling out registration paperwork while Nathan rested his head against Uncle Jet's firm shoulder. Nathan knew exactly what Uncle Jet was feeling, and he shivered while remembering how the Ash Being had affected his own mood. That feeling of being okay with your own death. Uncle Jet's shoulder rose and fell with his deep, heavy breaths. Nathan could hear Uncle Jet's slow heartbeat.

Nathan wanted to make a joke to lighten the mood and pretend like things were normal. It would be better for Uncle Jet to change the subject and talk like none of this was happening, so that it wasn't so heartbreaking.

Would it, though? Because if Nathan did that, he would be doing the exact same thing that Nali was doing, that his father did during the divorce. If he were to pretend and ignore what was actually happening, like the adults did, he would have done it because he was scared of hurting Uncle Jet further. Was that what the adults did? Try to protect him from further pain and sorrow by pretending and ignoring? Nathan didn't want to do that. And he would appreciate it more if the adults talked with him about stuff like this instead of awkwardly pretending like everything was okay when it clearly wasn't. This was something that had to be faced head-on.

"Uncle Jet, I love you," Nathan said.

"We both do, son," Nali said.

"I'm so tired of feeling this way," Uncle Jet said.

Nathan knew that Uncle Jet's negative emotions were being amplified by the Ash Being. "You need the N'dáá."

"I'm not sure—" Uncle Jet said.

"You said you'd try. Remember!" Nathan said.

Nali pulled Uncle Jet into a hug with Nathan in between them. "N'dáá will help you. It'll cure you."

She sounded again like she firmly believed the ceremony was going to miraculously cure him.

She said, "You don't have to be this way, shiyáázh. You can smile again. You have to try."

"I've been trying. For so long," Uncle Jet said.

"K'ad, níká 'o'olwod. You have help now. Niye', Nathan, is right here."

A male nurse walked to them and said, "Jet Todacheenie? We are ready for you." The nurse motioned for the three of them to follow.

The three of them stood and were led through dirty vinyl hallways to a small, boxy room.

In the room, Nathan noticed a pamphlet selling antidepressant medication. It read "You can smile again" and showed a white woman smiling with bleached teeth. Uncle Jet sat on the examination table. He looked weak, scared, and exhausted.

Not long after, a white doctor came into the room and sat down. He had a name tag with a picture of his bearded face. He interlaced his fingers and leaned back in his chair.

"Hello, I am Dr. Williams." He extended his hand to Nali's.

"Louella," Nali replied, shaking his hand. It always sounded weird to Nathan whenever he heard her actual name. To him, she was Nali.

Dr. Williams said, "I understand that you're seeking help, Jet. That was a very strong thing to do. It's not easy to ask for help."

Uncle Jet didn't respond.

"What's going to happen to my uncle?" Nathan asked.

"Well, we're going to put your uncle—that's you, Jet—under constant surveillance. Realistically, we're looking at least six days. In the meantime, we'll begin therapy and we'll start a regimen of antidepressants. Part of full integration will require restricting visits from family and friends."

Nathan's heart dropped. Uncle Jet was going to be alone here for six days!

"I can't see him?" Nali asked.

"Mrs. Todacheenie, we'll have him under constant observation, and we'll use every tool available to help your son. He is—you are"—he looked at Uncle Jet—"in good hands."

"He needs the N'dáá," Nali said. "It'll cure him."

"An In-Dah?" Dr. Williams said. He looked at Nali through his round glasses.

"Doctor," Nali said, "all summer, we've been planning for a ceremony that will fix him. It's in less than five weeks. Once he has it, he won't need antidepressants. He'll be cured."

Before the doctor could respond, Nathan turned to Nali and said, "Nali, N'dáá isn't going to fix him."

She looked shocked.

"He needs both the ceremony and the treatment," Nathan continued. "The N'dáá will help get rid of the thing that is making his emotions and his habits worse. But it isn't going to cure his emotions and fix his habits. He needs therapy and anti-depressants for those. He needs to walk both paths to wellness." Nali seemed to finally hear him.

"Okay," she said.

"Yes. It's my experience that, with the Navajo population, when patients have traditional ceremonies in addition to long-term medication and therapy, the patient has a dramatically increased chance of recovery. But after the ceremony, Jet needs to be in therapy."

"Hágoshį́į́, shinálí. Okay, Dr. Williams," Nali said. "I'll make sure that after the N'dáá Jet keeps up his therapy."

"You're doing the best you can, as any great mother would," the doctor said.

That was all that was needed to send Nali into tears. Dr. Williams handed her a box of tissues. After a few more minutes of talking, Dr. Williams took Uncle Jet away and Nali and Nathan walked to the truck, holding each other.

Nali took Nathan to a burger restaurant. He ordered a green-chili cheeseburger and fries for a late lunch. Her ringtone chimed through their quiet meal. She opened her flip phone and said, "It's your dad." She took off her glasses and massaged her forehead.

"Hi, Justin," she said. "Yes, he's under constant surveillance. For the next three days, then probably another three after that."

Nathan grew anxious to talk to his father.

Nali said, "Yes, we're eating at Grandpa's Grill. Okay. That's wonderful. We'll see you at home."

Nathan's ears perked up. Was his father coming to the mobile home?

Nali said, "Hold on, here he is."

Nali handed Nathan the flip phone. "Dad," Nathan blurted out. His desire to be stoic shattered. It was like he had been standing for so long, ignoring the ache in his knees and ankles, and now, finally able to sit down, felt every pain at once.

"Nathan? Hey, hey, it's all right."

"Uncle Jet, he—" The words weren't coming out of his mouth. Simple sounds and squeaks escaped his throat, but they didn't make any sense at all.

"Nathan," his dad said. "Everything will be all right. I'm coming."

All the images of Uncle Jet floated to the surface. This time, Nathan didn't push them away. It felt okay to let go when he was around both Nali and his father. It felt safe to let the two of them take control. "Okay, Dad."

"I'm entering Holbrook. I'll see you guys at Nali's, okay? Nathan, everything is going to be fine. What you did for Uncle Jet was brave and strong."

"Uh-huh," Nathan said.

"I love you, son," his father said.

"I love you, too, Dad," Nathan said, nodding even though his father couldn't see him.

"Everything is going to be fine," his father said. "When Uncle Jet gets out of the hospital, I'll bring you back to Phoenix, okay?"

"What?" Nathan asked. Nathan couldn't go back to Phoenix, not now.

"Yes, you're coming back to Phoenix with me," his father said, his tone happy.

Nathan was too shocked to respond.

Naadiin Dóó Bi'ąą Díį́

TWENTY-FOUR

EARLY THE NEXT MORNING, NATHAN lay in his bed
and worked on the protection song that Pond was teaching him.
But his worrying muddied his concentration to the point where
he couldn't even remember the melody. In his mind, he repeated
scenarios of telling his father he was going to stay. Each ended
with an argument, and with Nathan being forced to go back to
Phoenix. But Nathan had to go to the Third World. Pond was
growing weaker with each passing day, and he only had one
more braid of sweetgrass to help with the radiation poisoning.
Nathan went back to mentally singing the water monster lullaby.

Nathan heard his father saying hi to Nali in the living room,
where he had slept. He felt his heart unfold and expand, glad
that his father was actually here in person. So often Nathan had
heard that his father would be at one of his school events only to
be told that work had come up. And what's more? No Leandra.

Nathan walked into the living room. "Hi, Dad."

"Good morning," his father said, yawning and massaging his lower back.

"Thank you for coming, shiyáázh," Nali said. She sat down at the kitchen table. Nathan and his father made their way over to her.

"I had to. He's my little brother. Mom, I'm taking both Jet and Nathan back with me."

"Excuse me?" Nali said. She looked confused.

"Once Jet is out of the hospital, he's going to need support. A lot of it. Gallup has some decent people working there, but down in Phoenix, he can have the best care."

"I don't understand," Nali said, shaking her head.

"There are many great therapists in Phoenix for him."

"Why can't he be with me? Are you saying I can't do it?"

"You can come with us as well. But I think he needs to be in Phoenix. He's my baby brother, Mom."

"I don't know about me going there. It gets too hot for me," Nali said.

It looked like Nali was considering it. Nathan said, "What about my science experiment?"

"Son, you can do another science experiment."

"No, I can't," Nathan said. "It's already halfway done." Nathan was desperately thinking of ways to convince his father that he had to stay.

"How about Jet's N'dáá?" Nali said. "A member of the family has to help plan it. I can't plan it by being in Phoenix."

"Does he need it, Mom?" his father asked.

"Yes!" both Nathan and Nali said.

"Okay. Okay. The N'dáá is important. I understand that. But I am bringing Nathan back with me, Mom." His dad took a sip from a bottle of water, then spat out the water after tasting it. "Ugh, it's hot. I can taste the plastic." He placed the bottle on the table.

"Yes. It's about time for Nathan to go back to Phoenix. I can finish his science experiment, do the measurements, and send it to him," Nali said.

Nathan's heart rate increased as if he were sprinting. They were going to force him to go back! No way. Pond was still sick. He had only one option to ensure that he stayed. And that was telling both of them about his journey to the Third World.

"I can't," Nathan said, loudly and firmly. "I'm staying."

His father looked at him like he had never seen this side of Nathan.

"I'm not really sure how to say this to both of you," Nathan finished.

His father said, "I'm listening."

"All right. Don't say anything until I've finished talking. Either of you," Nathan said. He took a deep breath. "So, one night I got lost in the desert following some sassy little horned toad that was stealing my seeds and found Pond, who's a water monster and also my friend. Okay, here's where it gets real. Pond is sick, so I'm helping him get better. He's been poisoned by radiation from the nearby uranium mine, and I made a promise."

"Nathan?" his father said.

"I'm not done. Okay, I discovered that an Ash Being is messing with Uncle Jet, and he has to have an Enemy Way to get rid of it. I know that the Ash Being is back because I saw the eyes, and it keeps saying things like 'You're worthless' to Uncle Jet. We'll get back to that. But I made a deal with the Holy Being; oh yeah, First Turkey was there who was the boss of the little horned toad—its name is Seed Collector. Long story short, I made a deal with the Holy Beings in return for their help with Uncle Jet, so I have to go to the Third World for some medicine for Pond, the water monster. They've been helping Uncle Jet by making it so that he can have his N'dáá this year. I need to do my part by going to the Third World."

Nali looked like she was thinking.

"Third World. Like First Man, First Woman," his father said.

"Yes. Exactly."

His father's mouth made a familiar twitch. His father was not taking him seriously.

"You don't believe me," Nathan said, disappointed.

"No, I don't. All this talk of fairy tales."

"They're not fairy tales!" both Nali and Nathan said.

"Traditional stories, then," his father said.

"Shinálí, you really have been aiding the Holy Beings?"

"All summer."

"And that's why everything has been so easy for Uncle Jet's N'dáá?" Nali asked. "And you are supposed to go to the Third World? Where Mother Water Monster lives?"

"Yes. I need the bow guard, Nali. I have to learn the rest of the songs," Nathan said.

"I want to believe you, Nathan," Nali said.

But she didn't. Nathan thought for sure that Nali would believe him.

"Why don't you believe me?" Nathan asked.

"They're nothing more than stories," his father said. "Stories that grandparents tell their grandkids."

"They are more than stories," Nathan said. Nathan grabbed the warm water bottle and, in his mind, thought the words of the water monster lullaby. He imagined the water bottle freezing. He was so desperate he almost sang a few of the words. He hoped the act of thinking the song would affect the water bottle.

"Well, I don't see how you can go to the Third World if there is no Third World," his father said. "Wherever it is you think you're going, you're not. Because you're coming back with me to Phoenix, Nathan."

Nathan stopped signing in his mind. "I made a promise to a friend and I have to help him. I'm going to the Third World. With or without your permission." Nathan handed his father the water bottle that he had frozen completely solid. Both his father and Nali looked at the bottle in utter surprise. Tiny frost crystals had formed on the outside. "But it would be wonderful if you could, at least once, believe in me."

Nali looked at Nathan. "You need your nálí hastiin's bow guard?"

Nathan said, "I'll take good care of it."

"But you haven't earned it yet. It'll be yours when you graduate from college."

"I'll give it back after the Third World. *And* I promise to graduate."

Nali pulled her glasses down and looked right into his eyes. "Not just from high school. You'll have to promise that you'll keep reaching higher and higher in your education. You're going to get your bachelor's, your master's, and your PhD. Only then will I let you wear the bow guard."

"I promise, Nali. I'll get good grades and graduate from high school, college, and those other schools you said." Nathan raised his pinkie to Nali.

"Deal." She locked her pinkie with his, and they shook. Nathan looked back at his father, who was still dumbfounded by the frozen water bottle.

That night, Nathan finished tying the bow guard on his wrist. He took a huge whiff of the sweet, perfumed night air. The bugs chittered and the stars twinkled. He'd have to come back next year, even if it was only for a few weeks. He walked through the cornfield. The modern rows were almost as tall as he and the traditional were about three inches shorter. Round squash hid underneath large broad green leaves. At the edge of the cornfield, there was a swirling dust devil.

"Hi, Wind Being. I'm ready to go meet Pond and Darkness," Nathan said.

"You've got your communication stone back," Wind Being

said. Nathan thought he heard contentment in Wind Being's voice.

The little dust devil flattened into a trail. Nathan knew what to do and stepped onto Wind Being's back. In moments, he was again zooming through the desert. It was such a freeing feeling, whether on Wind Being's back, or on Pond's back, to be traveling at this speed.

Wind Being slowed down and Nathan's feet pressed against the soft earth. Before him, Pond struggled to get up while Wind Being spread the moon sands out. Nathan hurried over to Pond's side and grabbed around his shoulder to help hoist him up. Nathan practically had to carry Pond to the center of the sand painting. The closer they got to its center, the more Pond was able to use his own strength.

"I trust that there will be no more disruptions," Darkness said. "We are far behind in your teachings."

"Yes. I'm ready to learn all the songs," Nathan said.

"We've wasted enough time with the protection song. Tonight, we need to get started on the water monster songs. After you sing the lullaby back to me."

"I can sing it. I was able to freeze some water today!" Nathan said proudly.

"What?" Pond said. Both Wind and Darkness gasped. "Did you sing out loud?"

"No. Only in my mind. And I told the water to freeze and it did," Nathan said.

"That's incredible," Pond said, his jaw wide with surprise.

"Humans normally can't do that. The water monster lullaby is the foundation of all water monster songs. Melodies and phrases are expanded and deepened in the other songs, which gives the singer better influence over water. But still, you must have been feeling very strongly to have frozen water with the water monster lullaby."

Nathan nodded. He had been desperate. If he hadn't, then he probably would be going back to Phoenix in the next few days.

"Okay, back to the songs," Pond said. "Sing the lullaby, which you learned with the bow guard. Then we'll start the two water monster songs, and then we'll go back to the protection song, which you learned without the bow guard."

Confused, Nathan said, "Sing it, and I'll learn it."

Pond coughed, clearing his throat. Then he sang. The melody of this song was deeper and much slower than the first song. Nathan picked out more words here and there.

A sparkle caught his attention. He lost his concentration and noticed that as he exhaled, he could see his own breath. Nathan looked around and saw that the plants around them had a white blanket of sharp frost. When he looked up, he saw tiny sparkles in the sky like the tiniest of fireflies. Nathan had read about this; it was called diamond dust. It was so cold that the moisture in the atmosphere had frozen into icy crystals. In between the lines of the moon sands, the diamond dust fell onto the desert floor and into sparkly piles. This must have been how Pond had created snow.

Even though it took Pond two hours to complete the song,

Nathan did not feel his body temperature drop at all. When he finished, Pond slumped to the floor. "Oh! My head!"

Nathan went to him and pressed his thumbs into either side of Pond's scaled head and massaged. He noticed that Pond was shivering, which was weird, because his scales were very hot. Nathan helped Pond use the last sweetgrass. Once this braid was done, Pond would have nothing to diminish the effects of the radiation poisoning. Nathan devoted all his concentration and brainpower to learning the songs. But a small seed of doubt grew in the depths of his mind: he wouldn't be able to learn the songs and save Pond.

Naadiin Dóó Bi'ąą 'Ashdla'

TWENTY-FIVE

ELEVEN DAYS LATER, THE MOON was at three-quarters waxing. After breakfast, Nali drove the two of them to the primary ceremonial site where the N'dáá was going to take place. Nali mentioned that the site had hosted many ceremonies throughout the years. There was already a large chaha'oh to house everyone who was going to participate. It was high in the Chuska Mountains, a few miles away from Devin's mobile home. The N'dáá was scheduled to begin next Monday, which was in five days, but there was still a lot of work to be done.

For all the talk and struggle to get Uncle Jet to commit, Nathan realized he had no idea what the ceremony was, apart from the fact that it was seven days long. Needing a break from the repetition of singing in his head the first phrases of the fourth song, he asked, "Nali, what is an N'dáá and what happens?"

"The First 'Ana'í N'dáá was conducted for the Warrior Twins

after they killed all the Human-Eating Enemies in this world. The spirits of those Enemies attached to the Twins and made them sick. The First N'dáá rid the Twins of those spirits.

"Nowadays, if a person interacts with Anasazi, or any ancient civilization, ruins, or pottery, they have to have one. I once heard of someone who went to Pompeii in Italy and, when he came back, he needed N'dáá. The idea is that the spirits of the ancients will attach themselves to you. But it's more common that our people go into the military and complete a tour of duty. When they are discharged, they'll need one.

"You're not supposed to talk about N'dáá outside of ceremonial settings, so I'll say what I can. It's spread out over seven days. The first day is always on a Monday and both families meet and discuss important details. Tuesday and Wednesday, we do preparations. On Thursday, we construct a special item. Friday, we give it to the recipient family. Saturday, the female returns the item. Then Sunday is the actual event. After that, Monday morning we sing to the sunrise and it is complete. Does that make sense?"

"It'll have to do." Nathan understood that Nali wasn't able to share more than that about the ceremony. He wanted to know more, but for that to happen, he would actually have to participate in it. By the time the N'dáá started, Nathan would already be in the Third World. His heart raced when he thought of that. Nathan had done his best to learn what he could. He felt confident enough with the lullaby and the first water monster song, which he discovered allowed him to move water around like he was telepathic. But he did make mistakes here and there. This fourth and final song allowed him to change water from liquid to gas and to solid. But he worried at the rate they were going, that they wouldn't be able to return to the protection song, which he hadn't learned in its entirety.

"You're going to the Third World soon, aren't you?" Nali said.

Nathan shuddered in fear. "Yes."

"Do you know how long you're going to be gone?" Nali asked.

"I don't know," Nathan said.

After a few seconds of silence, Nali said, "I want to have hataałii bless you before you go. I'll call and set that up. I just . . . I don't know what more I can do."

"You've already done enough, Nali. You believed in me."

She drove the truck up a steep hill, and at the top Nathan saw the ceremonial site. A large number of males, some a little older than he, some older than his father, and many in between, worked on a chaha'oh that was much bigger than Nali's. It was as long as Nali's mobile home and twice as wide. The chaha'oh was split in two with a wall of plywood. The older men were placing freshly cut oak tree branches with dark green leaves on the roof and the side walls.

Nali parked the truck and they both stepped out. Nathan followed Nali into the eastern entrance of the large chaha'oh. Inside, a teenage boy was hanging light bulbs on an oak beam that ran across the ceiling.

Someone tapped his shoulder. Nathan turned around, about to scream. Then he saw Andrea standing in front of him.

"I thought it was you," she said.

"Andrea!" he said, not really sure what else to say.

"Hey, do you want to play on my Switch?"

"You brought your Switch?" Nathan yelled louder than he had intended. Pretty much everyone working on the hut looked at him. But Nathan didn't care.

"Nali, can I hang out with Andrea?" Nathan asked.

"'Ałtsé, let's find her mom first," she said, scanning the back of the chaha'oh.

"She's over here. Come," Andrea said.

Andrea led them to the other section of the large hut. At the back end, she opened the flaps to a large camping tent. There, Andrea's mom was folding fancy and expensive-looking Pendleton blankets into a tall tower that reached to the plastic roof.

"Mom, where's my Switch?" Andrea asked her mom.

"Not now, honey," she responded.

"But I want to play with Nathan."

"You're always playing that video game system!"

"You're the one who bought it for me," Andrea said.

"And I'm the one who can take it away." She finished folding and grabbed a nearby chair. She brought it to Nali. They hugged before Nali sat down.

"Yá'át'ééh," Nali said to her.

"'Aoo' yá'át'ééh. Haash yit'éego sindá?" Andrea's mom said to Nali.

"So where is it?" Andrea said.

"Go chop wood, then you can play it," Andrea's mom said.

"But, Mom!"

"Go be helpful! There's a lot of work to get done."

"Mom!"

"Andrea Denehtsoh Yazzie, don't you raise your voice at me. Woods. Now," Andrea's mom said sternly.

"Go chop wood with her," Nali said to Nathan.

"Sure," Nathan said.

"Shoot, just like that?" Andrea's mom said.

Nathan followed Andrea to the woodpile that was behind the large shade hut. Surprisingly, there was already a decent amount of wood chopped and stacked. It didn't look like there was much more to do.

"They're making us busy so they can talk 'adult stuff,'" Andrea said. "You stack. I chop."

That was fine with Nathan, because his chopping wasn't nearly as efficient as Nali's yet. He didn't want to embarrass himself with his imperfect chopping technique. Andrea grabbed the ax and soon got into a rhythm of chopping, stumping, and tossing firewood.

Nathan picked up the pieces by the armload, walked them over to the woodpile, and placed them neatly on top of one another. When he turned around, he nearly screamed. There was a horned toad standing on its hind legs, like Seed Collector. But this horned toad wore furry plant roots as bracelets and even a necklace of sweetgrass. It seemed not to notice Nathan and walked through the wood chips.

Nathan stared at the horned toad. It was walking in broad daylight! Seed Collector would have been hiding in the shadows, darting from one hiding spot to another. Then this Holy Being walked right up to Andrea and yelled her name. Andrea didn't notice. Nathan walked to the two of them and watched the Holy Being call her.

"Andrea," Nathan said. "I think this assistant wants your attention." Nathan pointed to where it stood.

The horned toad looked at Nathan, its eyes wide and its mouth open in shock.

Andrea looked at Nathan. "You can see Plant Healer?"

It spoke in Navajo, looking right at Nathan. Andrea's ears perked up.

"What did it say?" Nathan asked.

"Plant Healer is surprised you can see it."

Plant Healer walked up to Nathan and examined him. It walked around him, its eyes scanning Nathan from head to toe. This one had no fear whatsoever!

"You're lucky. I can barely see it anymore. Where is it?"

Nathan pointed at it. "Right here. What does it want?"

Plant Healer walked back to Andrea and then spoke loudly again. Andrea responded, leaving Nathan to guess what was being said. After some back-and-forth, Plant Healer walked away from them, right into the busy chaha'oh. No one suspected a thing.

"I'm helping it to gather plants with healing abilities. And it wants me to find some yucca root. It says you're the one that's been healing the water monster."

"You know about that?" Nathan said. Did the Holy Beings talk with each other?

"Lots of Holy Beings are paying attention to you."

"Oh, I have so many questions! When did you start seeing or hearing them? Are we the only ones who can see them?"

"Adults can't see them. Most other kids don't, but sometimes they can hear."

"How come this one walks in daylight? I thought they could only walk at night? There's one that kept stealing some seeds from my nálí's cornfield. I think sunlight harms it."

"I think it has to do with who they are assisting and whether that Holy Being operates during the day or night." She shrugged. "Plant Healer freaks out when the sun sets."

"Nathan!" he heard Nali shout. It must be time for them to head back.

"One more quick question. Why can we see them?" Nathan asked.

"We believe in them," Andrea said. "Also, we're Changing Woman's grandchildren, but mostly because deep down we believe in the Holy Beings. Your grandma looks like she needs you. I'll see you around, healer of the water monster."

She grabbed the ax and chopped again. Nathan walked to Nali. Nathan was relieved that there was another person who could see Holy Beings. He could ask her all the questions that had been bubbling up in his mind like shaken soda. Mostly, when the time came, Nathan wanted to ask Andrea to take care of Pond when he returned to Phoenix.

Naadiin Dóó Bi'ąą Hastą́ą́

TWENTY-SIX

POND FORCED HIMSELF TO SING the final phrases of the fourth song, grunting and groaning the whole time. His health was fading fast.

Pond finished the song and winced. His elbows jutted out at awkward angles as he lowered himself down onto the cool sands. Then several scales, glittering from the moon sands below, fell off his green body. Nathan could see vertebrae and his rib cage.

Nathan hummed the third song he learned, which he called the Move song. He soaked the sands beneath Pond's body with the bottle of water he had brought. He then commanded the water to form a cradle under Pond's neck. "It's almost over, Pond. You'll feel better soon."

"Thank you, my friend," Pond said.

Nathan smiled and patted his shoulder. The radiation pulsated through his fingers.

"You have done extremely well, Nathan," Darkness said. "Given how little time you had to learn the water monster songs, Wind Being and I are honestly surprised."

"It wasn't easy," Nathan said. His brain actually ached from how often he practiced the songs on his own!

"Finish learning this song as quickly as you can. You will be leaving for the Third World in three nights," Darkness said, shocking Nathan.

"Three nights!" Nathan said. A shiver ran down his entire body. His heart pumped so hard that he felt the rush of hot blood flow to his head. Nathan forced himself to breathe long, slow breaths. "I haven't even finished the protection song."

"That'll have to be adequate. The water monster song is of higher importance right now. Make arrangements to ensure you are prepared for the journey," Darkness said.

Wind Being floated to Darkness's side and said, "We must tell him of the obstacles."

Nathan's ears pricked up. No one had mentioned that before. "Obstacles?"

Darkness shrank to the height of Nathan and looked at him. "When your ancestors traveled from the Third World, they had to overcome four obstacles before the trials of the Fourth World."

"What are they?"

Wind Being and Darkness turned their human-shaped forms

toward each other. Wind Being said, "We don't know."

"What? Didn't you two come from the First World all the way through to this world?"

Wind Being said, "Yes, we did. As Holy Beings, we have a multitude of duties to make sure the worlds do not fall apart. We don't bother ourselves with history. It has been the responsibility of beings of thought, your ancestors through to you, to remember the histories and share the stories out loud, so we, Holy Beings, are able to remember."

"Unfortunately," Darkness said, "your generation is less concerned with learning the stories as well as sharing them, and more concerned with modern conveniences. As such, we are losing our memories." Darkness's hand rubbed its temples. "I'd hate to think of what will become of me if I were to lose all my memories."

"And you can't remember any of the trials?" Nathan asked. Wonderful! In addition to Mother Water Monster herself, there were four trials.

"We do not know what we'll encounter," Wind Being said. "Our best guess is that the songs Coyote learned from the infant he kidnapped from Mother Water Monster saved the First Beings as they traveled between the two worlds."

"It was my decision not to worry you with the four obstacles, Nathan," Darkness said. "I needed you to focus on learning the songs with as few distractions and as little stress as possible."

"How long will it take for me to get down there?"

"We estimate a few days," Wind said.

"Are you serious?" Nathan said, not even bothering to hide how annoyed he sounded. He wanted them to know.

"Time flows at a different rate in the Third World," Darkness said. "You may live through ten days, but when you return, you will only have been gone for seven up here. As such, you must make your preparations. Humans need sustenance for such a prolonged journey."

Nathan had to absorb this news. Obstacles. Different time flows. He thought he was only going to be gone for four days max. He was going to completely miss Uncle Jet's N'dáá. Feeling downtrodden, he said, "Wind Being, please take me home."

"You can do this, Nathan," Wind Being said.

"I'd like to go back now, please." Nathan said. "To prepare, you know. I'll also tell Spider to be ready."

"Yes, please do," Darkness said.

Wind Being's human form unraveled and stretched into a long stream of air. Nathan stepped on and began to move. As he ran, a three-quarters-full moon was slowly descending against a vast canvas of multicolored stars.

Nathan crawled into his window, and before he took off the bow guard, he grabbed a gummy bear and held it up to the ceiling.

"Spider!" Nathan said.

"Good evening, Nathan!" Spider rappelled down from the ceiling into the light of the stars and moon that shone through his window. Her bulbous abdomen had grown from the size of a golf ball to a racquetball.

"Here you go," Nathan said.

"Thank you," Spider said, grabbing the gummy bear with her front legs.

"We leave in three days. Do you have enough webbing?"

She hung in midair and said, "Yes. With these pieces of sweets, I've been able to capture and consume many bugs! I have miles and miles of strong web that we can use as a safety line. I'm so excited. But also a little scared."

"Me too," Nathan said.

"Get some rest, friend."

"Thanks," Nathan said. It took him only a few minutes to pass out completely.

In the morning, the smell of fire and cooked eggs wafted into his room. His stomach growled.

After watering both corn groups, he made his way over to the eating area, where Nali was sitting. Her back was turned to him. She slurped her tea. Nathan sat next to her and gathered some food.

"Good morning, Nali," Nathan said, hoping she would respond in a happy mood.

"Good morning," Nali said with a flat voice that was hard to read.

"The food tastes good," Nathan said.

"Yes."

Nathan's appetite disappeared. She was angry.

"Tell me more about your doings with Diyin Dine'é," Nali said.

Nathan told her about his journey to the Third World in three days. Nali sipped on her tea, staring into space. Her empty expression terrified Nathan. He finished telling her about how it might take him a few days to complete the journey, and then said, "Are you mad? Please don't be mad."

"You're not going to any Third World."

"I have to."

"It's dangerous."

"I got help."

"You're not going, because I'm going," she said. She stood up and poured more hot water into her cup. "If anyone is going to talk to Mother Water Monster, it's going to be me, a mother!"

"Nali, you can't go. You don't know any of the songs."

"If I can't go, then you can't, either." She sat down and blew a little too hard on the steaming water. Some of it spilled on her hand. "Ow!"

"I have to go to the Third World and I'm going to find the medicine for Pond. And when he gets better, it'll rain, and you'll be so glad!"

Nali poured the water into the fire. The water sizzled and the embers dimmed out. "You must understand, shinálí yázhí, that I'm going to worry about you even when you're an adult. You'll understand when you have your own kids. And when your own kids say that they're going to do something dangerous, you won't simply sit down and allow it to happen."

Nathan went over to her and gave her a hug. "I can do these things. I'm able to be strong because of you." He started to walk back to the mobile home. If he emptied his backpack, then he might be able to carry whatever he needed to bring with him. What would he need?

Late that afternoon, Nali parked her truck in front of Devin's hogan. Black smoke floated out of the ceiling into the scalding afternoon air. If it was already hot outside, it was going to be unbearable inside.

Both Nathan and Nali stepped out of the truck and entered. Devin was sitting in front of a bed of embers looking into its neon orange hue. Beads of sweat fell off his forehead and sizzled into steam after touching the glowing sources of heat. He looked up at them and smiled.

"Dah nidá," he said and pointed to his side.

"He said sit down there," Nali translated for Nathan.

Nathan was wearing the bow guard, but because it was still pretty bright outside, it wasn't working. Nathan helped Nali sit down next to Devin.

"When do you leave, young one?" Devin said.

"This Saturday," Nathan said. "I might be gone for seven days. At least that's what they said."

"You'll be missing your uncle's N'dáá," Devin said.

"I know," Nathan said. "But this is the deal I made with them."

"I still don't understand why I can't go instead of you," Nali said.

"It's not our place to question the design of Diyin Dine'é', shimá. Nathan, I have to admit I'm a little jealous!" Devin chuckled. "I wish I could see the Holy Beings! I wish, when I was your age, they had asked for my help! You are very blessed to be at their service."

"Doesn't feel like it at times."

"Oh, it is. It may be difficult. It may feel impossible. You are the only one who can do this. Otherwise they would have gone with someone else. You are more important than you know. Not only to Diyin Dine'é, but also your nálí 'adzą́ą́, and your uncle."

"Hataałii," Nali said. "Is he going to be okay?"

Devin looked at her and smiled. "Of course he is! That's why we are here. With your prayers, shimá, he will be safe and fine."

"My prayers? I want you to do it for him."

"I will do the songs. But grandparents' prayers for their grandkids are the strongest kind. So, ní, you pray and sprinkle tádídíín on him."

"Okay," Nali said.

"Shimá," Devin said to Nali. "Don't be scared. Trust in the Holy Beings. They wouldn't put your nálíyazhí in danger without the tools and means to protect himself. He's no longer a baby. He's growing into a man."

"I know, I know."

"The Holy Beings will protect him. Your son Jet needs you.

Nathan will be fine. Focus on Jet."

"I'll try."

"Nathan, may you travel safely and return to us quickly." Devin reached into a beaded pouch and pulled out a handful of cedar. He sprinkled the cedar on the bed of embers and its mountain smell filled the entire hogan.

It was happening. It was happening. Nathan's heart began to beat. Nathan was going to the Third World!

Naadiin Dóó Bi'ąą Tsosts'id

TWENTY-SEVEN

THE EVENING OF HIS DEPARTURE, Nathan watched the tall stalks of corn sway in the wind. There were fully grown ears, some ready to be picked. As big as Nathan's forearms, the ears pulled the proud stalks of the corn into a downward bend, almost as if they were bowing with respect to Nathan himself. The height difference between the traditional corn, planted in a spiral, and modern, planted in a square, was minimal. When he returned from the Third World, he would record his final measurements.

Nali walked to him, carrying the bow guard, deep in thought. Her skirt billowed in the winds that were growing in strength.

Nathan bent over to pick up the backpack by his feet. During the morning, Nali had cooked food and helped to fill his backpack with anything that could be of use. He did not feel at all confident with the protection song, which he wasn't able to learn completely. But there was no time left. He had to go with what he knew and hopefully that was enough. He tightened the straps of his backpack. Its weight pulled his shoulders. Nathan adjusted his stance.

"Shinálí, please return safely to me," Nali said.

"I will, Nali," Nathan said.

She smiled and rubbed her coarse thumb against his cheek. "You're growing up way too fast. Going on adventures without me!" She laughed, though she sounded fearful. "Let me tie this for you." She held up the bow guard.

Nathan lifted his arm, and Nali muttered in Navajo while she tied the bow guard to his wrist. The sun fell behind the sandstone rocks and the shadows grew darker. Then Nathan could understand what she said: "Changing Woman, protect my heart. Watch his steps. Guide his steps back to me safely. I put my trust and my faith in your design. Please, Changing Woman, protect my little one, my heart." She finished tying the deerskin string.

"Nathan!" a voice said at the far end of the cornfield.

Nathan turned and saw Jet Stone Boy waving at him. He could feel Spider tapping excitedly against his calf muscle. It was time to go.

"Okay, I got to go," Nathan said.

"Go. Save your friend, then come right back."

Nathan hugged her one last time before jogging to Jet Stone Boy.

"Spider, you can come out now," Nathan said. He felt her tiny legs crawl out from his jeans and then her body moving up on top of his jeans to his shoulder and then into the backpack.

He finally reached Jet Stone Boy and was breathing heavily. "I was calling for such a long time and you didn't hear!" Jet Stone Boy said.

"I'm sorry, Jet Stone Boy. I can't hear you until it is dark." Nathan tapped his bow guard.

"Well, that's inconvenient," Jet Stone Boy said. "Let's go."

"Okay. How do we get out there?"

"Have you ever traveled by rainbow path?"

The Warrior Twins used rainbow paths during the time of the Enemies of the Fourth World. Was that how he was going to travel? "I've heard of it."

Jet Stone Boy started to sing and pulled an arrowhead the same texture and color of his body out of a pouch that hung at his right hip. A glowing rainbow began to float in the air like ribbons from the tip of the arrowhead. With deep concentration, Jet Stone Boy gently pressed the tip against the surface of the earth. Whoosh! A bright rainbow rose up toward the evening sky into an arch, traveled across the sky, and landed somewhere far away.

"Give me your hand," Jet Stone Boy said.

Nathan grabbed his hand and felt the ground beneath his feet disappear and the force of the wind pull the skin on his face back. Nathan saw the ground fall away from him. The mobile home became smaller and smaller until it was a dot against an expansive landscape. Then he began to fall.

He gripped Jet Stone Boy's hand harder and screamed.

"Calm yourself! Nothing will harm you!" Jet Stone Boy said.

Nathan kept screaming anyway until they slowed down and Nathan was standing in front of Jet Stone Girl. She smiled at him. Pond lay at the base of Darkness's body to his left about ten feet away.

"Nathan!" Pond said. He struggled to lift his head and smile. His breathing was shallow. Nathan could feel the unnatural warmth from where he stood.

"Pond," Nathan said. He walked over to him. The heat grew and grew the closer he got, until it felt like he was standing next to an open oven.

Jet Stone Girl and Jet Stone Boy held each other's hands and were staring at the stars that were appearing in greater and greater numbers by the second. The full moon rose in the eastern horizon. Jet Stone Boy pointed out a constellation to Jet Stone Girl.

"What are they doing?" Nathan asked.

"They are using the stars to pinpoint the destination," Seed Collector said, to the right of Pond. It folded its arms across its body. "Don't you know anything?"

"Seed Collector, we will need to cooperate," Wind Being said, its human body forming from strands of sand and flat discs of flower petals.

"Young Spider," Darkness said.

"Yes!" Spider said, climbing out of Nathan's backpack.

"Are you ready?"

"Yes. I am," Spider said.

"Me too," Nathan said.

"Good. The time is now," Darkness said.

"Thank you, everyone," Pond said.

"Pond, we'll be back quickly. Rest," Nathan said.

Wind Being bent over to speak to Pond. "I would enjoy the return of moisture and the plants that grow here. Yours is a life worth saving."

"We're ready," Jet Stone Girl and Jet Stone Boy said, pointing to a cluster of stars in the northern sky. The two of them sang and touched the earth with their arrowheads. A rainbow trail emerged and shot straight into the sky. It arched, then landed somewhere very far away. Jet Stone Girl placed her foot onto it; her body zoomed into the sky and out of sight. A second later, the rainbow disappeared. Jet Stone Boy kept his arrowhead pressed against the ground.

"That's so cool. How do you do that exactly?" Nathan asked.

"Inside the arrowhead is pure sunlight. When the tips touch the earth, the sunlight refracts and creates the ribbons of color. Through song, I control the ribbons and weave them into a rainbow and then a path that will travel almost as fast as light. One of us must remain on the ground while the other may travel. Jet Stone Girl went ahead to set up your landing site. After we go there, she will return here so that we may bring you back when you are finished." The rainbow reappeared in the sky and then fell down to where Jet Stone Boy was holding the tip of the arrowhead.

"If you're done wasting time, we should be on our way,"

Seed Collector snapped. It raised its hand to Jet Stone Boy.

"Join Spider in Nathan's backpack," Wind Being said to Seed Collector.

"What? No! I would never hitch a ride from this thief!" Seed Collector said.

"Seed Collector," Darkness grumbled. "I might have to have a chat with First Turkey about replacing you!"

"Bah!" Seed Collector said, then jumped into Nathan's backpack. "It stinks in here!"

"Nathan," Darkness said, "bring these moon sands as a gift to Mother Water Monster." It reached into its dark body and pulled forth the pouch containing the moon sands. Nathan grabbed it.

"You have done well, Nathan," Darkness said. Pond moaned loudly and was shivering violently. He curled his body into a fetal position. "Now go! Time runs short."

Jet Stone Boy extended his hand to Nathan. Spider and Seed Collector slid deeper into Nathan's backpack. Wind's human body unraveled and disappeared. Nathan turned to Jet Stone Boy and grabbed his hand.

They zipped up into the night sky. Nathan's eye drank in the scene of the massive desert. The sagebrush, exposed stone, and dry washes turned into a blurry mosaic. Off to his left, Nathan noticed the lights of Gallup. Nathan and the Holy Being streaked across the sky. They were so high up that they plowed right through clouds. As they did, the cold mist collected on Nathan's hair and exposed skin.

They descended into a rocky canyon. Earthen spires rose out

of the ground, and they slowed gently as they reached the bottom, at the entrance of a dark cave. The light of the rainbow reached only so far into the rocky throat of the cavern. They stepped off the glimmering rainbow trail as its light faded away.

Jet Stone Boy and Girl stood next to each other and said in unison, "We'll await your return here."

Seed Collector emerged from Nathan's backpack. "Too dark! Is everybody here useless?" It reached into its pouch and held a small white quartz crystal to its mouth. It muttered some words that Nathan couldn't hear, and then a tiny fire curled into life. With the light, Nathan was able to see into the mouth of the cave.

Nathan stared at the petroglyphs carved into the sides of the canyon walls. There were hands, animals, spirals, and depictions of Holy Beings. There were other pictures, too, that Nathan felt didn't quite fit the style of the rest of the petroglyphs. They looked like jagged rows of rectangles, and a zigzag line that meandered through the mazelike arrangement. Next was a picture of a fish. After that was a picture of someone sleeping on the floor. And last, there was a picture of two rocks that were pressed against each other. These four pictures seemed oldest, and somehow more urgent. It was like these images were trying to talk to him.

"It's beyond the maw of that cave. From there, I'm sure we'll find the entrance," Wind Being said, forming its human shape from the sands around it.

"Whoa, you weren't with us on the rainbow!" Nathan said.

"I have no need to travel by rainbow when there is air

everywhere," Wind Being said. "Let's begin."

They walked into the mouth of the dark cave, guided by Seed Collector's shining quartz crystal. Nathan glanced back at the Jet Stone Twins. Jet Stone Girl touched the earth and stepped onto the rainbow trail that appeared. In an instant, she was gone. Jet Stone Boy noticed Nathan was looking at him and waved at the troupe as they walked farther into the cave.

"Should I begin the safety line?" Spider squeaked out.

"Not yet," Wind Being said. "We'll need every inch of your silk. This entrance doesn't divide or split. It appears to be a straight path to the seal."

Spider crawled into the backpack.

Seed Collector squirmed as Spider crawled by it. It grabbed Nathan's ear and held on to it for support as it raised the light source as high as it could.

"Stop that. It's hurting me."

"Oh, it's hurting you? Would you rather I not hold the light and you can feel around in the dark?"

"Seed Collector," grumbled Wind Being.

"Such a bother!" Seed Collector said. It grabbed Nathan's hair instead. Not ideal, but it was way more comfortable.

The farther back they walked, the colder the temperature became. The ceiling started to dip lower and lower, to the point that Nathan had to hunch forward. Soon, Nathan had to go to his hands and knees and crawl on the cold, rugged stones. Even farther in, Nathan had to take off his backpack and crawl on his stomach.

"I'm not sure I like this," Nathan said. The sides of the cave pushed against his shoulders. He put the backpack ahead of him and pushed it forward and used the tips of his toes to keep moving. The passage was even smaller up ahead. Then it happened. Nathan was stuck. His shoulders were too wide for him to pass through. He pushed the bag ahead, hoping that there was some ledge he could grab. But there was only smooth, cold stone.

"I'm stuck. I'm stuck! Help! I'm stuck!" Nathan squirmed around and every inch of his shoulders, his stomach, and his hips rubbed up against the rock. The light source was on the other side of the backpack. He tried pushing himself backward, but it was no use. The rocks around his shoulders had him locked down.

"Nathan. Calm yourself," Wind Being said. "A little farther ahead the path widens."

"Come on, Nathan! You can do this!" Spider's voice said.

Nathan focused on his breathing to calm himself down. He pushed his hands to the sides of the cave and dug his toes into the floor. He counted to three, then pulled and pushed as hard as he could. He readjusted himself, grabbed, and used all the strength in his calves and forearms to inch forward. As he pushed his backpack ahead of him, it suddenly fell downward. And up ahead Nathan could see a large area. His fingers could feel a ledge! He pushed against the floor with his toes and then he was finally able to grab the ledge! His shirt tore, and the bare skin on his shoulders and stomach scraped against the stone.

"Ah!" he screamed, feeling more of the rock scrape against

his bare skin. He pulled and pulled and pulled and then his head came over the ledge. Three feet below him were Seed Collector and Spider. Using the last of his strength he pushed his stomach and hips, then plopped onto the floor below him.

"Took you long enough," Seed Collector said, holding the crystal fire above its head.

Nathan stood and looked at the bloody scrape marks. They were mainly on his shoulders and around his belly button. They weren't too deep, and they felt more like rug burn than anything serious. He put his backpack on, careful not to rub over his scratches.

"That was scary!" Nathan said. He noticed that he was standing in a round enclosure that looked like the inside of a hogan. At the opposite end stood a massive block of blue ice. Pillows of vapor flowed into the air around it. Seed Collector brought the crystal fire to the slab of ice and examined it.

"Nathan," Wind Being said, "this ice barrier was created by Mother Water Monster to prevent passage between the worlds. You'll have to sing for us to pass."

Nathan walked to the ice door and touched it. It was cold, but it didn't feel like natural cold. The ice expanded and shrank as if it were breathing. Nathan started to hum the melody for the Change song and then sang a few words, but the ice did not respond at all when Nathan instructed the water to melt.

"Try another song," Spider said.

"Okay, how about this one?" Nathan cleared his throat and began to sing the water monster lullaby. As soon as Nathan sang the first chorus, the ice block melted into a wide pool.

"This is where the real trials await," Wind Being said, hovering over the pool of water. Small waves in the water spread outward from Wind's body. "Spider, I believe we will need your safety line. Beyond this barrier, I do not remember anything of the obstacles ahead. Everyone, keep your bravery high and your mind alert!"

Spider jumped out of the backpack and onto a nearby rock. She tied a thick knot onto a protrusion. She then returned to Nathan's backpack, gently spooling out webbing as Nathan walked forward. Seed Collector lifted the crystal fire higher. The walls around them were covered in solid ice, and his footsteps crunched into the packed snow.

Nathan took one last look at the hogan-like space before walking into the passage that would lead them directly to Mother Water Monster herself.

Naadiin Dóó Bi'ąą Tseebíí
TWENTY-EIGHT

EVEN THOUGH ICE SURROUNDED HIM, Nathan didn't feel the temperature cool. He could see his breath, but his bare arms didn't have goose bumps. Nathan touched the ice on the wall to his side. It expanded and contracted like it was breathing.

"Wind Being," said Nathan, "do you remember how long this hall is? Or what the obstacles are?"

"I do not. I apologize," Wind said.

Up ahead, the iced walls and floor ended. Nathan stopped at the end of the hole and tried to see how far down the floor was. But the light didn't shine that deep.

Spider asked, "Are you going to climb down?"

"Don't have much of a choice, huh?" Nathan said. He tightened the straps on his backpack, lowered his legs over the edge, and found some ledges to step on.

"Be careful," Seed Collector said, extending the crystal fire so that Nathan could see his footing and how far below the ground was.

Nathan climbed and climbed until his forearms ached. Thankfully, before his arms gave out, his shoes pressed against solid floor. Nathan looked around. The path before him went in only one direction; the ceiling was an inch taller than his head. Wind Being's human form floated down beside him.

"Would it be too much to hope that that's one of the obstacles?" Nathan asked. He massaged his forearms to release the soreness from holding on for dear life.

"I don't think it is. However, we must be nearing the first. Keep steady and guarded," Wind Being said and floated ahead.

Nathan took a deep breath and stepped forward. Whatever was up ahead, he had to find a way through, for both Pond's and his own sake.

Nathan estimated that they had walked about half a mile. With each step forward, tiny finger-sized shards of white crystals embedded in the walls reflected the crystal fire. The farther he walked the larger these crystals grew on either side of a clear path down the middle. Like crowns, quartz crystals jutted out of the sides and the ceilings and even the ground, which made it difficult to walk on the path. The walls expanded away, and the ceiling rose. Nathan rounded a milky crystal as thick, round, and tall as a cedar tree and saw a grand gallery of clear white quartz crystals. They were standing in a massive geode.

The light from Seed Collector reflected and rebounded off

the million angles. At the top of the ceiling, like golden chandeliers, yellow-tinged quartz ignited in the same color as an evening sun. Some of the crystals were as massive as skyscrapers! Nathan wished he had his phone to take photos. It was breathtaking.

Powder from the massive crystals coated the floor like glistening snow. Wind Being collected these shimmering grains into its human form. Its body twinkled like a million tiny revolving stars.

"It's so pretty," Nathan said.

"For the first time, I agree with you," Seed Collector said.

Nathan stepped forward and saw thousands of reflections of himself, like a house of mirrors. He stopped and looked at his surroundings.

"What are you doing?" Seed Collector asked.

Nathan looked at the clearing on the ground. The path split into multiple directions. He wasn't sure which one was the real way out. "We're in a maze."

"Spider," Wind Being said. "We'll need your safety line the most in here."

"On it!" she said. She hopped off Nathan's backpack and made a secure point on a crystal edge. Done, she returned to his shoulder. "Don't walk that fast, please."

"You got it," Nathan said. He stepped forward. All his reflections did, too. He was so distracted by all the movement around him that he walked right into a crystal.

"Careful!" Seed Collector said. "You could have squashed me!"

"Oh, you're fine!" Spider said to Seed Collector.

Nathan rubbed his nose, surprised that blood wasn't pouring out of it. In the corner of his peripheral vision, Nathan spotted a reflection that wasn't rubbing its nose. Or at least that's what he thought he saw. When he turned to look at it again, all his reflections copied his movement. "Huh." He must have walked really hard into the crystal.

Spider crawled onto the handle of his backpack and they kept going. Nathan held his hands in front of him to prevent another face-plant. His fingers occasionally pressed up against the mirror-smooth texture of the crystals.

After ten minutes of walking, Wind Being said, "Take a break, Nathan. I'll see if I can find a path out of here from up high." Wind Being's form floated above them.

Nathan's stomach growled. Had he been traveling that long? He sat down and dug into his backpack for the trail mix of nuts, raisins, and chocolate that Nali had packed for him.

"There is no way for me to determine where the exit is," Wind Being said as it returned to the group.

"Wonderful. We're doing this the old-fashioned way," Nathan said. He stood and stretched his arms upward.

"If by 'old-fashioned' you mean walking aimlessly until we find the exit, then yes," Wind Being said.

Nathan walked for what felt like a mile. He was growing certain that there was no exit.

"Stop!" Spider said. "This isn't right!"

"What?" Nathan said, folding over, his hands on his knees. His knees were aching.

Spider hopped from the top of his backpack to Nathan's shoulder; then she jumped in front of them. She grabbed something invisible in the air and her body bopped up and down on a web.

"This web is from earlier." She crawled forward and then at a perpendicular angle. She looked at Nathan. "We've been here before."

"So we've been going in circles?" Seed Collector said.

Nathan sat on the flat surface of a chair-sized crystal and massaged his legs. He stared ahead, trying to think of a way out of here. Again, in his peripheral vision, there was a reflection that wasn't doing what he was doing. He looked at it, but like before, all his reflections repeated his motions.

"There must be a path that we overlooked," Wind Being said.

Seed Collector said something that Nathan didn't pay any attention to. It was probably a grumpy remark anyway. Nathan stared straight ahead. He then scratched his head with his right hand. There it was: a reflection that wasn't repeating his actions!

"What do you think, Nathan?" Wind Being said.

"I think we have to do nothing," Nathan said.

Nathan sat as still as possible. He focused his vision directly in front of him and waited to see what would happen.

"Well, that's the dumbest idea ever," Seed Collector said.

Nathan sat still, looking forward. He turned only his eyes to get a better look at the reflections. Then one of the reflections pointed left.

"Left!" Nathan said.

"What? Why?" Seed Collector said.

Nathan jumped up and walked to his left. His hands felt before him and then pressed against the surface of a crystal. Nathan felt to the sides, then up and down. Aha! There was an opening at the bottom that he could crawl through.

"Here!" Nathan said. He knelt down and first pushed the backpack down. Once he, Wind Being, Seed Collector, and Spider were through the opening, Nathan sat still again and watched that same reflection point in another direction. Nathan walked and then came across a junction. There were paths to his left and his right. The reflection pointed left and so he took the left path. Nathan followed these directions until he came to an enclosure. There was no other path.

"Huh? Did I take a wrong turn? No. I followed their directions," Nathan said.

He anxiously waited for any of his reflections to move. He didn't know he was holding his breath until he gasped for air. None of his reflections were doing anything. He was about to move and then suddenly, one by one, all his reflections pointed to the wall in front of him. The ones on top of him pointed downward. The ones to his left pointed rightward. The ones on his right pointed leftward.

"We have to go forward . . ." Nathan said. He reached ahead. The crystal was expanding and contracting, like the icy entrance.

"The lullaby!" Nathan said. He warmed his voice and throat by harmonizing. Then he sang the chorus and first four verses of the lullaby. The crystal bent and warped until it cracked and shattered into dust. Before them was a hallway like before.

"Well, how about that?" Wind Being said.

Nathan reached for a bottle of water in his backpack. His throat was scratchy.

"Good work," Wind Being said.

"Thank you," Nathan said.

"Save the sentiment! That was probably the easiest obstacle!" Seed Collector said.

"I think you did great, too, Nathan," Spider said.

"Thank you, but Seed Collector's right," Nathan said.

"I am? Of course I am!" Seed Collector said.

"That *could* be the easiest obstacle," Nathan said.

Nathan walked out of the crystal cavern and into the ice hall. The more steps he took away from the grand gallery of quartz chandeliers, the dimmer the light became. The room reflected less and less light until it was completely dark and silent.

Naadiin Dóó Bi'ąą Náhást'éí

TWENTY-NINE

NATHAN FINISHED EATING A MEAL Nali had prepared for him: a ham-and-cheese sandwich with a bag of Hot Cheetos. He hoped that the others didn't notice that he was taking his time eating. He initially thought that these obstacles were going to be one right after another.

Seed Collector had been walking impatiently in circles while Nathan ate his meal.

"He's done! Let's go now," Seed Collector said.

"Can we wait a few minutes? My legs are . . . they're jelly," Nathan said.

"We must keep our pace," Wind Being said.

"But I'm tired!" Nathan said, pushing down on his knees to hoist himself upward. Grabbing the bag, he trudged forward. Seed Collector used Nathan's hair at the back of his head for balance. Spider hung off the top handle of his backpack, threading their safety line.

"How do you do that? With the crystal?" Spider asked Seed Collector.

Seed Collector cleared its throat. "Well! When the Holy Beings assigned me my tasks, they taught me a set of skills that allowed me to search for seeds, which included a prayer that ignites fire in crystals. There have been plenty of times when I had to search in the middle of the night."

Nathan briefly remembered following Seed Collector away from Nali's mobile home. That was so long ago.

"The crystal fire is one of the ways from the First World," Wind Being said. "With that way, First Man and First Woman were able to find each other in the darkness."

"Wind Being, aren't you from the First World?" Nathan asked. Nali had mentioned that in the First World, some of the beings, such as First Man and First Woman, had different forms than they did today. Other beings, such as Wind Being and Darkness, maintained their same shapeless forms.

"Yes," Wind Being said.

"If we went far enough, do you think we could make it there? To the First World?" Nathan asked.

"For me, yes, it would be possible, because I don't require sustenance. But for humans? No. I do not believe it would be possible. Let's focus on the Third World," Wind Being said. "Do you hear that?"

Nathan focused his attention. He heard what sounded like the pitter-patter of heavy rain on glass. Then Nathan noticed that his skin felt moist. Nathan looked to the floor of the hall. Light was bouncing off small clear puddles.

"There's water," Nathan said.

"This will be to our advantage," Wind Being said. "To yours, specifically, Nathan."

Up ahead, the walls ended, and Nathan was able to see the next obstacle. The bottom was smooth, unnaturally so. It mirrored the ceiling when Seed Collector held the light higher. Nathan carefully tapped his toe on the surface, and multiple ripples disrupted the calm surface and went beyond the reaches of the light and kept going in the darkness.

"It's a pool," Nathan said. "How deep does it go? Seed Collector?"

"Yes?" Seed Collector said.

"Do you have another crystal? One I can drop into the water?"

"Fine," it said. Nathan could hear the disdain in its tone. After muttering some words, Seed Collector handed another crystal fire to Nathan. He held it above the surface of the water and let it fall. Nathan watched the crystal float down and down and down until it became a speck of nothing. And it probably kept on falling.

"It's deep. I don't know how large this room is. I don't think I can swim across it."

"Please don't swim!" Spider said.

Nathan thought he heard a muffled yawn. But from what he could see, there was nothing around except the deep pool.

"Let me try a song," Nathan said. He closed his eyes and began to hum the melody of the Change song. Then he sang the words. One chorus described the changing of seasons, from fall to winter, from winter to spring, and how water changes from water to steam to rain to snow. The air around his arm cooled. Ice formed at the base of a ledge near him.

Nathan concentrated and kept on thinking of water solidifying into ice. He lowered a foot down onto the ice. It held his weight!

"Keep singing, Nathan!" Spider said. Her terrified eyes looked at the dark water.

Nathan sang louder, and the ice spread out even farther. Snow fell around them. Growing more confident, Nathan walked forward with ice forming a path before him.

Nathan finished the first verse, which took fifteen minutes to sing. All around them, water stretched beyond the reach of the light. It was like he was walking on top of a massive ocean. He wondered if it was because of the protection of the moon sands that the song wasn't affecting the water in his body. Nathan kept singing. Then, for certain this time, he heard a yawn. He stopped singing. Thankfully, the ice held firm.

"Why did you stop?! Keep singing!" Spider said.

"What is it, Nathan?" Wind Being asked.

"Something's waking up," Nathan said.

"Well, I didn't hear anything," Seed Collector said.

"Keep going. Please, keep going!" Spider said.

"You're right," Nathan said. He remembered the last verse he sang and began again. He pressed forward.

Then a loud boom made the surface of the water shiver and droplets fall around them like rain. The moisture near Nathan fell and turned into slowly falling snowflakes. His instincts told him to stop singing and to look for whatever it was that had made that loud sound. But he kept singing anyway and picked up his pace.

The ripples returned and more moisture dropped from the ceiling. Then he heard a boom below them. The ripples increased in size.

"What has wandered down here?" a deep voice said.

Nathan looked below but he could not see beneath the ice underneath his feet. He stopped singing.

"Why did you stop?" Spider said.

"Shh!" Nathan whispered.

The crystal dust that made Wind Being's human form spun faster and faster. It floated on top of the waters. "We are not alone in the cavern."

Nathan got to his hands and knees and crawled to the edge of the ice sheet. He searched into the water's depths.

"Seed Collector," Nathan whispered.

"Yes?" Seed Collector said with a scared voice. Apparently, it understood they were in danger, too.

"Can you give me another crystal fire?" Nathan asked.

"Yes." Seed Collector handed Nathan a small lighted crystal.

Nathan dropped it into the water. It fell a long way. Then a massive shape about the size of a blue whale swam over the light source, creating a huge, dark shadow. Moments later, a loud boom erupted and instead of ripples, small waves lapped the edges of the ice sheet.

"I know that you are here," the thing said.

It must be blind, Nathan thought. It has lived here in complete darkness, and when he dropped the crystal fire, it didn't notice.

"Tell me where you are," the thing said.

As quietly as he could, Nathan hummed the Change song and tiptoed forward. The ice he was producing wasn't as thick as it was before. Every step created lightning-like networks that snapped under his weight. Nathan sang the words a little louder and the ice became thicker.

"It has been so long since I've had a decent meal," the thing said. It swam to the surface and dipped its mouth above the waterline. The ice bridge that was behind Nathan broke, and the ice that Nathan stood on began to spin. Nathan went to his hands and knees to regain balance. He spun in circles and lost his sense of direction. Still he sang the song. He had to keep moving and crawling.

"Ah!" Seed Collector screamed. Seed Collector fell out of his backpack and landed on the ice. It slid to the edge. "Grab me! Don't let me fall into the water!"

Nathan lunged forward and grabbed Seed Collector.

"There you are!" the creature beneath them said. Suddenly, puke-green bioelectric lights ignited on the sides of the thing's body. It was a huge angler fish. It jetted up toward them. Teeth like porcupine spikes poked out of its lower jaw. Its body launched above the water, a few feet from Nathan. Its head slammed against the ceiling and its body splashed back into the water, creating massive waves.

Nathan immediately sang and froze the wave before being pushed into the water.

"I've not heard that song in eons! You are human. Tasty and soft human!" the angler fish said.

"Hurry, Nathan! You have to move!" Wind Being said.

Nathan sang louder. And as he ran through Wind's body, Nathan heard his voice echo. The ice felt more solid underneath his feet and spread out even farther.

The angler fish had recovered itself and was swimming in circles. Nathan searched for something, anything, that he could use. If there was a rock, Nathan could trick the fish into swimming into it. There was water and the ceiling. Perfect for echoes! Then Nathan thought up a plan.

The angler fish zoomed forward toward Nathan. At the last moment, Nathan jumped to the side, and the angler fish's body launched above the surface, its head bumping against the ceiling again.

"Where are you? Where are you?" the angler fish said. "You sound very delicious!"

"Wind Being!" Nathan said. He stopped running. "I need you to create gusts and winds to push my voice. Make my voice louder by pushing the vibrations up against the ceiling to create echoes around us!"

"Will what you're planning work?"

"Yes, because it's science!" Nathan shouted. "Watch me. When I clap, push my voice as far and as loud as possible!"

"Okay!" Wind Being said.

The angler fish pointed its snout toward them. Nathan stood his ground and sang loudly. He increased the volume of his voice until he was shouting.

The angler fish glowed bright and then once more launched its body. Nathan looked at Wind Being. He turned his head and saw the terror in Spider's eight eyes. He was now shouting the words of the song at the top of his voice. His throat itched.

At the last moment, Nathan jumped to the side and clapped his hands. An enormous gust of wind, strong enough to push Nathan into the air, blew through the area. His shouts turned into impossibly louder and louder echoes.

The angler fish's body had fully emerged when ice formed beneath them. Nathan rolled out of the fish's way. The angler fish's large abdomen crashed against the ice, and surprisingly, the ice did not crack. The fish slid forward, gasping for water.

"No. NO!" it said. "Not this way." The lights on its body flashed on and off.

Nathan walked to its head.

"What are you doing? Let's be on our way!" Seed Collector said.

"But it's going to die," Nathan said.

"So what?" Seed Collector said.

"Nathan doesn't like that," Spider said.

Nathan saw its face, truly horrible and ugly. It had no eyes, and Nathan could see through its clear skin, right to its rapidly beating heart.

"Who's there?" the angler fish said.

"My name is Nathan," Nathan said. "Are you okay?"

"I'm in pain! So much pain!" the angler fish said, gasping loudly.

"Listen, I'll help you get back into your water, if you promise not to eat us," Nathan said.

"You would do that? How do you know that I simply won't eat you after I get back into the water?"

"Because if you try, I will freeze all the water and trap you inside it," Nathan said. Even if the angler fish had been trying to eat him moments earlier, it was wrong to let something die so slowly and painfully. Nathan sang the Change song again and instead of thinking of water solidifying, he thought of it lique-fying and transforming into mist. A pool collected underneath him. He directed his thoughts to melting the water underneath the angler fish. Then the water stopped melting underneath him, and the body of the angler fish began to sink.

Whoa, he thought. He could control where the melting and freezing would occur.

Eventually, the angler fish was fully back in the water. Nathan immediately thought of water turning to ice and focused his attention on the hole before him. Ice covered the opening.

"I thank you, human. Though delicious as you certainly are, I will honor your gesture. Follow me and I will show you the exit."

Underneath the ice, the angler fish glowed again. Nathan followed it and eventually saw the exit to another ice hall.

"Thank you!" Nathan said. The huge angler fish stopped glowing and disappeared underneath the ice. Nathan headed over to the ice hall. He had only two more obstacles left!

Tádiin

THIRTY

NATHAN'S FEET DRAGGED AGAINST THE bare stone beneath him. His whole body ached and burned. He was hungry and tired. He swayed so much that his shoulders bumped against the walls on either side.

"Nathan, it may be time for you to rest," Wind Being said. "Sleep here. You'll need energy for the next obstacle. I will go ahead and see how much farther we have."

"Don't have to tell me twice," Nathan said. His T-shirt stuck to him like a second skin from all the sweat. He peeled the backpack off and dropped it on the floor. Spider and Seed Collector were already fast asleep. He reached into the bag and pulled out a small blanket. Nali had thought of everything.

"Only for a few minutes. Then wake me up," Nathan said. He covered himself and then closed his eyes. "We have to keep . . ."

And he was asleep.

Nathan opened his eyes. He gasped because he was no longer in the cave with Spider, Seed Collector, or Wind Being. His mom and his father were in front of him, standing next to someone who was taking his picture. They both smiled at him. Something about their faces, maybe their eyes, disturbed Nathan and scared him. He turned around and saw his science project on background radiation and the golden first-place trophy for his category.

"Smile," the photographer said.

"First place!" his father said.

"I'm so proud of you!" his mom said.

Almost as he remembered.

He immediately knew this wasn't real and that this was an obstacle. He had relived this memory so many times that he could see the inconsistencies of this dream. It was like looking at a photo through a filter that amped up the colors. The photographer had blond hair but wasn't glowing. His dream mom and father were happy during the science fair but not this happy.

But it still felt good to hear his parents say that. He smiled and enjoyed reliving one of his happiest memories.

"All right!" the photographer said, letting the large camera he had used to take the picture dangle on his side. "Congratulations."

His parents walked over to him. They weren't arguing. They weren't mad. They were happy with him. And all three of them were finally together again. Nathan let himself get washed in nostalgia. He so wanted to re-create this moment, to have both his parents in the same space, happy and together. It was the whole reason why he wanted to win first place again in the science fair.

He enjoyed this moment even though he knew it was fake. But when he felt he had his fill of living in this moment, he said, "I'm ready to go back to the cave. Thank you for letting me have this moment again."

"What are you talking about?" both his parents asked.

"I'm in the cave with the others. And we need to go to the Third World to save Pond," Nathan said. The moment he said Pond's name he shuddered, remembering how sick Pond had looked. Skin stretched across his rib cage. Scales flaking off his body. Eyes yellow with red streaks.

His mom's eyes met his. "Stay here. We want you to."

"Both of us," his dad said. He wrapped his arm around her shoulders.

"This is not real," Nathan said.

"But it can be," his parents said in unison.

"What about my real parents? My real friends? Pond and the ones with me in the cave?" Nathan asked.

"Just dreams," his father said. "Simple dreams that will fade away."

"No. They aren't dreams. You are," Nathan said.

His father said, "I thought you wanted parents who didn't fight."

"I want"—Nathan stared at them—"parents who are happy! Even if it means they have to be divorced. Thank you for letting me relive this moment, but I need to get back to my friends."

The parents before him, along with the walls surrounding them, started to fall apart. The floor beneath him gave way, and Nathan fell down into what seemed like quicksand. At that moment he felt his stomach drop, and he let out a loud scream.

He was surrounded by darkness, much like when his communication stone was made. A dim light shone beneath him and he saw his body slumped on the floor. He was floating toward his body.

"Worthless." Nathan recognized that voice.

"The Ash Being," Nathan said. He looked around. But there was only blackness.

"You'll never be anything other than a drunk living off his mom," the Ash Being said.

"Uncle Jet!" Nathan called out. "Uncle Jet. Can you hear me?"

"Nathan?" Uncle Jet's voice said through the dark. "Is that you?"

"Yes, it's me!"

"Where are you?" Uncle Jet said.

"I'm on my way to the Third World. Where are you?"

"I think I'm sleeping. We are constructing something here for the N'dáá," Uncle Jet said. "I don't think I can go through with this. It's too much for me. I can't stand the way everyone looks at me. The songs, they hurt."

"That's because you are weak," the Ash Being said.

Nathan thought about this. Nali mentioned that they were going to construct an object on Thursday. He had already been gone for four days! "Uncle Jet! You have to keep going! Finish the ceremony! The songs are hurting the Ash Being, who is then hurting you!" At least that's what Nathan figured.

"It'd be easier if you were here," Uncle Jet said.

"Uncle Jet, ask Nali for help. Ask my father for help. It's not weak to ask for help!" Nathan shouted. Nathan could feel himself falling back toward his body. "You can do this! It's the only way to get rid of the Ash Being!"

Nathan gasped for air as he woke up in the long passage. Wind Being hovered above him.

"Oh, thank goodness," Wind Being said.

He hoped that Uncle Jet was okay. There was nothing he could do down here except trust and believe in Uncle Jet. Nathan's legs no longer seemed as though they were on fire, and he felt well rested but very hungry. He reached for his bag for another packed meal and devoured it. Seed Collector slept happily on the floor.

"Seeds. Seeds everywhere," Seed Collector mumbled, still deep in sleep.

Nathan gently picked up Spider, who blinked her eyes open.

"Huh? Nathan?" He placed her on his warm neck, and she leaned against him.

"Did you have a dream?" Wind Being asked Nathan.

"Yes. I think it was another obstacle," Nathan said.

"I'm thankful you overcame it," Wind Being said. "When you all lay down to sleep, I went ahead to gauge the length of this passage. I traveled for a long while and covered what felt like many miles until I turned around and saw that I had gone but a few paces away from your bodies. This passage is meant to tire travelers and lure them into a deep sleep. Once they sleep, they may sleep the remainder of their lives in a fanciful dream. The most self-centered and those who lack compassion will not pass."

"You didn't sleep?" Nathan asked.

"I don't sleep," Wind Being said.

"A sea of seeds!" Seed Collector said and smiled.

"Well, now that you are awake, I think it would be best to keep moving forward," Wind Being said.

Nathan picked up Seed Collector and tapped on its forehead. It looked at Nathan angrily and said, "Why did you wake me?"

"We have a job to do," Nathan said.

"Bah, let me sleep!" Seed Collector said.

"Seed Collector," Wind Being said.

Spider yawned loudly enough for Nathan to hear. He turned to look at her. Her legs were half-limp and trying to push against his neck.

"You ready?" Nathan asked.

"Yes. Walk and I'll spool." She stretched her legs into the air.

Nathan put his backpack on and walked forward with renewed energy in his steps. There was one more obstacle and then, Nathan thought, he would be standing in front of Mother Water Monster herself.

Tádiin Dóó Bi'ąą T'ááłá'í

THIRTY-ONE

NATHAN STOOD AT THE END of a corridor. There were rows and rows of boulders as tall as telephone posts. At the bottom of the floor was a thin layer of water.

"Why aren't you walking?" Seed Collector asked.

"I feel like the rocks want to hurt me," Nathan said. Then he had an idea to test his hunch. Nali had told him that during the Era of the Enemies of the Fourth World, there were Rock Beings that would sit at either side of a path, and whenever a human walked between them would smash together. Nathan took his backpack off and took out an empty plastic container. He tossed the container between two rocks. There was a loud crash and water splashed everywhere. As Nathan had expected, the rocks rushed together and destroyed the container.

The two rocks then slid back to their original bases. Nathan looked closely at the rocks. He searched the top of them and saw what looked like a face. There were definitely two hollow grooves that looked like eyes. Those grooves seemed to stare down at Nathan.

Nathan looked at the water on the floor.

"What do you have planned?" Spider asked.

"Um. Let me try turning this water to ice. Maybe they can't move if the water is frozen," Nathan said. He sang the Change song and turned the water to ice. Then he tossed another plastic container between the two rocks. They slid even faster than before! The resulting collision sounded like a thunderclap.

"They have eyes. They can see whatever is between them," Nathan said. "So, if we blind them? Seed Collector?"

"Yes, Nathan?" Seed Collector said.

"I'll need you to turn down the light."

"Okay," Seed Collector said.

Nathan sang the Change song again, and then, instead of ice, he thought of fog. The ice on the floor evaporated and quickly turned into thick fog that rose to the ceiling, covering the rocks' eyes.

"Let me try this again." Nathan tossed his last empty plastic container. It bounced and bounced, then slid across the floor. Two rocks slid toward each other, slowly, and pressed up against each other. But the two stones had missed the container.

"Okay," Nathan said. "I think these things can hear, but they rely on their sight to kill. So, be quiet, keep below the fog, and we'll be fine."

Nathan got on his hands and knees and began to crawl on the

floor, careful not to breathe loudly.

"Seed Collector," Nathan said, "dim the light a bit more. We can't be too careful."

Seed Collector dimmed the light to the point that it was hard to see ahead.

Spider crawled to Nathan's ear. "Take a right here," she said.

"You can see?" Nathan said.

"No," Spider said. "But I can smell something. It's coming from this direction."

"I feel it, too. There is a draft coming from somewhere," Wind Being said.

"Okay. Tell me where to go," Nathan said.

Nathan crawled forward. He felt a gentle wind brush against his arms. And he could smell the salty musk of an ocean.

"Here," Spider said. "And it should be directly ahead."

Finally, he came to the room's exit. Nathan quietly crawled through the corridor and into what he knew to be the last hall.

"Seed Collector, can you brighten it again?" Nathan asked.

The light brightened and instead of ice, or smooth stone, the walls had the porous texture of volcanic rock. Suddenly, Nathan thought of Nali and her rough palms. *Hold on a little longer*, he thought. The ceiling was high enough for Nathan to stand. He walked at a quick pace. If he finished quickly, he might be able to make it back for the last portion of Uncle Jet's N'dáá.

◊ ◊ ◊

"We passed all the obstacles, Nathan!" Spider said after they were deep enough in the hallway that the smashing rocks were far behind them.

"Yes," Nathan said. Now to get the medicine and then hurry back to Uncle Jet's N'dáá.

As Nathan walked, he was deep in thought about how to address Mother Water Monster. He didn't notice the ground had grown soft and sank underneath his shoes.

"Wait. What is that?" Nathan said. The wall to his right was green.

He stopped and pressed his palm against the wall. It was smooth like leather, and there were parallel lines on it that ran up and down. The floor beneath him was made of the same green material. Above him was a bright green tube that looked like a midrib of a large leaf.

"Is this a plant or something?" Nathan said.

Wind Being floated to his side. "This is the river reed that your ancestors used in their ascent. We are at the entrance of the Third World."

"Now to Mother Water Monster," Nathan said. He trotted down the passage. Up ahead it curved to the right and there was a faint blue radiance, like the sky of early night. The walls began to close around him, and Nathan had to duck low. The passage straightened. Nathan hurried to the end where light was shining through.

Seed Collector blew onto the crystal and the fire inside went out. Nathan approached the hole and crawled through.

Nathan's eyes had to take a moment to adjust to the amount of light around him, even though it was still pretty dim. When they finally did, he gasped at the sight.

A huge ocean stretched for miles in every direction. Little islands polka-dotted the smooth blue blanket of water. Gentle waves washed ashore on the beaches. He walked the length of the leaf to the massive central shoot of the enormous river reed. Nathan estimated that its diameter was as wide as Nali's mobile home. There was a path made of the long leaves that circled all the way down to the base of this plant, where there was a beach. He was standing where the First Beings had once stood all those ages ago.

A wandering cloud floated around them. When it cleared, Nathan saw rows of rock spires on the ceiling that pointed downward like fangs. Crystals also poked downward and glowed with a gentle blue light. Millions of blue lights twinkled on the ceiling like stars. This place was an eternal night ocean.

Seed Collector placed its crystal into a pouch. Nathan looked at the crystal and then back at the crystals at the top of the ceiling. The two crystals might be made of the same thing, Nathan thought. To his right stood a tall pine tree that did not touch the ceiling. To his left stood an oak tree about half the height of the pine tree. Farther down was the green blur of another tree that his ancestors had planted to exit the flooding of this world.

"Aha!" Seed Collector said. It jumped off Nathan's backpack and landed on the leaf he was standing on. It got to its knees and picked up a tiny round object. "It's a seed! Oh, would you look at this! I wonder what this will grow into." Seed Collector smiled and put it into its pouch. It walked on foot, zigzagging, scanning for extra seeds.

"Why are you collecting seeds?" Spider asked.

"It is my sacred assignment," Seed Collector said. "When humans completely ruin the Fourth World, it is up to us Holy Beings to start again."

"What do you mean?" Nathan said.

Seed Collector put various seeds into its pouch. "There is a kind of corn, not of Mother Nature's design, but of human making. It is the wish of certain humans to create a new strain of corn that is sweeter, to use for their products. They have achieved such a task with unnatural ways. They changed the corn, everything about it, including the pollen. Having been infused with alterations, the soul of the pollen eroded. The pollen of that plant has traveled across many mountains and valleys, and over bodies of water, by way of breezes, bees, and beasts. It is changing the sacred corn. How will all the people bless themselves when the pollen they use has been desecrated?" Seed Collector looked at Nathan. "That's my assignment, to preserve as many seeds untouched by human manipulation as possible for the next, Fifth World."

"I can help," Spider said. She jumped down, and the two of them darted back and forth on the massive leaf that was as wide as a car. Nathan peeked over the river reed leaf. It was going to take some time for him to descend to the sandy beach below.

Nathan took his backpack off and sat down. He reached into

his bag and pulled out a water bottle.

"Oh! Look at that striped one over there!" Seed Collector pointed, and it and Spider scuttled over to another leaf.

Wind Being hovered over the edge and looked at the entire world.

"Like you remembered?" Nathan asked Wind.

"Please tell your children of your time here, Nathan. I want to remember the splendor of the Third World," Wind Being said.

Nathan stood up and approached the edge of the leaf.

"Are you ready to bargain with Mother Water Monster?" Wind Being asked.

"It doesn't matter whether I'm ready or not," Nathan said. "But I think so."

"I wish all humans had your qualities, Nathan. The Fourth World wouldn't be in such a mess as it is now," Wind Being said.

Nathan blushed. Suddenly, there was a crack and the leaf buckled under his weight. The leaf was bending!

"Nathan! Jump back to the center!"

Before he could respond, there was a loud moan and the leaf beneath him gave way. Nathan's feet slid off the smooth exterior. Nathan's stomach sank as he fell into the air and toward the water. He let out a loud scream. He looked at the ocean. If he could sing the Move song, he might be able to save himself. But he couldn't think of any of the words. All he could focus on was how fast he was falling, and that these were going to be his last seconds alive.

Then a stream of water splashed around him and slowed his descent. He tried to breathe, but water entered his mouth. More and more water engulfed him, completely halting him before he could touch the ground. But now water was entering his nose and ears. He couldn't breathe. Then Nathan lost consciousness.

Nathan coughed himself back to consciousness. He could feel water deep in the middle of his chest moving up his throat and out through both his nose and mouth. Nathan couldn't breathe until the last drops of water flowed out. He sat up and saw a water monster staring at him. The designs on this water monster were very different from Pond's. Instead of the diamond shapes on Pond, there were aggressive triangles and zigzags on this one. Nathan pressed his palms into the soft beach sands to stand up. His bow guard thankfully was still tied to his wrist.

"You *are* human," the water monster said. Her voice sounded like a woman's.

"Are you Mother Water Monster?" Nathan asked. His head exploded in sharp, stabbing pain.

"Don't move so much, young one. You almost drowned. I am not my mom. She's in the waters at the moment. Please, tell me of the Fourth World. Tell me of my river. Oh, how I miss it so!" The water monster brought her snout to Nathan's eyeline.

"River?" Nathan was confused. There were so many rivers.

"You might know it by the name the pale people forced upon it. The San Juan River," the water monster said. "But its original name, my name, is Yitoo Bi'aanii."

"I'm sorry. I don't know," Nathan said.

"Please, any information at all? What became of my waters?" Yitoo asked.

"I don't know. I grew up in Phoenix," Nathan said.

"Phoenix? What is that? Oh, what does it matter? What are you doing here?" she asked.

"I'm here for Pond. He's a water monster, too, and he's very sick," Nathan said.

"One of my brothers is sick?" Yitoo asked. She lay down. "It seems like we all are becoming sick in the Fourth World."

"You're sick, too?" Nathan asked. The pain in his head finally calmed.

"Yes, I came back here so that I might recover," Yitoo said. "In human words, I've been here for one hundred and fifty years."

A gust of wind blew around the two of them.

"Nathan! You are all right! Thank goodness!" Wind said. It wrapped Nathan in a funnel of warm winds.

"Is this Wind Being?" Yitoo asked.

"Yes. It is I," Wind Being said.

"Welcome back, Holy Being," Yitoo said. "Please, tell me about my sibling. Why wasn't he himself able to come down?"

"He has radiation poisoning. He's physically not able to do much and—and . . ." Nathan couldn't finish because saying it out loud made it feel real.

"He's near death," Wind Being finished for Nathan. "His symptoms are such that physical exertion is out of the question.

Nathan here is your brother's representative."

"Do you know where I can find Mother Water Monster?" Nathan asked.

"Touch the water with your bare hand. She will sense you are human and will come for you," Yitoo said.

Nathan turned to Wind Being. "Where are Spider and Seed Collector?"

"They are still on the reed."

"Can you tell them that I am fine?" Nathan said. "I will meet up with you when I am done with Mother Water Monster."

"If that is what you desire. I will wait with them." Wind Being floated up into the air and disappeared from view.

"So, all I have to do is touch the water?" Nathan asked Yitoo.

"Yes!" she said, smiling at Nathan and leading him to the edge of the water.

Nathan walked to the edge of the beach. This was it. He quickly reviewed the first three water monster songs and as much of the protection song as he knew. He hoped that he wouldn't have to sing much of the protection song.

He leaned down and touched the water with a single finger. A deafening roar shook the surface of the water, creating thousands of waves. The water at the beach frothed and receded.

Far in the distance, a creature of titanic proportions rose from the water. Waterfalls cascaded from its scaly body. A tidal wave rose in front of Nathan to three times his height. The wave stilled and held. Nathan felt that, at any moment, the force that was holding this wave would let go and crush him.

Water cleared from the face of the creature, and a pair of bloodred eyes stared at Nathan. The beast exhaled. Nathan could feel the air around him warm even though he was so very far away. Mother Water Monster took a step with her enormous foot. A wave rose and crashed on a nearby island. All the greenery was stripped away from the force of the water.

"A human in my domain?" Mother Water Monster growled.

"Mother, listen to this Navajo youth!" Yitoo cried out to her.

"Be gone, daughter! I will deal with this intruder how I see fit."

"Good luck!" Yitoo jumped into the tidal wave and swam away.

"My . . . my name is Nathan!" Nathan yelled. Mother Water Monster took ten steps and was towering over Nathan. Nathan arched his neck back to look up at her. Her head was almost touching the ceiling. She lowered her head and tilted it so that a great red eye could look at him. Nathan saw his own terrified expression staring right back at him.

"Are you here to steal another of my children?" Mother Water Monster snarled.

"No! I am here because I represent one of your children!" Nathan shouted, maintaining his ground. "He is sick!"

"Sick? Explain!"

"Pond, that's what I call him, has been poisoned by uranium," Nathan said. "He is in great pain and needs medicine."

"That's preposterous!" she said, her breath pushing so much air that Nathan could feel the force pressing his head downward.

"All my children, when they are of age, are sent with medicine bundles to wherever they choose to live."

"He's used up all his medicine! He has no more. And this is a new sickness."

"Human, how do I know you are who you say you are? How do I know you truly represent one of my children and are not an impostor? What proof do you have?"

"He taught me some of his songs!" Nathan yelled. His neck was aching from looking up. He could feel his knees shaking. It took everything in his power not to run to the reed and start climbing.

"His songs? You mean my songs," Mother Water Monster said. "Very well, prove it."

Nathan closed his eyes and cleared his throat. His hands also began to shake. She could easily step on him as if he were nothing more than a bothersome bug. Nathan breathed in and out. He shut out all distractions and heard his own heartbeat. He listened to it and told it to slow down. His heartbeat slowed, and the words to the Water Monster's lullaby appeared in his mind. He began to sing.

He sang as loud as he could until his throat was sore and dry. But he finished. And every word was perfect, as far as he knew, at least. He opened his eyes after the last word and looked up at Mother Water Monster. Her eyes were no longer red, but a calm blue like a deep aquarium.

"So it is true. You do represent a child of mine," Mother Water Monster said. Water poured out of her ears, eyes, nose, and mouth. As the water left her body, she shrank until she was able to walk on the beach without crushing Nathan. She was still as tall as a pine tree, but definitely a lot less scary.

Nathan reached into his backpack. "I have a gift. These are moon sands. I was told to give these to you in exchange for the medicine. I guess that doesn't make it a gift and more like a payment." Nathan held the pouch out toward her.

"Moon sands? Why, we haven't had the sun and moon in our world for many ages." An arm made of water extended from the ocean and grabbed it. Then it disappeared into the depths.

"His condition must be dire if he sent a human," Mother Water Monster said. "Very well, what I have to offer is at the bottom of my ocean. It is shaped like a rock. Once in the Fourth World, its exterior will crumble. My son will know what to do next." Mother Water Monster lowered the tidal wave and the water softly rushed up to Nathan's knee.

"It would be wise for you to protect yourself. There are many creatures that would love a tasty little morsel like you as a snack," Mother Water Monster said.

Nervous, Nathan said, "I know a protection song."

"Is that all?" she asked.

"And two other songs. One I call a Change song because I can change the form of water, and the other is a Move song that I can use to make water move with my mind," Nathan said.

"Let's hope they are adequate protection." Mother Water Monster looked at Nathan. The ocean parted, leaving a path that led downward. Nathan followed Mother Water Monster. He couldn't hear her singing. She must have been so powerful that she didn't need to do anything to influence the waters. "Shall we?"

"Yes, ma'am," Nathan said.

They walked and went deeper below the ocean line. Nathan looked back and noticed that the path behind them was gone, and that above them were the dark shadows of massive creatures. To his side were giant glowing jellyfish that lit their surroundings with their streaming tails. Fish as big as houses with sparkling scales darted away from the jellyfish creatures.

"You might want to sing that protection song. I see a lot of hungry eyes looking at you," Mother Water Monster said.

Nathan cleared his throat. He shook off his nerves and began by humming the melody. The words came to his lips and he began to sing. To his left, a giant crab-like creature walked over them and into the dark depths at their right. Its thick and long legs were as large as pine logs.

"The song is protecting you. So don't stop," Mother Water Monster said.

Nathan nodded and did his best to ignore his nerves. Once he sang what he knew, which was half of the song, he quickly started the song again, hoping that it would continue to work because that was all he knew.

Nathan was happy when Mother Water Monster stopped near a bed of rocks that nested on a tangle of seaweed. She pointed at it with her snout. Nathan walked over and pulled out a rock and placed it into his backpack. He held his breath, afraid that merely breathing on the rock would spoil its healing effect.

"Keep singing."

Nathan nodded and restarted the song from the beginning. The crab creature passed overhead again. He was ready to go back to the Fourth World. Pond was going to be okay!

"Let's go," Mother Water Monster said.

Nathan restarted the song from the beginning again. A crab creature was staring directly at him from the distance.

They were about a third of the way back when Nathan restarted the song a fourth time. Mother Water Monster turned to him and said, "Is that truly the entire song?"

"No. I don't remember the rest," Nathan said.

"You better run," Mother Water Monster said. Immediately, she darted forward, the water before them clearing and the water behind them closing in. Nathan had to sprint at top speed to keep up with her. He didn't have any idea how long he could keep this up. But when a giant claw pierced the air bubble they were in and snipped at his neck, Nathan doubled his pace.

The giant crab creature groaned behind him. Nathan looked up and saw the pincers coming down. Nathan ducked. The claw snipped a few inches above his head. He felt the air move from the claws.

Nathan began to hum the Move melody and belted out the words as best he could between deep inhales. About midway through the first verse, Nathan tested his ability and saw a fish the size of a car swimming near them. He spun the water around the fish and easily turned it upside down.

Up ahead, the glowing jellyfish flashed like lightning. Nathan commanded the water to push the jellyfish toward the creatures behind him.

Singing demanded a lot of oxygen, and his sprinting needed as much. The edges of his vision were growing faint, fuzzy, and black. He forced himself to stay alert and to keep shouting. He focused and made the water push the jellyfish. And it was working. He concentrated harder and the jellyfish was moving quicker.

Five claws reached into the air bubble they were in and jabbed toward Nathan. Then the claws retracted, and the massive creatures scuttled away from the encroaching jellyfish. Mother Water Monster slowed to a halt.

"You command water?" she asked.

"Yes, ma'am," Nathan said.

"Who could have imagined a human doing this with such ease," Mother Water Monster said.

"Can we slow down? Need to catch my breath," Nathan said. He reached his arms above his head. His lungs were aching for as much oxygen as they could hold.

"Do what you must," Mother Water Monster said.

They broke above the ocean surface a little later. Nathan loosened the straps on his backpack. They were rubbing against his shoulder, and he was certain he had friction burns in those areas. All his muscles, even ones he didn't know he had, were sore. He wasn't sure if he could make it back, not without a few days of rest.

On the beach, Nathan sat down, exhausted. Mother Water Monster stood in the ocean and said, "You may drink my waters to regain your strength. Then be on your way, Nathan."

"Mother Water Monster!" Nathan said.

"Yes?" Mother Water Monster said.

"Thank you!" Nathan shouted.

"You're welcome. Now leave. I have little patience for humans, even if they do represent one of my children," Mother Water Monster said, diving back into the waters and disappearing from Nathan's sight.

Nathan sat up and crawled to the edge of the water. He cupped some water and drank. It wasn't salty, but instead sweet and tingly. He felt his soreness disappear and his muscles become invigorated. The water moved from the center of his stomach to his legs, to his arms, to his ankles, to his wrists, to his toes, and to his fingers. It felt like he was glowing. He stood up, feeling rested and ready to vigorously run a marathon.

Nathan made sure that the stone was placed securely in his backpack. Yitoo's toes moved into his vision. Nathan looked up and she smiled at him.

"She blessed you?" Yitoo said.

"What?"

"She allowed you to drink her water," she said.

"I guess so. Yes," Nathan said. He stood up, looking at the tall reed and searching for his companions.

"By drinking her water, you'll be able to sing water monster songs without it harming you," Yitoo said. "Looks like your involvement with us is not over yet."

"Nathan!" Spider said. Spider was on top of Seed Collector, who was running toward Nathan on the sandy shore.

Wind Being hovered over Nathan. "Were you successful?"

"I have the medicine!"

"You're safe!" Seed Collector said. It jumped onto Nathan's leg and squeezed gently.

"Whoa!" Nathan said, surprised at Seed Collector's hug. "Did you find more seeds?"

"Yes, but unfortunately, my pouch is already full of seeds that had fallen off First Turkey. I may have to make another journey on my own," Seed Collector said.

"We should head back, everyone. Pond is still waiting," Nathan said. He scooped up Seed Collector and put it into his backpack.

"For my younger brother's sake," Yitoo said, "I will show you the shortcut we water monsters use to travel between the worlds."

"Really?" Nathan said. Hopefully the shortcut was indeed very short. He could still make Uncle Jet's Enemy Way.

"Whenever you are ready," Yitoo said.

Nathan took one last look at the Third World. He hoped that after puberty he would be able to remember everything about this amazing place. "We're ready," Nathan said.

Yitoo created a platform of ice that Nathan stood on. She

pushed the platform to the ceiling and into a pathway that snaked its way upward into a round opening in one of the crystal spires. It felt like riding a very fast and dark elevator.

Hold on, Pond, Nathan thought, *we are almost there.*

Tádiin Dóó Bi'ąą Naaki
THIRTY-TWO

THE SHORTCUT WAS ONLY ONE-WAY and didn't deviate. Nathan hoped that this wouldn't take them too far from the entrance of the cave system. About an hour later, the ice platform finally slowed down and stopped. Nathan stepped forward as Seed Collector held out its crystal fire. They were in another hogan-like dome. At one end was an ice door. Nathan ran over and sang the first words of the lullaby. The ice door immediately melted.

They stepped through and Nathan found that they stood opposite the entrance in the canyon. Moonlight shone on everything, but Nathan couldn't see where the moon was. Up ahead Jet Stone Boy stared up at the sky, singing to the stars.

"Jet Stone Boy!" Nathan shouted.

"Nathan?" Jet Stone Boy looked around for them.

"Over here!" Nathan shouted and waved. He rushed into the

moonlight. Nathan took a look back and saw that the shortcut entrance had transformed back into rock. "How long were we gone?"

"Let's go! Let's go! Pond's health is fading fast!" Jet Stone Boy said, waving them over.

Nathan hustled over to Jet Stone Boy, who was already pressing the tip of his arrowhead to the earth.

"I will meet you all there," Wind Being said. Its human form disintegrated, and the crystal sands zipped through the air.

A rainbow appeared and arched upward. Nathan grabbed Jet Stone Boy's hand, and they instantly streaked across the night sky. Nathan looked at the moon. It was half-full. Nathan estimated they had been gone seven days at most.

They landed in front of Darkness and Pond. Pond! His eyes were closed. It looked like he wasn't breathing. Darkness bowed its head over Pond's still body.

Nathan pulled off his backpack. Seed Collector and Spider leaped to the ground to let Nathan pull out the stone.

"Pond! Pond?" Nathan said, holding the stone in front of his face. The exterior began to dry and crack.

Pond's chest lifted then deflated. He was still alive.

"Pond, we have the medicine! Wake up!" Nathan said. He placed the rock on his lap and pushed against Pond's searing shoulders.

"It may be too late," Darkness said. "Nathan. Look at me."

Nathan looked at the top of Darkness's form. "We just got here. Come on, Pond! You have to tell us what to do with the medicine!" Nathan shouted.

Pond's eyes opened. Tears dripped down his face. He looked at the rock that Nathan had taken out of his backpack.

"I see you brought me a little sister," Pond said. Groaning, he forced a smile, even though it looked like it caused him great pain. It was the smile that Nathan was familiar with. His parents, Nali, even Uncle Jet, did it. It was a smile meant to hide suffering.

"What?" Nathan said. He held the rock in both his hands. The volcanic texture turned into soft sands and sifted away, revealing a smooth oval egg.

"It is a water monster egg—my little sister," Pond said. "It's a sign that I am beyond saving. I am to die. My mother must have known."

"Don't say that! That's not true." Nathan looked at the others. Wind Being and Darkness bowed. Spider walked to Nathan, but Seed Collector held her back, shaking its head.

"No! No. You can't die," Nathan said.

"Nathan," Pond said. "My friend, it's all right. Everything has an end. I'm no different."

"She said this would help! I know, I'll go back and demand she give me medicine. Wait. I'll be back as quick as I can!" Nathan said. Tears were streaming down his face.

"Nathan," Darkness said.

"It's okay," Pond said. "You've already done everything in your power."

Nathan wrapped his arms around Pond, who groaned in

response. "You can't die. We all tried so hard. Please. It's my fault. I should have focused on learning the songs. I should have been quicker. I should have been smarter. I wasn't fast enough. It's my fault."

"It is not your fault, Nathan," Darkness said. "You didn't interact with uranium, the remains of the Enemies of the Fourth World."

"You must teach the songs to my baby sister," Pond said. "When she is of age, she can bring the rains back to the desert. Can you do that, Nathan?"

Nathan forced a smile. "I'll sing the songs with her. I'll make sure that she learns and remembers them."

"When you bury the egg, make sure she is in a safe place," Pond said.

"Okay." Nathan gently cradled the egg in his hands. "Can I hug you until . . . ?" Nathan couldn't say the word "die" out loud.

"I would love that, my friend," Pond said.

Nathan placed the egg into his backpack and safely wrapped it in the blanket. He crawled over to Pond and held his neck. "Thank you, Pond, for being my friend."

For ten minutes, Pond's body rose and fell. Then Pond's breathing slowed until finally there was no breath. And the heat from Pond's skin cooled in the night air. Pond was no more.

"Pond!" Nathan said. The sky was brightening and turning dark orange.

"Nathan," Seed Collector said. "I'm afraid I must leave. I

was not made for daylight." Seed Collector walked to his side and held one of Nathan's fingers. "I wish you well. Hopefully, our paths will cross again." Seed Collector then crawled under a nearby shadow. The first ray of sunlight raced across the sky. Darkness shrank into the shade of a nearby sagebrush.

"I'm going to bury Pond," Nathan said.

"All right," Wind Being said.

Nathan used his hands to push and move sand on top of Pond's body. He dug into and pulled the sand away. His arms were dusty and tired when he was done. Standing, he patted the mound in front of him.

"I'll carry you to where you want to bury the egg," Wind Being said.

"Can you take me to Nali's cornfield?" Nathan asked, wiping his nose.

Minutes later, Nathan stood in his cornfield. He looked at the spiral shape of the traditional group and the square shape of the modern group. He pulled the egg out of his backpack, knowing where he wanted her to eventually hatch. He got onto his knees and dug again with his hands, in between the spiral and the square.

Done, he stood up. In the distance, the morning rays were barely touching the tips of the sandstone mesas. Suddenly, his grief over Pond's death overpowered him. It wasn't fair. After all that effort Nathan had put into saving Pond, it wasn't enough. He wasn't enough.

"My sweet grandchild, my heart," a feminine voice said.

Nathan looked up and saw a butterfly with rainbow wings fluttering. The colors on the wide wings changed and moved. "You have been brave and strong to go to the Third World and back. I'm so very proud of you."

"Thank you. Who are you?" Nathan asked, wiping away his tears.

The butterfly hovered in front of him. Its wing colors changed to blue and purple, then to yellow and white. "I am Grandmother of all."

"Changing Woman?" Nathan asked. Nathan couldn't believe that the most beloved of all Navajo Holy Beings was talking to him.

"I have answered to that name, yes," she sweetly said.

"Nice to meet you, my grandmother," Nathan said. He bowed his head.

"Be confident that your efforts were enough, my heart. Very little could have been done to save your friend."

"So, everything I did was worthless?" Nathan asked.

"You gave Pond a great pool of hope, for his own health and for the return of the rains. Hope is a very powerful medicine and can give every minute we have alive a great deal of meaning and worth. There is someone else, my heart, who you have given hope."

"Uncle Jet."

"Pond will always be a part of your being, through the songs he taught you, and through the rain you will bring back to this land. Your uncle, my other grandson, still needs you. Can you be there for him, for me?"

"Okay, my grandmother."

The butterfly landed on Nathan's nose. Its lovely wings flapped, and the gentle waves of air it created caressed Nathan's eyelids. "Thank you, my heart." The butterfly flew straight upward and disappeared from sight.

"Wind Being? Can you please take me to my uncle's Enemy Way Ceremony?" Nathan asked.

"Of course," Wind Being said.

Nathan's foot touched the ground in the middle of a cedar forest that was near the ceremonial site. He was no longer on Wind Being's back. In the distance, he heard drumming and singing.

"Thank you, Wind Being," Nathan said. With that, Wind Being disappeared.

Nathan wiped away the tears on his cheeks and walked to the source of the singing. The trees cleared, and before him was a line of men wearing turquoise jewelry, blue jeans, velvet button-down shirts, and red moccasins. A drummer stood in the middle and gently tapped on the deer-hide drum under his right arm. They were singing facing the east, where the sun was still behind the horizon.

In front of the singers, wrapped in fine fabrics, jewelry dangling off his arms and neck, Uncle Jet was standing next to Andrea's mom. A beautiful gray-white-and-blue Pendleton blanket wrapped his midsection, and a black-red Pendleton blanket around her shoulders. They both stretched their arms to the rising sun. Their exposed skin was covered in something dark.

Nathan ran to the singers. He wanted to be a part of them. The men looked at Nathan but kept on singing. He didn't feel out of place as he stood in their midst. In the corner of his eyes, he saw Nali, his father, and Leandra. Nali was holding her hands over her mouth. She looked relieved.

Rays of sunlight grazed the tops of the trees. Nathan touched the bow guard and could no longer understand what the singers were saying. But he listened and picked up on the verses and chorus. He sang alongside them for a few minutes.

The men stopped but Nathan wanted to keep singing, because it felt like he was learning songs from Pond again. He wanted to keep on feeling like Pond was still teaching him. So, he sang the protection song, which he hadn't been able to fully learn. Since it wasn't specifically a water monster song, the people around him shouldn't be in danger from it.

Nathan sang the first verse and the chorus. Uncle Jet turned slightly and saw him singing. Nathan could see that Uncle Jet was surprised. The singers joined him when he returned to the second verse. Nathan was surprised at how quickly they picked up the song. When Nathan led them to the chorus, they were in time and sang the exact words.

But soon, Nathan came to the part of the song that he didn't know. He would never be able to finish this song because Pond had died and couldn't teach him. He started to cry again. Even though he had felt the life leave Pond's body, it still felt like

Pond was in the desert and was going to teach him another song. He stopped when he couldn't remember any more.

Then one of the singers rubbed his shoulder and continued the song. The other men sang along. They already knew the song! Nathan listened to the song and remembered Pond singing these exact words. He closed his eyes and focused on the words and the rhythm. When the singers returned to the chorus, he sang along with them. The song finished and Nathan felt complete and full again, even if for a minute. The singers and drummer dispersed.

Uncle Jet turned around and gave him a hug. He was smiling. Nathan listened closely, and that voice was no longer pestering his uncle. Nathan couldn't see the eyes of the Ash Being in Uncle Jet's shadow.

"Where did you learn to sing like that, Nathan? You don't even speak Navajo!" Uncle Jet said.

"My friend taught me," Nathan said.

"What friend?"

"The water monster." Nathan ran toward Nali and his dad. They both wrapped him in long hugs. When they were done, Nathan went over and hugged Leandra.

"Whoa, this is unexpected," Leandra said.

"Nathan," his dad said, pulling him into a hug. He could smell his dad's shampoo. Nathan yawned.

Nali approached him after his dad let go. "He's tired. Let him rest."

He was ready for a very long rest after a hot meal.

Tádiin Dóó Bi'ąą Táá'
THIRTY-THREE

NATHAN WAS IN HIS ROOM at the mobile home, folding his clothes and then arranging them in his duffel bag. He zipped up the bag and then went to pack his backpack, which still smelled like an ocean, even though he had returned from the Third World three days ago. He placed his communication stone in a secure zipped pocket. He then slid in his notebook that had all his notes on the cornfield experiment. For his final measurements, the modern corn was taller. But there were more plump ears on the traditional corn. Nathan didn't feel that this was a good enough experiment because there were too many different factors. Not to mention, the traditional seeds had been planted in a different pattern, and that may have influenced water distribution and pollination.

There was a knock, and Uncle Jet leaned against the door. Nathan looked at his shadow and listened very closely. No sign of the Ash Being.

"Your dad says he's ready to leave. You packed?" Uncle Jet said.

"Yeah," Nathan said. "I'm craving Hot Pockets."

"Listen," Uncle Jet said. "I want to thank you for that day back in Nali's hogan."

"Huh?"

"I think you oughta know that," Uncle Jet said, "well, you saved me. Without you, I don't think I'd be where I am right now. And to be honest, I was a little upset that you didn't show up for the actual ceremony. But something happened, I think it was Thursday night. I went to sleep, and in my dreams I heard you calling out for me."

Nathan remembered when he was in the third obstacle, a dream space that re-created desires. He had talked with Uncle Jet then. "Yes, I remember."

"You were for real. All this time, you were for real. About the water monster and the thing that kept telling me I was worthless. All this time, I thought I was never going to get better."

"It's gone, Uncle Jet. You confronted it with the ceremony and got rid of it."

"I still feel, well, like nothing has changed," Uncle Jet said.

"When the Ash Being was messing with me," Nathan said, "it was making all the bad feelings and thoughts I already had worse."

"Yeah. Devin said that N'dáá helps to get rid of the things that are holding on to me and that therapy is going to help me let go of things that I'm holding on to."

"Keep at it, Uncle Jet. You promised me you'd try, remember?" Nathan said.

"About that. When your dad took me down to Phoenix, and you were still up here, I kind of took over your room."

"Really?"

"Yeah. I was kind of hoping I could borrow your room until I can save up enough money for my own place."

Nathan jumped up and laughed. "That would be awesome!" Nathan's thoughts ran a million miles an hour. With Uncle Jet in Phoenix, they could hang out! They could watch movies! They could play video games together! And Nali could . . . wait. "What about Nali? She's going to be alone until the school year starts."

"She knows and is fine with it," Uncle Jet said. He patted Nathan's shoulders. "Thanks for everything." Uncle Jet left the room.

Nathan went to the corner where Spider was.

"Spider!" Nathan said.

Her hairy front legs pulled her round abdomen out of the shadows. Nathan smiled at her and extended his hand. She crawled onto it.

"I will see you in November, okay?" he said, hoping that she could understand him.

She turned around, then raised her front legs at Nathan.

Nathan reached to the ceiling and she jumped off his hand and crawled back onto the ceiling. Nathan grabbed his bags and left his room.

He pushed the front door open. His dad and Leandra were already putting their things into the SUV. Nathan walked on over. The sun warmed his skin gently. The scorching days of summer were ending, and the days were becoming more comfortable. But still, it was so very dry and dusty.

"You ready to head back, Nathan?" Leandra asked him.

Nathan looked at her and said, "Yeah. I think I am."

Nathan placed his luggage by his dad's leg. "Hey, Dad, where's Nali?"

"She's in the cornfield," his dad said.

"Let me say goodbye to her," Nathan said.

"Take your time," his dad said.

Nathan approached the cornfield. Nali stood between the traditional and modern corn groups. Nathan walked to her. The lively green husks brushed up against his shoulders and arms. The sweetness of the kernels perfumed the air around them.

Nathan leaned his head against Nali's shoulder. A sudden sadness bloomed in him.

"This is where the egg is at?" Nali said, looking at the slight mound in the middle of both corn groups.

"Yeah. It's a she."

"A baby water monster in my cornfield. Never in my life," Nali said. In her hand was a cup of lavender and sage tea. She sipped. "Sháh! I don't know nothing about raising water monsters."

"Me neither." Nathan chuckled. "You don't have to raise her.

But she does need to learn songs."

"I can take her to Devin."

"No. I don't think we'll know much about how to raise her until she hatches. So, um, are you going to be here during Thanksgiving?" Nathan said.

"What are you thinking?"

"I want to check on her."

Nali smiled and said, "We'll meet back here for your Thanksgiving break." She sipped her tea.

"'Ahéhee', shinálí," Nathan said. "'Ayóó' 'áníínísh'ni."

"'Aoo', 'aoo', 'áníínísh'ni, shinálí hastiin."

Nathan hugged her and she sighed deeply. "I'm going to miss you, Nali."

"Shidóó, that's me, too. Call me when you get back. Hágoshį́į́?"

"I will." Nathan stood with her until he heard his dad call his name.

Nathan sat in the back of the SUV and looked at the desert around them. He imagined what this entire place would look like had it rained. The greenery that was hiding underneath the sand and was waiting for moisture of any kind. Flowers. Grass. Bushes. And the animals that would return if the plants returned. The small critters and the predators that fed on those. But all around them was sand, stone, and sun.

He was so close! He could have saved Pond and brought the water back! But he was too slow and too dumb. He stopped his thinking right there. He wasn't slow. He wasn't dumb. He did his best and he wasn't done trying. He was coming back for his November break to check on Pond's sister.

He and the Holy Beings hadn't succeeded, at least not yet.

His dad slammed the door shut and put the SUV into drive. Both he and Leandra talked about the ceremony. Uncle Jet sat quietly looking out the window. But when they got to the highway, Leandra had fallen asleep.

The tires drove onto the smooth pavement, and their speed increased as his father drove them into traffic. This road would take them all the way back to the Phoenix valley.

"Leandra? You awake?" his dad said. She didn't respond. She was out cold.

His dad turned the rearview mirror to look at him. Nathan smirked.

"Hi, Dad," he said.

"Okay. Tell us everything. From the beginning."

"I wanna hear everything," Uncle Jet said.

"It started when I got lost in the desert following Seed Collector. It had dropped a pumpkin seed." While Nathan talked, both his dad's and Uncle Jet's attention were completely on him. And it felt great.

Nílch'its'ósí

NOVEMBER

UNCLE JET WAS COOKING SOME flank steaks on an open-fire grill, while his dad chopped wood to keep the fire going. The chill of the late-November air flowed through Nathan's thick sweater. Nali sat by the fire sipping her tea, bundled in a blanket. With the sun setting, the coldness of the air would eventually sting.

The sun settled into the western horizon. It was time! Dark shadows lengthened and covered more than half the land. Nathan slid on a ring that securely held the communication stone and started toward the cornfield.

"Nathan," Nali said. He turned around and looked at her. "Don't stay out too late." She handed him a flashlight.

"I'll be back quick," Nathan said, and turned the flashlight on.

"You're going to let him wander the desert alone?" his dad asked.

"He's not alone. He has the Holy Beings," Nali said.

Nathan jumped into the cornfield. The corn had been harvested and now the field was once again empty. He ran across the ground. In the middle, his shoes stepped on eggshells.

At the other end of the field, he raked his fingers through the sand. He felt around, then pulled up a tiny thread of spider silk. He followed it through the desert.

The spider silk ended before the rise of a large dune. Nathan sat down and looked into the shadow of the dune.

"Hello, it's me again," Nathan said, pressing his thumb against his communication stone.

A tiny lizard, about the size of his palm, crawled out from beneath the sands. Her forked tongue tasted the air. She recognized Nathan and excitedly ran to him and curled up on his lap.

"Let's sing the lullaby," Nathan said. "It's very important for water monsters to know."

The tiny lizard raised her head and looked at Nathan. She nodded. Together, they hummed the melody to warm up and then sang the song.

Far above them, a lonely little black cloud amassed. In its dark belly, moisture swirled and condensed into droplets. A tiny pearl-sized bead of rain fell to the desert floor.

GLOSSARY

I have decided not to include pronunciation in this because some Diné accents and sounds just don't have a phonetic equivalent. But if you wish to hear the Diné language and perhaps some of these very words, please check out https://navajowotd.com, as they have a wonderful library of Diné words pronounced.

Family Relationships

There are multiple variations of family terms, and certain contexts determine proper designation or colloquial usage. Let's take 'análí, for instance. In colloquial Navajo, which often is mixed with English words, 'análí is used with a possessive prefix such as shi- (my), ni- (your), or bi- (his/her/its). Shinálí, ninálí, and binálí, respectively. In English conversations mixed with Navajo words, it's common to say my nálí, your nálí, or his/her/its nálí.

Navajos also use clans to determine family relationships outside of blood relationships. For instance, Nali is related to Devin as his clan mom. Through the clan system, Nathan's father and Uncle Jet would consider Devin a brother. And last, Nathan would refer to him as uncle and should treat him as such. There is no Navajo word for "clan relative" because that relationship

would be as real as a blood relationship. In the story, Devin calls
Nali shimá (my mom) and she calls him shiyáázh (my son).
Often Navajo kids will know who their blood relatives are at a
very young age. When older family members indicate the existence of another relative, the kid will assume it is a clan relative
and not some long-lost relative.

nálí (full spelling: 'análí)
Literal meaning: paternal relationship. Contextual: some
Navajo children will address their paternal grandparents as
simply nálí. Nathan's name for Nali references this.
shinálí: my paternal relationship
nálí 'adzą́ą́ (full spelling: 'análí 'adzą́ą́)
paternal grandmother
shinálí 'adzą́ą́: my paternal grandmother
nálí hastiin (full spelling: 'análí hastiin)
paternal grandfather
shinálí hastiin: (older to younger) my adult grandson,
(younger to older) my paternal grandfather
nálíyazhí
little paternal relation; in this story, often means "your young
grandson."
shinálí 'ashkii: my young paternal grandson
shinálí yázhí: my paternal grandchild
niye'
Literal meaning: your son. In Navajo culture, brothers of the
father are considered fathers of the kid and their offspring

are considered siblings not cousins. Sisters of the mother are considered mothers of the child, and their offspring are considered siblings, not cousins. Jet is the brother of Nathan's father, and culturally Jet and Nathan would refer to each other as father and son.

shiyáázh: my son (female speaker: mother to son, maternal aunt to maternal nephew)

shiye': my son (male speaker; father to son, paternal uncle to paternal nephew)

shimá: my mom

shitsilí: my younger brother

zhé'é (full spelling: 'azhé'é) father

nizhé'é: your father

shizhé'é yázhí: literal meaning is little father; actual meaning, paternal uncle

Numbers

t'ááłá'í	one
naaki	two
táá'	three
dį́į́'	four
'ashdla'	five
hastą́ą́	six
tsosts'id	seven
tseebíí	eight

náhást'éí	nine
neeznáá	ten
ła' ts'áadah	eleven
naaki ts'áadah	twelve
táá ts'áadah	thirteen
díį' ts'áadah	fourteen
'ashdla' ts'áadah	fifteen
hastą́ą́' ts'áadah	sixteen
tsosts'id ts'áadah	seventeen
tseebíí ts'áadah	eighteen
náhást'éí ts'áadah	nineteen
naadiin	twenty
naadiin dóó bi'ąą t'ááłá'í	twenty-one
naadiin dóó bi'ąą naaki	twenty-two
naadiin dóó bi'ąą táá'	twenty-three
naadiin dóó bi'ąą díį'	twenty-four
naadiin dóó bi'ąą 'ashdla'	twenty-five
naadiin dóó bi'ąą hastą́ą́	twenty-six
naadiin dóó bi'ąą tsosts'id	twenty-seven
naadiin dóó bi'ąą tseebíí	twenty-eight
naadiin dóó bi'ąą náhást'éí	twenty-nine
tádiin	thirty
tádiin dóó bi'ąą t'ááłá'í	thirty-one
tádiin dóó bi'ąą naaki	thirty-two
tádiin dóó bi'ąą táá'	thirty-three

Words and Phrases

'ałk'idą́ą́	a long time ago
'abínídą́ą́	earlier this morning
'Adzą́ą́ Nadleehí	Changing Woman
'ahéhee'	thank you
'áłtsé	wait
'aoo'	yes
'ayóó' 'áníínísh'ni	I love you.
'éí biniinaa	this is the reason
'éí dooda	Literally: this is no. Understood meaning: nope (firmly)
'iishjáshįį	we'll see; wait and see
chaha'oh	Literal meaning: shade. However, also refers to a traditional rectangular structure constructed out of pine trees for the frame and oak branches for walls and ceiling. Modern interpretations use plywood for walls and ceilings.
Cheii Chizh	Grandpa Firewood

cheii (full spelling: 'acheii)	Literal meaning: maternal grandfather. Also refers to horned toads. Often when spoken with English, it's common to say and spell cheii without the 'a- at the beginning. When a Navajo comes across a threatening animal, it is common to address the animal as cheii (grandpa) or masani (grandma) in hope that by referring to the animal as a loving relative the animal won't harm the person.
chizh	firewood
da'ósą	eat (direct command)
dah nidá	sit down
Dibé Nitsaa	Mount Hesperus
Diné	Navajo
Diyin Dine'é	Holy Beings
Dook'o'oosłííd	San Francisco Peaks
ha'át'íílá	No equivalent English translation, but loosely translated it's an exclamation that can mean the following things: What the heck?/ What's wrong with you?/What in the world!/What in the dickens! Can be used in a teasing manner, can also express frustration.
hágo	come over here; get closer

hágoónee'	goodbye
hágoshį́į́	okay, as in agreement
Hash 'akót'é?	Is that right?
hastiin	man
hataałii	medicine man/medicine woman
hózhó náhásdlį́į́	There is beauty around me.
Hwééldi	Literally: where they suffered. Actual meaning: Fort Sumner, New Mexico, where Navajos had been relocated between 1863 to 1868.
N'dáá (full term: 'Ana'í N'dáá)	Enemy Way Ceremony. Very common to just use N'dáá in conversation.
naadą́ą́'	corn
Nááts'íílid Dine'é	Rainbow Being
nahałtin	rain
ní	you
Níłch'its'ósí	November
níníł'į	Look at that.
nizhoní	good
Sháh!	No equivalent English translation. Expression of light frustration, sometimes used jokingly.
shidóó	Me too
shił łikan	Literally: this tastes sweet to me. Also used to say this is delicious.
shooyá	expression of tiredness or accomplishment

Sis Naajiní	Mount Blanca
skoden	This isn't Navajo but rather a contraction of the phrase "Let's go then." Sometimes spelled "skodan."
sǫ'	star
Sǫ' Náhookǫs	Northern Star
tádídíín	corn pollen or corn pollen pouch
Tsoodził	Mount Taylor
txį'	let's go; come on
yá'át'ééh	hello
Yaa!	Expression of mild frustration. Never used jokingly.
yaadilá	No literal translation. Closest English equivalent is: Are you kidding me?
yé'ii	a specific type of Holy Being
yiską́ągo'	tomorrow

Sentences

'Áyóo nanitł'a.	It's going to be very hard.
Ch'iyáán 'adaal'įįgi bóhoo diłáał.	I'm going to teach you to cook.
Dichin nísin.	I am hungry.
Díí shinálí 'ashkii, Nathan.	This is my grandson, Nathan.

Doo 'ájínída'!	Don't say that!
Háájí Jet?	Where's Jet?
Haash yit'éego sindá?	How are you doing? (Person being asked is sitting.)
Hastóí lą'í.	There's a lot of men.
Hazhóó'ógo, shinálí.	Literally: "Easy, my paternal relation." In context: "There, there, my grandson."
Jó Vegas go diniyalá.	You're going to be in Vegas now.
K'ad ałtso.	We are finished.
K'ad amá 'idiiłjii bí'oh díneshdlį́į́. T'ááshí ako.	Right now, I have to accept that I wasn't a good enough mother.
K'ad, níká 'o'olwod.	You have help now.
K'adí. 'Ałtso tsídé tsą́ą́.	That's enough. I've heard enough.
Kwe'é sikéhíjíí.	Right here where we sit.
Na'ahyílá.	He's drunk right now.
Ni' 'at'ééd niba'.	Your girlfriend is waiting.
Ni'dó 'ahéhee'.	You too, thank you.
Níléidi chizh ła' nidiijah shinálí.	Over there, grab some firewood for me.
Sha'awe'. Hazhóó'ógo.	My baby. Take it easy.
Shighandí 'ałwosh.	At home, he's asleep.
Shinálí, ch'iiyáán 'adeiilníł.	My grandson, let's cook dinner.

Shiwos neezgai.	My shoulder hurts.
Shiyáázh Jet shá bik'é jidlíído'.	Bless my son Jet wherever he may be.
Yá'át'ééh shik'is, Nathan. Ni dootł'izhii shą́?	Hello, my friend Nathan. Where's your turquoise?
Yá'át'ééh, shiyáázh!	Hello, my son!

ACKNOWLEDGMENTS

I want to thank first and foremost shimá Paula White dóó shizhé'é Tom White, Jr., my mom and dad, for all their support and prayers. I know it wasn't easy seeing me struggle for so many years, but I am capable because of your patience and teachings.

Thank you to all my professors at Columbia University's School of the Art's fiction writing staff, who taught me the unique strengths of literature. A special thank-you to my workshop professor, Joshua Furst, who demanded the highest amount of effort, critical thinking, grammar, and evocation of all my stories and of me.

Thank you to the three individuals who wrote recommendations for my application to Columbia's MFA program: Theodore Van Alst, Shelly Lowe, and, of course, Sarah Tames. You all believed in me and that has been the fire in my drive to complete my program.

Thank you to all my colleagues in my MFA program who provided feedback to both my short stories and to what would become *Healer of the Water Monster*. Special thanks to Shelby Wardlaw, whose wisdom and feedback have been incredibly helpful.

Thank you, Dan Mandel, my agent. You were the first yes

out of hundreds of noes and without you, I wouldn't have had this opportunity. Here's to more stories!

Thank you to my editor, Rosemary Brosnan of Heartdrum. Thank you for your patience with all my grammar and spelling mistakes! Your amazing insight has made Nathan's journey all the more clear and emotive. I am so very grateful that you saw potential in me and in Nathan.

Thank you, Cynthia Leitich Smith! You have done so much work in building up Heartdrum so that authors like me can sing our stories loudly and proudly. Even outside Heartdrum, your professional guidance has dispelled the fears and uncertainties many authors have about being published.

Thank you, Laura Pegram of *Kweli* journal. Your support and continued enthusiasm for *Healer of the Water Monster* has always ignited my inspiration to polish Nathan's journey for readers of all ages! Thank you for giving me and other authors of color a platform for connecting and building family.

Thank you, Corinne Duyvis, for first suggesting that people use #OwnVoices on Twitter. Thanks to your intellect and bravery, authors such as myself can be seen and heard. I originally was able to get forty agents to look at the second draft of my book when I used the OwnVoices hashtag. Because of that, I was able to see that my story was something I should invest my whole being into.

Thank you, Beth Phelan, for all that you have done for #DVpit on Twitter. I am filled with hope because you are doing the incredibly important work of connecting unagented BIPOC authors with agents. I wasn't able to secure an agent when I pitched my second draft, but because of your efforts, I was filled with hope and motivation to work on *Healer of the Water Monster* for as long as it took.

Thank you, Weslee and Steven, for letting me use your names as those of Nathan's best friends. We have been best friends since second grade, and I don't see that changing any time soon. Steven, I'm sorry you never got the chance to read my book. Every time I pitched this book to someone, I had to clarify that this was set in present times, because everyone always assumed that Native people exist only in the past, and I had to describe the Emergence Story. When I pitched to you, you told me, "Brian, I know what water monsters are, and why are you telling me it's set in current times—we are in current times." I miss you, Steven, and every time I read your name while editing, my heart ached and I wanted to call you so I could hear your laugh.

Thank you, Tiffany Tracy, for your guidance and your knowledge of the Navajo culture. You have always been someone I admire for traditional knowledge and adherence. Thank you for telling me what was appropriate representation.

'Aadóó 'ahéhee' Diyin Dine'é.

AUTHOR'S NOTE

Yá'át'ééh, Brian Young yinishyé. 'Ahéhee' for reading *Healer of the Water Monster*. I know that stories such as mine are exceptionally rare in mainstream publishing and extremely important for young Navajo readers who have nothing written for them. I know how important a book like this can be because I was that young Navajo reader who could not find a single story that had characters who resembled me and who lived in my environment. So, this book is for you, 'ashkiiké dóó 'at'ééké. Your experiences and your existence are important.

Healer of the Water Monster is the culmination of years of imagining, discovering my characters, wording their experiences, and growing as a storyteller. This book began as a dream I had when I was living in Albuquerque, New Mexico, working as a meat cutter for Whole Foods, barely able to pay my undergraduate loans. In my dream, I saw a young Navajo boy running into a cornfield to meet with a lizard. The two sang and suddenly it began to rain. From there, that dream would surface in my consciousness while I was dicing red meats and parting chickens. I immediately knew that the boy wasn't a listener or a learner. He was the teacher.

When my daydreams of *Healer of the Water Monster* started to take firmer form, I knew that Nathan would get lost in a desert and find a water monster, and that the water monster was sick. I originally had Pond stricken with coal mine dust lung disease because of the extensive coal mining that occurs on my homelands. Mining, whether it be of uranium or coal, is a source of income for the Navajo Nation. But often, resource extraction contracts do not favor my Navajo people. Peabody Energy, then Peabody Western Coal, bribed my nation into a contract that would allow PWC to purchase one ton of coal for one penny. The contract between my nation and PWC has since expired and the hills where pine forests once stood are now flattened expanses devoid of greenery.

I vaguely knew about the uranium mines on my homelands that may have supplied the uranium for the atomic bombs that were dropped on Japan, but I was more aware of coal mining because one of my best friends from school had been relocated from his hometown due to coal mining. Watch the 1985 documentary called *Broken Rainbow* for more information on this topic. In the end, I chose the uranium mine because many coal mines are near big towns and roads. Had I gone with coal mining, the scene where Nathan gets lost in a desert would have been forfeited.

The uranium mine in *Healer of the Water Monster* is real. It is the United Nuclear Corporation Church Rock. On July 16, 1979, a dam holding the disposal waste pond collapsed. Its toxic by-product spilled into the Puerco River, which flowed into the larger Navajo Reservation. To this day, the area surrounding UNC Church Rock remains significantly radioactive from uranium mining exploits.

This book is about the relationship between Nathan and Pond, and metaphorically about the relationship between humans and the forces that control weather elements. Global warming is a topic that I don't outwardly name but constantly reference. Often Native Homelands, not only mine, deal with the tangible effects of global warning. For instance, when I was around Nathan's age, I spent my summers with my maternal grandparents herding cows in Nazlini, Arizona, one of the most isolated areas in the continental US. It is a large, open valley, and when I described Nathan getting lost, I used Nazlini as my desert. Nowadays, the entire valley is a giant bowl of dust. The gentlest of breezes turns its dusty floor into a sandstorm. Back when I was herding cows, there used to be grass that my cows would nibble on. My cheii's cornfield was able to produce corn as thick as my forearm. Even further back, my grandma said that the entire valley was covered in dark grass that was as tall as her ankles. The paths where I herded cows were once filled with cool streams of sweet water. Global warming and the draining of water to urban areas has turned Nazlini into a barren dust bowl. I want to talk more about this topic, and my next book will delve deeper into this issue.

My nation, like many other Native nations, has stories that can be told only during specific circumstances. Even more so, there are certain Holy Beings who cannot be replicated in drawings, writings, or films. Merely saying the names of certain Holy Beings outside of their ceremonial circumstance could diminish their healing abilities. I chose to draw upon the Emergence Story as inspiration for *Healer of the Water Monster* because it is a story that can be told anytime during the year. The Holy Beings depicted in this book have been chosen because, to my knowledge, they do not have those restrictions on their depictions. I have asked many members of my community who participate in cultural activities, even my own medicine man, to find out if the depictions are okay. While those surrounding me have said yes, I do anticipate that other Navajos will not agree with what I depict. I encourage you to listen to them and their concerns. Part of being in an oral tradition culture means that, from family to family, there are variances on small details in the stories as well as restrictions of those stories.

Another aspect of an oral tradition is that the spelling of Navajo words also has variances depending on the dictionary being employed. I am so very thankful for my translator, who has helped provide me with more accurate words as I myself am not fluent. We referred to the *Diné Bizaad Bínáhoo'aah: Rediscovering the Navajo Language* by Evangeline Parsons Yazzie and Margaret Speas, as well as *Navajo-English Dictionary* by Leon Wall and William Morgan for the spelling of Navajo words.

I originally did not want to provide translations and a glossary for the Navajo language. My initial hesitation stems from an expectation in academia, book publishing, legacy media, and beyond that knowledge should be provided easily and readily. That expectation is emblematic of a colonized mindset where the default is to take without considering the worth or giving something back to the source. With Navajo culture, knowledge is earned. Nali demonstrates that when she says that if Nathan does chores, she will tell him more traditional stories. I have decided to include the translations because I imagine a few Navajo readers might find value in it and be inspired to learn Navajo.

Non-Navajo creators who wish to use the Navajo culture in their stories, please don't. Just because I draw upon my culture in this context in no way gives you permission to use my people's culture for your creative expression. My culture has been decimated by relocation, by boarding schools, by Bible-based religions. My generation is putting the pieces of our culture together. The Navajo culture isn't only my culture. These aren't only my Holy Beings. The culture and Holy Beings depicted belong to a nation of people. It would be disrespectful to my people and the Holy Beings (not to mention selfish and stingy) if I implied that I am the final authority on Navajo culture and that all its contents belong to me because of that authority. So please, respect that these stories and the Holy Beings have a home and a context that is attached to their representation. I hope that I have done enough to demonstrate that I both cherish and revere the Holy Beings and the stories from which they originate.

Traditionally, these stories should be shared between people, in person, not through a book. It is my belief that the life of the stories is in the interaction between two generations that the stories foster. My people's history and traditional stories have primarily been passed down orally. And it's very interesting to hear other versions from my friends in the hometown where I grew up, and even in different sections of my reservation, because there are always little differences. I grew up believing that we currently are in the Fourth World, while one of my friends from grade school believes that we are in the Fifth World. I bring this up because I, too, have molded my own version of the creation story. In all versions of my people's creation story, water monsters remained in the Third World. I made the creative change to the story to say that water monsters followed my ancestors into this current world and that they protect bodies of water. This is my idea. I emphasize this because I want it clearly known where my creative interference intersects with the traditional stories. If you have the curiosity to learn more about my people's creation story, I referred to Aileen O'Bryan's *Navajo Indian Myths* and *Amá Sani dóó Achei Baahane'* from the Office of Diné Culture, Language, and Community Services while writing this book. Both have helped me become knowledgeable about the different interpretations of my traditional stories and provide a foundation for building my fictional additions to my culture.

I hope *Healer of the Water Monster* was enjoyable. Truly, 'ahéhee' for reading my book. And even my author's note! It still feels unreal that I am published. It's been a long, heartbreaking and joyous journey to get to this point. For young Navajo readers—or young at heart!—tell your stories, because they can be as big as the sun. Surpass what I have been able to accomplish.

Dear Reader,

I wouldn't be surprised if you had something important in common with Nathan.

Maybe you've been bullied at school. Maybe you're navigating divorced parents or trying to figure out how you fit into your own culture. Maybe you feel a strong connection to the natural world or love and respect your grandmother, or maybe someone you care about has a drinking problem like Nathan's uncle, Jet.

Nathan's uncle reminds me of one of my uncles by marriage. A big man with a big laugh, who called me "Cindy Lou" and loved to play Santa Claus. He wasn't one of my Native uncles— he was a white man—but like Uncle Jet, he had served in the military and struggled with alcoholism. He needed and benefitted from spiritual support. His family dearly loved him.

Alcohol can poison the body, trauma can poison the heart, and radiation can poison the planet. Yet hope abounds. This heartfelt, humorous, page-turning story by Navajo author Brian Young reminds us that, both separately and together, we can work toward healing ourselves, each other, and the Earth itself. We can seek out and embrace help when we need it most.

The novel is published by Heartdrum, a Native-focused imprint of HarperCollins Children's Books, which offers stories about young Native heroes by Native and First Nations authors and illustrators. I'm deeply honored to include this book on our list because it's so thoughtfully and skillfully crafted, because so many of the characters—like Nali, Spider, Seed Collector, and Pond—absolutely captivated me, and because Nathan is an ordinary kid playing a vital role in the future of his life, his family, his people, and this precious planet we all call home.

He's an everyday young hero, and that's something I know he has in common with you.

Mvto,

Cynthia Leitich Smith

Author and filmmaker BRIAN YOUNG is a graduate of both Yale University, with a bachelor's degree in film studies, and Columbia University, with a master's degree in creative writing fiction. An enrolled member of the Navajo Nation, he grew up on the Diné Homelands but now currently lives in Brooklyn, New York. As an undergraduate, Brian won a prestigious Sundance Ford Foundation Fellowship with one of his feature-length scripts. He has worked on several short films, including *Tsídii Nááts'íílid—Rainbow Bird* and *A Conversation on Race with Native Americans* for the short documentary series produced by the *New York Times*. Brian is currently working on another book for young readers. In addition to film and writing, Brian also works as a personal trainer, both online and in person.

CYNTHIA LEITICH SMITH is the bestselling, acclaimed author of books for all ages, including *Rain Is Not My Indian Name*, *Indian Shoes*, *Jingle Dancer*, and *Hearts Unbroken*, which won the American Indian Library Association's Youth Literature Award; she is also the anthologist of *Ancestor Approved: Intertribal Stories for Kids*. She was named a NSK Neustadt Laureate, which honors outstanding achievement in the world of children's and young adult literature. Cynthia is the author-curator of Heartdrum, a Native-focused imprint at HarperCollins Children's Books, and serves as the Katherine

Paterson Inaugural Endowed Chair on the faculty of the MFA program in Writing for Children and Young Adults at Vermont College of Fine Arts. She is a citizen of the Muscogee (Creek) Nation and lives in Austin, Texas. You can visit Cynthia online at www.cynthialeitichsmith.com.

In 2014, We Need Diverse Books (WNDB) began as a simple hashtag on Twitter. The social media campaign soon grew into a 501(c)(3) nonprofit with a team that spans the globe. WNDB is supported by a network of writers, illustrators, agents, editors, teachers, librarians, and book lovers, all united under the same goal — to create a world where every child can see themselves in the pages of a book. You can learn more about WNDB programs at www.diversebooks.org.